SLIGHTLY IRREGULAR

Rhonda Pollero

G

GALLERY BOOKS

New York London Toronto Sydney New Delhi

Gallery Books
A Division of Simon & Schuster, Inc.
1230 Avenue of the Americas
New York, NY 10020

First Gallery Books trade paperback edition April 2012

GALLERY BOOKS and colophon are registered trademarks of Simon & Schuster, Inc.

For information about special discounts for bulk purchases, please contact Simon & Schuster Special Sales at 1-866-506-1949 or business@simonandschuster.com.

The Simon & Schuster Speakers Bureau can bring authors to your live event. For more information or to book an event contact the Simon & Schuster Speakers Bureau at 1-866-248-3049 or visit our website at www.simonspeakers.com.

Designed by Jaime Putorti

Manufactured in the United States of America

10 9 8 7 6 5 4 3 2 1

Library of Congress Cataloging-in-Publication Data

Pollero, Rhonda.
 Slightly irregular / Rhonda Pollero. -- First Gallery Books trade paperback edition.
    pages cm
1. Legal assistants--Fiction. 2. Law firms--Fiction. 3. Missing persons--Fiction. 4. Beauty contestants--Crimes against--Fiction. 5. Dating (Social customs)--Fiction. 6. West Palm Beach (Fla.)--Fiction. I. Title.
 PS3616.O5684S58 2012
 813'.6--dc23

                                          2011048288

ISBN 978-1-4165-9073-6 (pbk)
ISBN 978-1-4391-0099-8 (ebook)

To Katie Scarlett, who reminds me to love; for Bob, who reminds me to laugh; for Amy, who reminds me to sit in the chair; and for Donna, who reminds me to hyphenate everything.

SLIGHTLY IRREGULAR

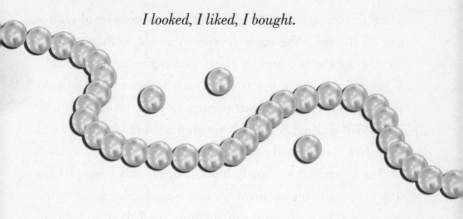

I looked, I liked, I bought.

one

Freedom was three hours away. Technically, only two hours and fifty-one minutes of work time, if I subtracted any time I'd be away from my desk. So, five minutes to answer my summons from the fourth floor; two minutes to go through the motions of straightening my office—we have a cleaning crew and it isn't me; then two minutes to gather my belongings, hit the elevator, stroll through the lobby, walk out the front door, and unlock my practically brand-new, champagne pink Mercedes CLK convertible. Since it was Friday, I might even be able to shave a few minutes off my exit plan.

Fridays are the only days of the week when Maudlin Margaret Ford, firm receptionist and all-around pain in the ass, did not get her feathers in a twist when I ducked out a few minutes early. Any other day of the week and she'd be sounding the alert to the senior partner. I could practically hear her voice in my head. "Mr. Dane! Finley left the building at four fifty-five!"

Margaret was passive-aggressive—with an extra order of aggressive on the side. She was a fifty-five-year-old woman with no life outside the law firm of Dane, Lieberman and Zarnowski. Technically speaking, it was now Dane, Lieberman, Zarnowski and Caprelli. It's a small but prestigious firm just off Clematis Street in West Palm Beach, where, until a few months ago, I was exclusively a trusts and estates paralegal.

The elevator door finally blinked open, and I stepped inside the small compartment. A one o'clock command to the executive floor rarely results in anything good about to happen. A summons used to have me shaking in my Jimmy Choos, but not so much now that Tony Caprelli occupied one of the partners' suites, and he was the one who'd requested my presence.

I sighed and fiddled with the cloisonné clip holding my blond hair off my face. Before leaving my office, I'd carefully checked my lipstick, added some Stila gloss, and smoothed the front of my vintage Lilly Pulitzer dress. The pale periwinkle and spring green dress with ribbon and lace accents was—if I did say so myself—one of my finest bargain moments. I'd come across it on antiquedressing.com, and talk about a find. Classic Lilly, circa 1960, with the metal zippers and original labels, is well beyond my meager means (made more meager since I was now carrying a hefty mortgage and most of my credit cards were near their limits). The catch? The hem was faded and dirty. A disaster for most women, but since I'm just shy of five-four, it was a snap for me to have the seamstress at my cleaner's turn up a new hem without destroying the line of the dress.

I'd turned bargain hunting into an art. Short of an inspection by Tim Gunn and Heidi Klum, no one, not even my best friends, would ever know that I was a walking, talking tribute to gently worn, factory damaged, and slightly irregular. And I wanted to keep it that way.

The elevator opened into a circular lobby. *The* secretary sat sentry at her desk. She glanced up at me over the tops of her reading glasses, then pressed the button on her Bluetooth.

"Miss Tanner is here to see you," she said. "Yes, thank you." She lifted her head and met my gaze. "You may go in."

I quelled the urge to salute her, but c'mon, the woman was so stiff she'd be a natural at Buckingham Palace. We'd worked together for more than eight years and never evolved past the point of addressing each other by last names.

"Thank you, Mrs. Greenfelder," I acknowledged before pivoting to the right and heading toward Tony's office.

My heart rate climbed with each step. Tony had joined the firm a little more than a month ago, and in that short amount of time, he'd generated quite a bit of interoffice buzz. And while everyone else was buzzing, I was actually training to work at his side.

No, I didn't like balancing the continuing education classes on litigation, evidence, witness preparation, or police procedure with the renovations on my new cottage. But I did like Tony. And not in an employer-employee way. The guy was hot and polished and, well, perfect. He was over six feet tall, with dark brown hair and eyes the color of rich imported chocolates. He wore tailored suits, monogrammed shirts, and a top-of-the-line Rolex. A perfect man with a perfect watch. What more could a woman want in a man?

A date.

I sucked in a breath and let it out slowly. Therein lies the rub. I'm almost thirty, not thirteen. I know when a man is interested in me. I've caught Tony watching me when he thought I wasn't looking. His fingers have brushed the back of my hand a few too many times for it to be accidental. He's interested. But he's also my boss. There are times when sexual harassment laws totally get in the way of good old-fashioned get-to-know-you dating.

Maybe I should slip into the ladies' room quickly, paint ASK ME OUT in liner on my lids, and then spend the whole meeting with my eyes closed. Naw, too desperate. Then again, I am on the precipice of desperation. Since I'd dumped Patrick after wasting two years of my life on him, the only men in my life were the ex-convict who was still doing some minor finishing work on my house, and Sam, my dear, dear friend, who had worse luck with men than I did.

Oh, and Liam.

Kinda.

A shiver ran along my spine as I conjured his image. Liam McGarrity is everything I never wanted in a man. Very little polish and way too much testosterone. But one look into those piercing blue eyes and I start to think I can rework him into the man of my dreams. The practical part of me knows better. The libidinous part of me doesn't care.

The only way I've been able to avoid the lure of those incredible eyes has been to keep my distance and screen my calls. So far, I've been successful, but who knows what will happen the next time we have to work together? Liam does a lot of the PI work for my firm. I won't be able to avoid him forever. I'll worry about that when . . .

"Sorry," Tony said as his hands bracketed me, keeping me from falling on my butt.

He smelled good, so good that for a second his cologne rendered me mute. Or maybe it was the feel of his large hands gripping my arms. My sweater had slipped, so the heat from his palms was against my bare skin.

"Is everything okay?" he asked.

"Yeah," I said, stepping back so I could pick up my sweater and the pad I'd dropped when I'd accidentally run right into him. "Sorry, I must have zoned out there for a minute."

Zoned out? I grimaced inwardly. *Zoned out? Really? What kind of dumb blonde thing is that to say to your boss-slash-lust interest?*

"Not a problem," Tony said, stepping aside to allow me to enter his office first. He looked good enough to eat in a dark well-cut suit, crisp creamy shirt, and dark blue tie. Very *GQ.* Very much the opposite of shaggy, rumpled Liam. Both men are sexy, but they're polar opposites in appearance. Both men, however, sent my pulses racing and my libido into hyperdrive.

Tony had a great office. Used to belong to Mr. Zarnowski, but he was gone now, too bad for me. Zarnowski had liked me, unlike Vain Victor Dane, the managing partner who always treated me like some annoying insect bite he couldn't scratch but couldn't ignore. Or Ellen Lieberman. The woman—a term I'm using in the broadest possible sense—thinks I'm a slacker because I didn't go to law school. She seems to forget that I didn't *want* to go. I never wanted to be like her—working seventy hours a week with no life. And in her case, no access to proper hair care. She wears her red-and-gray curls pulled back in a rubber band—doesn't even bother with a scrunchie from the dollar store. Her dresses are little more than sacks with slits, and her signature look includes those god-awful Jesus sandals from Birkenstock. Ellen might be a great contracts attorney, but she is devoid of discernible estrogen. Still, Ellen was kind of taking me under her wing. I was her pet project of sorts. I didn't doubt that her awkward attempts at friendship were sincere. I just figured it was a new tack to get me to further my career.

I started to clear a spot for myself on Tony's couch when he reached out and placed his hand over mine. "No need. This is going to be quick."

Turning slightly so we were face-to-face, I smiled up at him. "What do you need?"

"You."

The room spun for a second as my brain tried to wrap itself around that word. "E-excuse me?"

He took my hands in his and gave a gentle squeeze. "I have tickets to *The Magic Flute* tomorrow night."

"Nothing like a Saturday night with Mozart."

Humor flashed in his eyes, and when he smiled, I was treated to a look at the near-legendary dimple on his right cheek. "Right, your mother was a singer with the Met."

"Yes, she was. Now she's a professional widow, divorcée, or bride-to-be, depending on when you catch her."

"Sorry?"

Reluctantly, I pulled away from his grasp. I waved one hand in the small space between us. "Bad joke. My mother is very fond of getting married. She just has a problem *staying* married. That said, she made sure my sister and I were exposed to opera from birth."

Why had I offered that up? Nerves, I guess. Still, it made me sound like a babbling fool. Not exactly the impression I was going for. I regrouped.

"How do you feel about *The Magic Flute*?" he asked.

"I liked the Kenneth Branagh movie version. Very stylized, like a Target commercial."

Tony glanced at his watch. "I've got to be at the courthouse in like ten minutes. Is there any chance you're free tomorrow night? I know it's short notice, but—"

"Short notice is fine."

"Great," he said on a relieved rush of breath. "Can you be at my place at about six?"

"Absolutely."

He reached into his jacket pocket and handed me a piece of paper with an address on it. I gave it a cursory glance, then tucked it under the blank pages of my legal pad.

Tony walked around to his desk and crammed some files into his briefcase. As he came around again, he gave my hand yet another squeeze. "Thanks, Finley. See you tomorrow night."

"At six," I called as he left in such a hurry that the collection of drawings piled on his desk fluttered.

I picked up the one that fell on the floor and placed it in the center of his desk. It was a pencil sketch of some sort of bird, but I didn't give it any attention. My entire brain was fixated on the knowledge that tomorrow night would be my first date with Tony.

♦

"*Just like that?*" *Becky* asked the next morning when we met at the Gardens Mall. "No preamble, nothing?"

"Preamble?" I asked, laughing. "He wasn't writing the Constitution, he was asking me out on a date."

We were standing outside the about-to-close Crate and Barrel, our usual meeting place. And also as usual, Liv was late. And since Jane was riding with Liv, Becky and I stood chatting while we waited.

Becky and I have been friends since college. We graduated from Emory together, then Becky went on to law school while I came back to Palm Beach and went to work for Dane-Lieberman even after I'd aced the LSATs. Becky joined the firm after earning her J.D., and I was thrilled to have my best friend back in town.

Becky works for Ellen in contracts, and until the surprise addition of a criminal specialist, everyone assumed she'd be the next and youngest-ever partner at the firm. I knew she was disappointed, but I also knew she'd get there eventually. Becky is a smart, savvy attorney, and clients love her—male clients especially. She's tall, attractive, and always put together. She's on a very bright rust-orange-amber binge right now. She wears high-end clothing in various shades of orange to set off her reddish-auburn hair. She softens the tailored look with fun, funky jewelry.

Jane, on the other hand, doesn't tone down anything. She was fifty yards away in the parking lot, and I could tell it was her. I met Jane at a two-for-one gym promotion. We pretended to be friends to get the better price. The friendship lasted. My membership at the gym did not. Jane exudes sensuality. She can't help it. She has long, dark hair and a toned body that most women would kill for. Everything up top is cut low, and everything down below is hiked high. And why not? She has a perfect body and somehow manages to show skin without looking cheap. She's an accountant, though to anyone getting their first glance at her, they'd probably think she was one of the Pussycat Dolls.

Liv was with her, handing something—most likely a generous tip—to the valet attendant. Liv makes the rest of us look like trolls. She's a very successful event planner. Almost no one hosts a party or a wedding on Palm Beach without hiring Concierge Plus to deal with the details. Liv is an exotic-looking woman. She has eyes that match the ocean, clear turquoise, with midnight black hair like a modern Cleopatra. The biggest perk in knowing her—aside from the fact that she's a great friend—is she can slip us into a lot of the über-rich parties on the island.

Once the four of us were together, we made a mandatory swing through one of the mall's two Starbucks. I was so excited about my first date with Tony that I'd had a hard time sleeping. Thank God for caffeine and MSC concealer.

"He just asked you out of the blue?" Liv asked as we waited for our coffees.

"Geez! Why does that seem to surprise all of you?" I asked, minorly irritated.

Jane passed me my skinny vanilla latte. "Men aren't usually that spontaneous. Think about it, Finley. He e-mailed, asking you to come to his office so he could ask you out? Why not go to your office?"

"Or for that matter," Becky said, "why run the risk of asking you out at work and leaving a paper trail to do it?"

"The e-mail was harmless, and what risk?" I asked.

Becky rolled her eyes. "We all know there was no risk you'd

say no, but Tony didn't know that. A smart guy—and he is that—would call you after work so there could be no misunderstandings."

"Like?"

Becky took a long sip of her chai tea. "Like asking while at work could be construed as harassment. You could claim you felt pressured to go out with him because he's your boss."

"That's ridiculous."

Becky's green eyes bored into me. "You'd better hope Dane and Lieberman don't hear about this. Especially Ellen. She'll freak out if she thinks he's creating a hostile work environment."

"Anybody ever tell you you're a major buzzkill?" I asked.

Becky raised her hands. "Sorry I mentioned it."

"Okay," I said, happy to have that bit of unpleasantness quashed. "It's got to be black. I'm thinking something subtle, but I don't want to look like a mortician. Shoes and a clutch."

"Um," Jane began cautiously, "where does this fit into the budget we did for you?"

"Whatever I get for tonight, I'll wear to Lisa's rehearsal dinner. That cuts the cost per wearing in half right there."

"How many little black dresses do you have in your closet?" Liv challenged.

"Not as many as you and besides, the LBD never goes out of style."

"And Finley never gets out of debt," Jane grumbled.

I looped my arm through hers. "Lighten up. I'm splurging this once, then I promise to return to living like mortgaged-to-the-gills Mary. Okay?"

"You're pulling equity out of your house. You have every

right to do that. I'm just telling you, in my capacity as your financial planner, what I think."

"Fine. Then be my friend, not my financial planner."

Jane smiled. "Well, in that case, I say we go to Nordy's and find you *the* perfect dress."

"And shoes," Becky said.

"And a purse, and maybe some new jewelry," Liv weighed in.

Three hours and four lattes later, I had a stunning BCBG Max Azria, belted, one-shoulder sheath dress. It was fitted jersey and fully lined and, according to the saleswoman, required nothing but a thong.

I'd found the perfect shoes in a matter of minutes. Stuart Weitzman silk-satin platform sling backs with a wrapped heel. The saleswoman raced over and grabbed the matching clutch as I yanked my debit card from my wallet. I found a stunning Judith Jack double-strand pendant necklace and chandelier earrings to go with my new ensemble, finishing it off with three skinny bangles.

As I drove home, I didn't have buyer's remorse so much as paid-full-price remorse. If Tony had given me a week's notice, I could have put something together online, and even with expedited shipping, I wouldn't have spent nearly two thousand dollars. Then again, it was worth it. If I parceled the cost between the Tony date and the rehearsal dinner, it didn't seem so bad. If I could think of another occasion to wear it, I could keep dropping the CPW—cost per wearing—down to a more reasonable number.

Who was I kidding? I looked, I liked, I bought.

I stopped on the way home for a polish change and a brow

wax. Add another fifty dollars to my ever-growing debt. By two thirty I was on my way over the bridge to Palm Beach. Thanks to selling my soul to the devil—that would be my mother, the only living heart donor—I owned a very modest cottage on the beach. Thanks to my friend Sam, it was a showplace. It was sleek and beachy, comfy and posh all at one time. Handyman Harold still came by almost every day to tighten something or hammer something else, but for all intents and purposes, my home renovations were finished and stunning. And had me several hundred thousand in debt. Oh, Liam helped too, but I wasn't in the mood to give him credit for anything. Not after he'd kept Patrick's secret. And was still taunting me about the whole "three wishes" thing. It was silly, really. Liam had come to my rescue and pulled some lame *I Dream of Jeannie* thing, telling me he was now entitled to three wishes. I figured he'd used up more than three wishes by hiding the fact that my boyfriend was cheating. Well, maybe cheating was an understatement. At any rate, I wasn't playing.

My mother sold me a shack on primo land. I couldn't wait to see her reaction when she finally decides to accept my standing invitation to see what I've done with the place. She's currently back in Atlanta helping my sister get ready for her enormous wedding. In two weeks, Lisa will be walking down the aisle to become Mrs. David Huntington-St. John IV. Actually, she'll be *Dr.* Mrs. David Huntington-St. John IV. Except that David is a doctor too, so I guess they'll be Drs. David Hunt—oh, who gives a shit.

Don't get me wrong, I adore my little sister, and I'm happy she found the man of her dreams. But her dreams are amazingly dull. David is nice enough, but he's a nontalker and a big rich geek. Of course my mother loves him. He's rich, he's a doctor, and his family is old money. They are pillars of Buckhead, the tony suburb of Atlanta. Like my sister, Lisa, David is an oncologist. He and Lisa met on one of those Doctors Without Borders things.

I'm all for humanitarianism, but do you have any idea what it's like to have to compete with a perfect sibling? Lisa went to med school. Managed to finish the first seven years of academic work in three and a half. Lisa made something of her life. My mother considers me a failure. Maybe I am uninspired, but I'm happy in my mediocrity. Lisa never looks happy. Maybe you can't be a pediatric oncologist and be happy. Who knows?

But that wasn't the real reason I resented David and found fault whenever I could. If I was being totally honest, I was suffering some sibling envy. It was bad enough to be second on my mother's list, but once David was part of the family, I'd drop down to a distant third. Hence, I kept trying to find something, anything, wrong with my sister's fiancé. So far all I'd come up with was slightly large lips. And by slightly I'm talking millimeters. But I'd take what I could get.

I lingered in my spa tub, allowing the warm water to relax me. First dates always make me tense. It's like opening a can and not knowing whether there's a diamond in the bottom or if a dozen springy fake snakes will explode out of the top.

Tony didn't impress me as the fake-snake kinda guy.

Post soak, I carefully applied my makeup, savoring every second of the anticipation building in the pit of my stomach. I wasn't looking forward to sitting through *The Magic Flute*, but imagining all the delicious ways the evening could end made the notion more palatable.

I was really pleased when I finished dressing. The only thing that would have made it perfect would be a pink oyster-face Ladies DateJust Rolex. Unfortunately, I didn't own one. Yet.

I was well on my way, though. Since I couldn't afford the actual watch, I'd begun collecting parts on eBay. To date, I had several links, the screw-down crown, an authentic box, and a pending bid on the watch face. At my current rate, I should have all the parts for my build-it-from-scratch Rolex by the time I'm thirty-five.

Grabbing a black pashmina from my closet, I took my keys and headed out to my car. It was a beautiful night but there was no way I would sacrifice my perfectly coiffed hair by putting the top down. I punched Tony's address into the onboard GPS, and after a second a map appeared and a cheerful male voice with a touch of a British accent began giving me instructions.

I exceeded the speed limit on I-95 north since I hadn't bothered actually to look at Tony's address; I didn't realize he lived in Hobe Sound, seventeen miles north. I had eighteen minutes to make the twenty-five-minute trip.

I made it too, hitting the Bridge Road off-ramp with six minutes to spare. Making a left on Federal Highway, I went a few miles, and then followed the signs to the Falls at Lost Lake. I wouldn't have pictured Tony as a golf-course-community kinda guy, but as I scrolled through the keypad at the gate, I quickly came to "Caprelli" and pressed the button.

"Yes?"

"It's Finley," I said, my heart pounding in my ears.

There was a beeping sound, and then the gate swung open like a horizontal mouth of an alligator.

The British voice told me to turn right at the stop sign, and then Tony's house was the third one down on the left.

I pulled into the driveway and parked next to a vintage red Porsche. I'd never seen it at the office, so I figured it had to be his "fun" car. I couldn't imagine being so flush with cash that I'd have a car for work and a car for recreation, but I'm sure I could get used to it.

I tucked my keys into my clutch as I walked past the garage and up a pathway to what was easily a five-thousand-square-foot house. Like all the other homes in the community, the stucco was painted a shade of beige—in this case peachy beige—and the trim was fresh and white.

I went up one tiled step, took a deep calming breath, and then stood in front of etched glass doors as I pressed the doorbell. I mentally reminded myself not to look overly excited. Be cool and collected.

I heard a playful chuckle just as the door swung open. I lowered my gaze maybe an inch and found myself looking into a pair of big chocolate brown eyes. The mini-Tony had to be the daughter, Isabella. She wore rolled-just-below-the-knee sweatpants that were turned down at the hips, and double tank tops. Her long dark hair was pulled up in a ponytail, and when she snarled at me, I saw that she had inherited her father's right cheek dimple as well. Attitude and a killer dimple—dangerous combination.

"I'm Finley. Your dad is expecting me."

I heard the giggle again. It wasn't from the daughter. Maybe she had a friend over.

Isabella rolled her eyes as the sound got closer. I looked past Isabella, expecting to find another child.

Wrong.

Very wrong.

A goddess of a woman dressed in a strapless red Prada gown came around the corner giggling into her champagne flute. Tony was right behind her, looking dapper and handsome in a tux. His eyes met mine. He scanned me up and down as all the humor drained out of his face.

I took in his uncomfortable expression, the woman dangling from his arm, and then replayed the invitation in my head:

"Are you free Saturday night?"

"What do you need?"

"You."

"E-excuse me?"

"I have tickets to The Magic Flute *tomorrow night."*

"Nothing like a Saturday night with Mozart."

"Is there any chance you're free tomorrow night. I know it's short notice, but—"

"Short notice is fine."

"Great. Can you be at my place at about six?"

"Absolutely."

"Thanks, Finley. See you tomorrow night."

Ohgod, ohgod, ohgod. He'd never actually asked me out. I wasn't his date. I was the freaking *babysitter.*

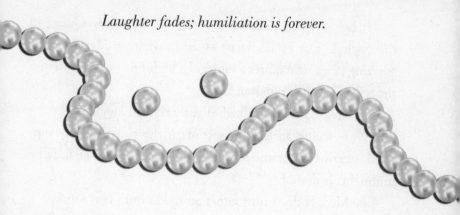

Laughter fades; humiliation is forever.

two

"Finley, meet Pepper. Pepper, Finley."

The statuesque woman put down the champagne and dangled an arm in my direction, making it impossible for me not to notice the gazillion-carat tennis bracelet on her wrist. Well, I had one thing on her: at least I didn't have a name better suited for a parakeet.

"My pleasure," I lied, shaking her hand. "Excuse my attire, I hurried here from a private cocktail party on the island." Kinda true, I'd had a glass of wine at my place. And I did live on the island.

The date stealer's artificially plumped lips lost a little of the curve in her superior smile.

"Have you seen *The Magic Flute* before?" I asked, fake sincerity dripping off each syllable.

"No." She tightened her grasp on Tony's arm. "I'm looking forward to it."

"It helps if you understand some German. The Queen of the Night's "Der Hölle Rache kocht in Meinem Herzen" is an amazing piece. It requires a range of a high F6—a true rarity on the scientific pitch notation."

I ignored Isabella's muffled, slightly choked laugh.

"We're seeing an English version at the Kravis," Tony supplied, steering the statue toward the door. "I should be back by midnight. Is that okay?"

I nodded. "I don't turn into a pumpkin until two a.m."

"Night, Izzy," Tony said as he placed a kiss on the top of his smiling daughter's head. "Behave."

"Always," she said, with teenage boredom. As soon as Tony and his arm candy left, Izzy glanced at me and grinned broadly. With one earbud dangling from her purple-encased iPhone, she slowly shook her head. "You like totally slammed her, and she didn't even know it. I'm going to have to try that on Lindsey Hetzler."

"I didn't slam her." *Much.* "I was just making polite conversation."

"Right," Izzy said, placing one hand on one budding hip.

"Who's Lindsey?"

"The queen bitch of the eighth grade."

"Are you supposed to use that kind of language?"

She shrugged. "Only when my dad can't hear me."

I tossed my clutch on a chair, noticing the decor for the first time. Midcentury modern. My guess was original Herman Miller. Unlike me, Tony didn't impress me as a knockoff kinda guy.

"Welcome to the 1950s," Izzy said on an expelled breath. "I hope you like chrome and molded plastic."

"Not so much," I admitted as I tossed my pashmina on my clutch.

"Me either. But my dad had a decorator do this. It's what happens when you tell some stranger you are all minimalist and junk."

"So what do you want to do?" I asked, spying a fifty-two-inch flat screen in the adjacent family room. Hopefully, my charge was a TV freak and I'd be able to use the computer I saw sitting on a bisymmetric glass-and-walnut table while she vegged out in front of the massive TV.

"He said you liked board games."

"He?"

"The friend of Dad's. The hot guy with the black hair and blue eyes. He works with you guys," she prompted. "Liam."

"When did you talk to Liam?"

"He set Dad up with that lanky chick. He's the one who suggested my dad get you to babysit. Not that I need a babysitter. My dad still treats me like I'm three instead of thirteen."

That bastard. "Tonight was orchestrated by Liam?"

Izzy smiled. "You look seriously pissed."

Pissed didn't begin to describe the fury boiling in the pit of my stomach.

"You can leave. We can tell my dad something like you had a major family thing or some other excuse."

"Oh no. We're going to play board games until we get freaking carpel tunnel syndrome from throwing the dice."

She shrugged. "Whatever."

Four hours later Izzy was kicking my butt at Scrabble. Again. The kid was like a thirteen-year-old dictionary. I thought

I'd finally gotten the best of her when I'd placed "camphors" on the board. What does she counter with? "Benzoxycamphors," for a flipping point total of 1,593. Apparently, it's some sort of chemical, but I had to Google it. I felt totally outclassed. Especially when we moved on to Trivial Pursuit, the Pop Culture Edition. She kicked my butt in that too, so quickly that I tossed in the pie-shaped pieces when she was beating me four to one.

"How are you at eBay?" I asked.

"But eBay isn't a board game."

"It's better than a board game," I insisted as I swiped the Scrabble tiles into their brown cotton bag and folded the Trivial Pursuit board. "It's a real competition. No benzoxycamphors bullsh . . . *stuff*. I'm a master, and I will dazzle you with the finer aspects of the Web site."

"I like shopping," she said, grabbing a cute Coach purse from a bar stool and pulling a matching wristlet from inside. From that, Izzy produced a credit card with her name imprinted on it. Somehow I knew she had a higher credit limit than I did and probably wasn't even close to maxing it out. Yeah, well, I had PayPal Buyer Credit.

I stood and shook my foot, which had fallen asleep during hours of sitting cross-legged on the floor. Silently, I added that to my list of reasons to find some way to make Liam's life miserable. No, not miserable. Unbearable. Painful. Excruciating.

"Have a log-in?"

She shook her head. "Nope. But I can set one up."

"Are you allowed to shop online?"

"I'm allowed to do anything but date," she whined.

"Tell me what you like."

Izzy's head dropped to one side, and she pinched her lips together. "There's a dance at school in a few weeks. Everyone says Lindsey Hetzler does a solid color theme, so I guess I'd like something totally not that."

"Betsey Johnson," I said with confidence. "Her new teen collection has an adorable pink bunny dress."

"What's that?" she asked, skeptical. "I don't want to look like a bunny."

"Come here." I quickly typed in the URL and showed Izzy the dress. "There's a pretty bow accent in the front, and it's short, which will show off your long legs."

"But it's strapless. My dad will have a coronary."

"So we get a chiffon sweater and you just leave it on until you get to the dance. He'll never know."

"Then let's buy it," she said, passing me her credit card.

"No, no, no. We look for it on eBay and save a ton of money."

"But I don't have to save money."

Jealousy washed over me. "But if you save on the dress and the sweater, you can buy the perfect shoes and a purse and still not spend as much as full retail. It's called shopping smart."

"More like shopping cheap. What if it's been worn?" she asked, her nose scrunched.

"Then you have it cleaned. What size are you?"

"A two, I think."

Now I was majorly jealous and feeling chubby in my size four. I satisfied myself with a mental reminder that she wasn't done growing yet. "Create a log-in, and let's get to work."

We found the dress and the sweater, and I showed her how

to place an initial bid, then clued her in on the finer points of eBaying. The dress was a "buy it now," but instead of the full price of four hundred twenty-eight, Izzy got it for three hundred eighty-nine. The sweater was more of a bargain. Gently worn and offered at half of the normal two hundred thirty-eight. Izzy would just have to watch the site in two days to make sure she wasn't outbid at the last second. "To be extra careful, do you have a laptop in addition to this desktop?"

"Yeah."

"Log in on both computers just in case one has a hiccup in the last minutes of the auction. Now for accessories."

"This is pretty cool," Izzy said. Her tone was now soaked in enthusiasm, and the snarl had morphed into a smile.

Freaking took long enough.

Once we'd theoretically saved her a bundle, we went looking for shoes and found a killer pair of kitten-heeled gladiator sandals with an adorable feather accent. Of course I practically commanded her to buy the matching hobo bag, insisting that it was necessary to stash the sweater she needed to fool Tony into thinking she was wearing a more modest dress. Unfortunately, neither was on eBay, so she had no choice but to buy them off BetseyJohnson.com, where she paid close to six hundred dollars for the accessories. To make up for the extravagance, I showed her my favorite funky online jewelry store, where she found a necklace and earrings to complete her look.

"That was seriously fun," Izzy said as she took pages out of the printer and clipped the images like paper dolls.

"And you're sure your father won't get pissed? I can't afford to lose my job."

"If he does, I'll play the mommy card."

I watched her, finding it hard to keep my jaw from dropping. The girl obviously had no respect for the dead.

"Get over yourself," she groaned, obviously reading the expression on my face. "It's hard to mourn someone you don't even remember. I was like eleven months old or something when she died. But everyone thinks I should have like issues or whatever."

As cold as it sounded, the girl's logic was flawless, and if anyone could understand that feeling, it was me. We left the computer area and sat on the hideously ugly—in my opinion—mustard yellow sofa with chrome armrests. I sat at one end, kicking off my expensive shoes and tucking my legs under me. Izzy did the same with her fuzzy slippers. She looked so comfy dressed in fuchsia Victoria's Secret Think Pink sweatpants and a pair of spaghetti-strap tanks. The bottom one was also fuchsia, while the top one was a pale pink. With her jet black hair, even darker brown-black eyes, and flawless olive complexion, she was stunning. Tony would have his hands full when she got older. No wonder he didn't want her to start dating.

"Do you have both your parents?"

I shrugged. "Not sure."

Izzy's Brooke Shields-like brows pulled together. "Huh?"

"My mother's alive. My birth father is a wild card." I'd just told an underage virtual stranger more than I shared with most of my adult friends. Great, when did a thirteen-year-old girl become my confidante?

"Did you lose touch? Lemme guess. He married someone else and like tossed you aside."

I shook my head. "Nope. As far as I know, he has no clue I exist."

"Wow. That's like beyond weird. Ever try to find him? You know, Google him or something?"

Again I shook my head. "Don't know if it's Mr. Finley or Mr. Anderson."

"Has to be Finley. Why else would your mother name you that?"

"Finley *Anderson* Tanner."

"Wow, that *is* weird. And it spells 'fat.'"

I rolled my eyes. "Thanks for pointing that out."

"It's better than Pepper," she said with unchecked disdain. "I mean, like what kind of parents name their kid after a spice?"

"How long has your dad been seeing her?"

"Counting tonight?"

I nodded.

"Twice."

"Think it'll get serious?"

"Only if her IQ goes up like a hundred points. I think my dad just needs to get laid."

"Izzy!"

"Oh, c'mon. Like you aren't thinking the same thing."

"Yeah, but I'm not his teenage kid."

"Haven't you ever gone out with a hot guy just for the sex?"

"I'm not having this conversation."

She laughed. "You're like all blushing and stuff. Which *so* means you have."

I glanced down at my acceptable Liz Claiborne watch. "It's almost midnight. Do you have a bedtime?"

Izzy groaned. "It's Saturday night."

"That doesn't mean you don't have to go to bed at a certain time." As evidenced by the third yawn she'd swallowed in the past three minutes. "Besides, how will it look to your dad if he comes home and you're still awake? He'll think I'm a failure."

"Whatever," she said, standing. "Wanna see my room?"

"Sure."

"It's like the only room without plastic."

"That's good," I said as I followed her up the plushly carpeted staircase. In complete juxtaposition to the living room, the artwork on the wall was French Impressionist, yet somehow it worked with the stark furnishings.

"Good God," I muttered, before I could check my reaction.

"Tell me about it," Izzy said on a groan. The room was Pepto-Bismol pink, dominated by a bed that was a replica of Cinderella's glass coach. The dressers and end tables were bright white, and my eyes immediately homed in on the framed photograph on the left nightstand. It was Tony and a stunning woman who looked a lot like a young Sophia Loren holding an infant.

"That's the shrine," Izzy said.

I moved closer. "Your mother was beautiful."

"I guess," she said, with a shrug of her shoulders. "At least it got scaled back when we moved here. In New York my grandparents made me a whole thing, complete with a rosary, a candle, and a crucifix made out of resin."

"I'm sure they meant well."

Izzy hopped into the bed-slash-coach, slipping beneath the pink fuzzy spread. "Yeah. They used to spend hours telling me all about her. Dad said I had to listen, or at least pretend to. Liam told me to nod every now and then, and when I'd had enough, I was supposed to tell them I had a thing and leave the room."

"Liam is big on *the thing*," I said, my irritation with him coming back full force. "How long have you known him?" I asked, hoping I sounded casual.

"You hot for him or my dad?"

Hope dashed. "Neither."

"That's like a total lie." She raked her hair with her fingers, each nail painted a different shade of neon polish. "Liam and Dad met when Dad taught classes at Quantico. Liam took the classes, and the two of them became friends. Liam would visit us in New York. I think they bonded over the whole wife thing."

"Liam's wife is alive." *And probably draped over him as we speak*.

"I know. But he was getting a divorce then, so he and my dad used to drink beer and pretend everything was okay."

"What'd you do, eavesdrop?"

"Totally. I was like eight or nine, and I thought Liam was hot. Even if he is old."

"Thirty-seven is hardly old."

"To you," she said as she grabbed the book next to her bed.

"Want me to read to you?"

Izzy rolled her eyes. "I've been reading since I was like four."

"Excuse me. I'm a tad out of practice at this whole babysitting thing."

"It shows."

"Anyone ever tell you you're a bit of a snot?"

She shrugged. "We all have to have a skill."

"On that note," I began, as I backed toward the door, "I'll leave you to read."

Her expression suddenly grew somber. "Will you come back?"

"I'll come up in a little while to check on you."

"Not tonight," she said with a tinge of a whine. "I mean come back again. Maybe the night of the dance, to help me with makeup and stuff?"

"Sure," I replied, totally taken in by the pleading look in her eyes.

I was almost out the door when she added, "I had a good time tonight, Finley."

I surprised myself with my own response. "Me, too."

As I descended to the first floor, I headed straight for the galley kitchen. Lots of stainless steel, and, judging by the lack of fingerprints, Tony had a damned good maid. I checked the time on the microwave: 12:17.

Tony had one of those one-cup-at-a-time coffeemakers that drew me in like a magnet. My caffeine level was dangerously low, and I needed a fix.

It took less than a minute for the mug to fill with strong, aromatic coffee. I was in my element. Well, except for the fact that I'd missed the end of an eBay auction I'd been nursing for eight days.

Coffee in hand, I went to the computer and silently prayed that even though I'd been inattentive, the Rolex watch face would be mine. My heart rate increased as I logged in with one hand while lifting the cup to my mouth. I still needed about seventeen more links and other assorted parts for my build-it-from-scratch Rolex project. Reaching my by-age-thirty-five goal was important to me. Even if I conned Vain Victor Dane, managing partner and all-around pain in my ass, into raising my salary, I still couldn't swing the thirteen thousand I'd need for the pink oyster-face watch.

An unpleasant image popped into my head. In the not-so-distant past, my cheating, former boyfriend Patrick had offered me the watch as a make-up gift. Like I'd ever forgive that sniveling weasel. Still, I was kicking myself for not taking the watch, then slamming the door in his face.

"Damn," I mumbled as I checked my account only to find that I'd been outbid on the watch face by a mere fifty cents. TimeBandit had bested me again. This wasn't the first time we'd gone head-to-head over a Rolex part, nor was it the first time he/she'd beaten me in the process.

I spent a few minutes searching new listings, stopping only to make another cup of coffee and to check the time: 1:05 a.m. The new vision in my head soured my already pissy mood. It didn't take two-plus hours to get back from the Kravis, so safe money said Tony was getting lucky.

I barely remembered the last time I'd had sex. I'd had a couple of near misses with Liam, but something always seemed to prevent us from consummating our complicated, frustrating, nonsensical relationship. Not that we had an actual relationship. No, it was more like mutual lust. Which was fine with me. Liam was not The Guy. In my twenty-nine years I'd finally learned that you can't fix a guy's faults by loving him. Hell, you can't fix a guy period. Nor, as it turns out, can you trust them. Two years wasted on Patrick proved that much. The next time I met a guy, I was running a full background check.

The sound of the door opening gave me a jolt. Enough of one that I sloshed coffee down the front of my brand-new Azria dress. It made the jersey fabric cling to my body, outlining my boobs. Great, just great.

Grabbing my pashmina, I quickly covered myself and used the edge of the fabric to dab up the few drops of coffee on the computer desk.

"Hi," Tony said, his bow tie untied, top button undone, and hair mussed. He might as well be wearing a sign that said JUST GOT LAID. "Sorry I'm so late."

"Not a problem."

"How did it go?" he asked as his cologne tickled my senses.

"Great." *As you'll find out when you get the Visa bill.* "Izzy is an amazing kid."

I got the dimple smile. Dimple smile plus mussed hair was a powerful combo. Right now it made me feel like a fool. I slipped on my shoes before I did something stupid like jump into his arms and offer to be his second conquest of the night.

"Sorry I was so late."

"Really, it was no problem," I lied, grabbing my clutch.

Tony reached in the front pocket of his pants and pulled out a small collection of bills. "Is ten an hour enough?"

"Enough for what?"

"Your time."

Lord knew I needed the money but not as much as I needed my dignity. Besides, if I made this a freebie, he owed me. It's always good to have a man in your debt. "Don't be silly. I'm not taking your money."

"I'm not comfortable taking advantage of you. Especially not when I inconvenienced you on such short notice."

"No inconvenience," I insisted. "Happy to help." I was impressed that I'd made that sound so sincere. There was an awkward silence before I added, "I'd better be on my way. I have a brunch tomorrow."

"You have quite the social schedule," he remarked as I moved to pass him in the hallway leading to the door.

Almost reflexively he pulled my pashmina up on my shoulder. The feel of his hand brushing my skin was enough to cause a jolt through my whole system. It was definitely time to make a speedy exit. "I'll see you on Monday."

"Thanks, Finley."

"You're welcome."

My shoulder still tingled as I slipped behind the wheel of my car. I toyed with the idea of stopping off at the Circle K for another cup of coffee, but my desire to get home won out. A decision I regretted when I turned into my drive and saw the battered Mustang parked in front of my cottage.

Liam sat perched on the step with a bottle of beer in his right hand. A surge of renewed irritation had me fantasizing about running over his feet, but I knew better.

After parking, I stepped from the car and made sure my face conveyed my feelings about babysitting and board games.

"Nice dress," he commented, then rose to his full height of six-three while his eyes ran up and down my body like a caress.

"Thanks. You can leave now."

He grinned, the sparkle of amusement visible in the slice of illumination from my porch light. "Not very hospitable of you."

"It's late. I'm tired, and you're annoying."

"And you suck at Scrabble."

How did he know these things?

"Izzy sent me a text," he said, as if reading my thoughts.

That explained why her cell phone was never out of arm's reach.

"Yes, I do," I agreed. I carefully sidestepped him as I dug out my house keys.

"So how was babysitting? Hope Tony paid you enough to cover the cost of that new getup."

Getup? A two-thousand-dollar head-to-toe makeover was not a *getup*. And how did he know it was new? I shook my head slightly, clearing away the thought. "I enjoyed myself." As I said the words I realized I'd meant them. But that still didn't get me past my anger over Liam turning me into a modern-day Mary Poppins. "Thanks for the referral." I'd make him pay later. Right now I just wanted to get inside. "Why are you here?"

"Just making sure you got home safely."

"I'm safe, so your job here is done. Don't you have a *thing* you can go to?"

"Yeah. I thought I'd come in for a drink."

"Well, you thought wrong."

"Anyone ever tell you you're sexy as hell when you're angry?"

"Not lately. Go home, Liam."

He reached out and gently closed his hand around my arm. I had no choice but to tilt my head back so our eyes locked. "Are you sure?" he asked, his voice deep, sensual, and way too inviting.

Hesitation was my downfall. Liam noticed it, so there was no point in pretending that, in spite of my better judgment, I was immune to his charms. "One drink," I said, more for my own benefit.

"That's all I'm asking for."

We went inside, and even though the contractor had arranged the space to give the illusion of grandeur, Liam's presence made it seem small and close.

"Beer, or are you going to make some girly drink?" he asked, offering a beer in my direction.

"Beer is fine," I said as I placed my purse and pashmina on the countertop.

Liam had been in my house for less than a minute and already the temperature seemed to be soaring. Maybe if I put some physical distance between us . . . ?

As I started to move away, he slid his hand around my waist and kept me close. Taking the bottle from me, he placed it next to his and took a half step forward. I should have put a stop to things right then and there but that was easier said than done.

My senses were overwhelmed. I felt the heat emanating from his body. Smelled the familiar scent of his cologne. Looked up into those hooded blue eyes. Everything came together, making my knees threaten to buckle under me.

When I felt his fingers splay at the small of my back, an urgent shiver danced along my spine. My stomach filled with warmth until it knotted with need.

Liam lifted his free hand and cupped my cheek. His palm was slightly callused, amplifying the sensation. I was drowning in a pool of desire. What few brain cells were still working insisted I put an end to this, but they were easily shouted down by the pure sensuality I read in his eyes.

What would it hurt? My brain reasoned. We were two healthy, consenting adults. Hooking up was perfectly normal.

His hand slipped lower, gently moving my hair away so his hand rested against my neck.

"Your pulse is racing," he said, his voice deeper and sexy as hell.

"That tends to happen when a man is about to kiss me."

He cocked his head to one side. "Ask me."

"Ask you what?"

"To kiss you."

"I'm standing here, aren't I?"

"Not the same thing." His fingers began making maddening circles as just the tips slipped beneath my dress, toying with the hollow just above my collarbone.

My whole body tensed with anticipation. "Kiss me."

There's a kiss, and then there's a *kiss*. Liam's lips brushed mine as he pulled me hard against him. I felt the hardness of thighs, his rippled muscles, and the broadness of his chest. Like a person about to fall off a ten-story building, I reached up and looped my arms around his neck.

As if acting of their own volition, my fingers couldn't resist raking through his thick, black hair. Liam deepened the kiss, urging my lips apart and teasing them with his tongue. I was a pliant and willing participant. At that moment I wanted nothing more than to feel him. Skin against skin.

Lost in the magic of his mouth on mine, I slid my hands over his shoulders and began working on the top button of his shirt. My hands were shaking, making it difficult to complete the rudimentary task. Finally, I managed to get it done and wasted no time slipping my fingers inside to feel the soft mat of hair. I could feel his heart pounding against his chest, and the knowledge that he was as turned on as I was made me feel powerful. And bold.

I quickly undid the other buttons and ran my hands all over his torso and back. Liam groaned against my lips as his fingers found my zipper.

Achingly slowly, he pulled the tab. I felt cool air against my overheated skin. My dress slid to the floor.

Liam lifted his mouth from mine and began trailing hot kisses over my neck and down to where lace met skin. He slipped a finger beneath my bra strap, and I saw flashes of light swaying on the wall.

It took my sex-starved brain a few seconds to realize I wasn't seeing flashes of ecstasy but rather the reflection of a flashlight's beam from the beach.

Leaping back, I snagged my heel in my dress and nearly tumbled to the ground. Liam steadied me, and his gaze lingered on my nearly naked breasts before glancing over my shoulder.

"There's someone out there," I said as I grabbed the fabric from around my ankles and did my best to cover myself. Panic quickly drained the passion from my system.

Liam moved over to the glass door and slid it open. I could hear teenage voices and lots of hoots and laughter. Oh God! It had to be the kid from two doors down. He was sixteen or seventeen, with a trust fund and apparently a thing for peeping in my window.

Liam yelled at him and his friends, and as I tried to rezip my dress, the beam of the flashlight moved off.

By the time he turned back to me, I was pseudo-dressed and, judging from the heat I felt on my face, blushing like a schoolgirl.

Our eyes met briefly. Liam said, "Guess the moment passed, huh?"

I cleared my throat. "Divine intervention," I mumbled. I raked my hair back. "It's really late."

He came a few steps closer. "Are you sure?" he asked.

Of course I wasn't sure. "I'm . . ."

"Forget it," he said, with an even tone that gave me no clue what he was actually thinking.

He took a long drink of beer and walked toward the Mustang; unlike me, he didn't look back.

Some mothers serve as a wonderful example;
my mother serves as a terrible warning.

three

"How humiliating was that?" Becky asked over the rim of the flute filled to the brim with mimosa.

Liv and Jane offered their condolences as well. Though all three had a sparkle of amusement in their respective eyes.

So much for sisterhood.

It was our welcome-summer splurge, brunch at the Breakers for a mere ninety dollars a head. Only thanks to Liv, we didn't have to pay full price.

Sunday brunch at the Breakers was a Palm Beach institution. There were a dozen serving stations offering everything from omelets to bazillion-calorie desserts. Waiters and waitresses wore crisp, white coats as they attentively topped off drinks and cleared plates when guests went in search of their next course.

"Was the kid tolerable?" Liv asked.

I nodded. "Actually, she's really smart and reminds me of . . . well . . . me."

"Finley Junior," Jane joked. "That I'd love to see."

I offered her a snarky smile. "Well, the next time Tony needs a babysitter, I'll give him your number."

"Pass, thanks. After the debacle with Paolo, I'm going slowly when it comes to men, marriage, and children."

"I'm starting to think that's the way to go," I said as I clinked glasses with Jane.

"What about Liam?" Liv asked as a waiter rushed over to refill her glass.

"He's too complicated."

Jane's brows arched. "You're writing him off?"

"He set me up to babysit, then came to my house to gloat," I continued, explaining how he'd manipulated my night of board games and teenage bonding. I left out the we-almost-had-sex part.

"When he came to your place, did you invite him in?"

"For a few minutes. Then I sent him on his way."

Jane ran one finger around the rim of her flute. "So he's back in the dating pool?"

I had to put up a decent front. I didn't want them to know how close I'd come to being a friend with benefits. Only Liam and I weren't actually friends. We were . . . Hell, I didn't know what we were. Safer just to pretend it never happened. "Yep. I hope he drowns in it."

"Seriously?" Becky asked, her eyes narrowed.

I raised one hand. "Swear to God. He can be someone else's problem."

"You two have chemistry," Liv injected.

"No, we have lust and . . . *whatever*. And a dose of manipulation on his part. Besides, I'm tired of his mixed signals. One minute he's screwing with my mind, and the next minute he wants into my panties. I don't want to have to work that hard."

"Your loss," Jane said.

"My sanity," I corrected. "Liam is too complicated. There's the *things*. Ashley, the not-so-ex-wife. The fact that he seems to know what's about to happen to me but never bothers to warn me. And let's not forget that he knew about Patrick before I did and kept his gorgeous mouth closed."

"Gorgeous mouth?" Becky repeated.

"Don't read anything into that. I can be frustrated with him and still admire his physical attributes at the same time. Can we change the subject now?"

My three friends let it drop. Becky was chasing a bite of prime rib around her plate. "Your mom comes back today, right?"

I nodded. "I'm picking up three orchids on my way home."

Liv laughed. "I swear, you're like a botanical Lizzy Borden."

Didn't I know it. As did my mother. She insisted on leaving me in charge of her plants even though I have the blackest thumb in the world. So I'd developed a routine—I took photos on day one, then after the plants committed flora-cide, I took the pictures to Ricardo at the local nursery and he'd give me exact replicas. I'm pretty sure my mother knew exactly what was going on, yet she still insisted I play plant-sitter, even though the concierge at her building would have gladly taken care of the penthouse vegetation. And he probably wouldn't get freaked out by the headless statues my mother collected.

"Why was she gone so long?" Becky asked.

"My guess is she had a little paint and bodywork done. Atlanta has some world-renowned plastic surgeons, and she was all freaked out over looking her best at Lisa's wedding."

"Geez," Becky groaned. "If your mother has any more face-lifts, her ass will be a hat."

That lightened the mood, and we spent the rest of our brunch overindulging ourselves on gourmet food and drink.

I was reluctant to end my time with my friends, but it was time to get back to the real world. For me that meant replacing plants, then settling in and studying for the Criminal Procedure final I had to pass on Tuesday night. It was the last class required for me to meet the strict conditions Tony had dictated when he'd yanked me from the relative comfort of trusts and estates.

Well, that was almost true. I'd still be doing trusts and estates, only now I got to add criminal work to my list of responsibilities. And there is nothing I loathe more than responsibility.

It took me a while to do the plant switch, then I drove back to my place on Chilian Drive. I recognized Harold the convict's beat-up pickup truck and Sam's shiny black BMW convertible parked in the horseshoe-shaped driveway. Something told me I should have answered one of the fifteen text messages Sam had been sending since this morning. Sam plus Harold meant only one thing—more construction. Which meant only another thing—more debt.

Shit.

I'd definitely shot my discretionary income on my babysitting outfit.

As soon as I stepped from my car, I heard the telltale sound of an electric drill. I walked through my house—actually, my shrine. Thanks to Sam's professional decorating skills, the cottage was a haven.

Every time I opened the door, I swear I heard the sound of a choir singing the Hallelujah chorus. My breath stilled as I marveled at the wide entry hall with its pale, coral-colored tiled floor and walls. A narrow, whitewashed table against the right-hand wall held a spray of sea grasses in a clear glass vase, reflected in an enormous mirror. Beyond the hallway was a great room with a wall of windows overlooking the ocean. I could stand at the front door and see the beach. Sam had given me pale teal walls to complement the floors in the same peachy-coral tile as the entry hall. The big, squishy, invite-all-my-friends-over furniture was covered in casual white slipcovers and a teal-and-deep-coral area rug felt soft under bare feet. Bless his heart, Sam had even tossed deep teal throw pillows covered with branch coral designs all over the sofas. Sam was all in the details. So frigging cool.

Only now my view was partially obstructed by some PVC project off to the left of the lap pool. Screw with my view? I didn't think so. I pulled off my shoes as I passed the kitchen. The white cabinets housed my entire Calphalon collection. In the stainless-steel appliances—unlike Tony's, mine had a few fingerprints and smudges. In the black granite of the center island, you could see light reflected everywhere. Sleek and warm. Perfect for sipping a glass of wine with the girls while sitting on the teal-and-white–patterned fabric bar stools.

"You're nuts!" I yelled as I yanked open the sliding glass

door, my voice raised half from irritation and half just to be heard over the drill or whatever power tool Harold had buzzing. "What are you doing?"

Sam came toward me. He looked kinda like a young, thin Nathan Lane. Maybe it was the blatant way he wore his sexuality, or maybe it was his dark hair—now rumpled by the sea breeze—and the excitement evident in his eyes. At that moment I didn't really care. My attention was fixed on the neat line of my cement patio that had been chiseled open like some surgical scar. "What are you doing?"

Sam Carter placed one hand on a hip and offered me an annoyed glance. "You'd know if you'd have answered at least one of my texts. I had a vision."

Harold's drill went silent, and he looked in my direction, nodding a brief hello. "Miss Finley."

"You envisioned tearing up my patio and playing Erector set in my backyard?"

Sam shook his head. "It isn't an Erector set, it's a cabana. Or at least it will be when we finish."

"It blocks the view."

"One foot of the view," he corrected. "Trust me. By this evening you'll be lounging out here like a princess."

"A princess eaten alive by insects."

"I thought of that. Naturally."

"Naturally," I muttered.

Sam picked up the smallest of the eight boxes piled off to one side of the patio. "This little gizmo will keep the bugs away."

It looked like a watering can.

"I'm supposed to drown them?"

"No," he replied impatiently. "You light this and smoke the area around the cabana. It'll keep the bugs at bay for hours."

Okay, that was cool, but it still didn't appease my irritation at having him build the rectangular thing. "Why did you dig up the cement?"

"We're going to add electricity to the cabana. That way you'll have a fan and lights in case you want to sit out here and study or whatever."

I walked over and looked at the skeletal structure. I'm not the kind of person who can envision a finished project, so I said, "Tell me about this thing."

Sam instantly became animated. "Once Harold has all the braces cemented into place," he continued as he took my hand and led me over to the boxes, "then we drape this ecru sailcloth around the poles. And once that's done, we hang the fan and the lights, and add the furniture."

Sam pointed to the pictures on the sides of three cartons. "There'll be a chaise, two accent chairs, and molded tables."

"Plastic tables?"

He rolled his eyes. "Anything else would mildew and/or stain the cement in a matter of a month. Knowing you, I went with practical."

"All done!" Harold called as he placed his cordless drill in his toolbox.

Even from a distance I could make out the prison tattoos on his left hand. Just below the knuckle on his left hand each finger had a crude letter and with his fingers together, they spelled out FUCK. Not his classiest moment.

I needed a few minutes to myself to take in this latest project, so I excused myself and walked inside to my bedroom, the pièce de résistance of my home. The only color in the room was the teal on the walls. Everything else was white, giving it the posh look of the finest hotel rooms in the world.

I stepped into my spacious walk-in closet—a complete renovation and replacement, given the mummified remains I had discovered in the original closet during my first walk-through—and considered my next ensemble. After looking at the offerings, I grabbed a bathing suit and sarong, then changed and leisurely removed my makeup. On my way back outside, I picked up my Criminal Procedure study guide. I loathed the idea of wasting the rest of my Sunday studying for my test, but I was starting to warm up to the idea of a cabana. Most of my neighbors had cabanas. Well, that wasn't *exactly* true. What they had was pool houses, but hey, a cabana worked.

As I stepped back out onto the lanai, most of my reservations were behind me. I'd tossed my study guide on the counter, and with my sunglasses dangling from my mouth, I was twisting my hair up. Harold started pouring concrete into the holes while Sam steadied the framing. Wires snaked out of the ground near the edge of the concrete. Sam paid me no attention as I went past him on my way to one of two teak lounge chairs at the water's edge. The creepy sensation of Harold's eyes on me quickened my step. Nothing like having an ex-con staring at your butt.

The June sun was bright and beat down on me relentlessly, forcing me to take frequent dips in the warm ocean to escape the heat. While I didn't relish the idea of walking past Harold on my way back up to the house, it wasn't long before I was desperate for a bottle of water. Luckily for me, when I stood, I realized he was no longer pouring concrete.

The poles were now braced with two-by-fours, and Sam was busy unpacking and assembling the furniture. My lanai was a mess of paper, plastic, and other stuff that I had to step over to get to the sliding door.

"Want some water?" I asked.

"Just got some."

"Make yourself at home," I teased. "What happened to Harold?"

"He went out for lunch."

I peered inside the house. "Lunch at three thirty?"

"The cement has to harden before I can drape the fabric."

"I thought it was quick set."

"It is, but I want to give it an extra half hour or so."

I swallowed a groan as I went in and grabbed my drink. I was still stuffed from brunch.

Sam stepped inside and said, "I'm going back to the store to replace the fan. Rattan will be more appropriate, and I want to get some potted plants as well."

This time I groaned aloud. "Plants?"

"Native plants. Minimum care and feeding."

"Maximum replacement."

He shook his head. "I'll pick up one of those automatic watering bulbs. You'll do fine."

"I doubt that," I mumbled.

"I heard that."

The house was quiet, at least for the moment, so reluctantly I decided to retrieve my book so I could continue my studying in air-conditioned comfort. No sooner had I grabbed the study guide than I heard car tires on the crushed-shell driveway. Not enough time for Sam to get to the store, shop, and return, so it had to be Harold. So much for peace and quiet. I tied my sarong up around my neck and was on the way to my bedroom when the chime from the doorbell startled me.

Peering through the narrow window on the side of the door, my heart stopped. A polished Bentley was parked on the grass. I felt the muscles in my shoulder knot as I retraced my steps and reached for the knob. Of course she had to pick today. My mind swirled as I indexed the things I would have done had I known she'd actually show up. Oh well, nothing I could do now.

Plastering a pleasant smile on my face, I opened the door wide. Standing regally on my front porch was Cassidy Presley Tanner Browning Rossi. My mother.

"Hi, Mom," I greeted, adding the customary country club air kiss on either side of her face. Well, not her face. She was wearing a scarf tied forward and giant dark glasses, so the only thing I could see was the tip of her nose and her newly—and overly—plumped lips.

"Finley," she returned, her mouth moving a lot like guppy lips. Not that guppies have lips, but the analogy was working for me.

"Welcome to my home," I said enthusiastically. My arm swung in a wide arc. "Please, come in."

As usual, my mother thumbed her nose at the hot afternoon weather by wearing a tailored green suit with a pale mint silk blouse beneath. I often wondered if she was the last woman in Palm Beach County to still wear panty hose. Slowly, she removed her scarf and glasses. Faded bruises around her hairline told me she'd had yet another thread lift, along with some collagen and Botox. Her vanity was unwarranted, given the fact that she didn't even look her true age. Then again, very few people knew her true age. She'd lied about it so often, and for so long, it was possible that even she didn't know she was about to hit fifty. Lisa's wedding created a problem; she couldn't shave a decade off her age with her daughters around. Quite the conundrum. She had been twenty-two when I was born and twenty-five when Lisa came along, so she'd have no choice but to own up to her fifty years.

She glanced around the great room, but thanks to the Botox, I couldn't gauge her reaction.

"When do you plan on decorating?"

Direct hit. No matter how old I got, her zingers still stung. "It is decorated, Mom."

"Oh."

"You hate it," I said, my spirits sinking.

"I just never would have considered decor best suited to an outdoor eatery. But then again, it makes sense. You and your friends are partial to those waterfront bars."

"Would you like something to drink?" *Arsenic, perhaps?*

"I'd like to see the rest of the cottage first."

"Follow me," I said, with a mental picture of holding a gun to my head and slowly pulling the trigger. In under thirty seconds my mother had me committing virtual suicide.

I got a lot of "uh-huh"s as we went from room to room, then what I hoped was the final noncompliment when we reached my bedroom.

"I had no idea you'd be napping in the middle of the day," she said, her puffy lips managing a scowl as she looked at my unmade bed.

"I had a late night," I explained. I detoured her away from the bathroom, where I'd left my brunch outfit crumpled on the floor. I wasn't usually such a slob, but with Harold here, the quick change was a must.

"Yes, I know," she said.

"You know what?" I asked as I led the way back toward the kitchen.

"About your second job."

It took me a minute to follow the winding path that was her logic. "I don't have a second job."

We returned to the great room. I sat on the sofa and offered her the chair across from me. She opted to stand.

"But Mr. Caprelli said you were a babysitter."

"Hang on. You spoke to my boss?"

"Of course, I needed Mr. Caprelli's address for the invitation."

"Are you having a party or something?" First I was hearing about it.

She shook her head as if I'd just suggested she vacation in Iraq. "I called him to ask if he would serve as your escort."

The hair on my arms stood up, and my skin tingled with dread. "My escort for what?"

"Well," she began as she lifted her scarf off her shoulders and began to retie it, "since you so abruptly ended your relations with Patrick, and even though I have a million things to attend to, I had to find you a suitable escort for the wedding."

Blood rushed to my head rendering me temporarily deaf. "So you called Tony?"

"He's successful. He's a lovely man. He comes from a very influential family in New York. Did you know his father owns one of the largest investment firms and is considered a financial genius? His mother is a member of the Daughters of the American Revolution. He's perfect as an escort. He'll photograph quite nicely, too."

"Please tell me you're kidding."

"I'm far from being facetious. The photographs are Lisa's keepsake memories that—"

My door opened, and Liam appeared. Normally, I would have been furious about him just bursting into my home, but I was stuck on planet Cassidy.

"You should not have done that," I explained, desperately trying not to grit my teeth or allow steam to come rushing out of my ears. I gave a sideways glance to Liam, who was wearing a grease-stained T-shirt and ragged jeans. His hair was mussed. "I already have an escort to the wedding."

My mother's spine straightened. "And that would be whom?"

"Liam," I said, pointing to the unkempt man near the doorway.

I thought for a moment that my announcement had the Botox draining from my mother's forehead. Botox or not, I knew there was a frown in there somewhere, but she rammed her sunglasses on her face and marched her heeled feet to the door. Sidestepping Liam, she waltzed out without another word.

I, on the other hand, was grinning, bordering on giddy. That moment ended when I remembered Liam's entrance. Standing, I asked, "Are the words 'my house' somehow confusing to you?"

"No, Ellen sent me. She's been calling you for the last two hours, and when you didn't answer your landline or your cell, she called and asked me to come check on you."

"It's Sunday."

"For me, too," he said. "I was working on my car."

"I hope you were working on pushing it off a bridge."

He cocked his head to one side. "Call your boss so I can get back to what I was doing."

As he turned to leave, I said, "Don't ever walk in my house without an invitation again."

"Speaking of invitations, I accept."

"Accept what?"

"I'll escort you to your sister's wedding."

I was still staring at the closed door five minutes after he left.

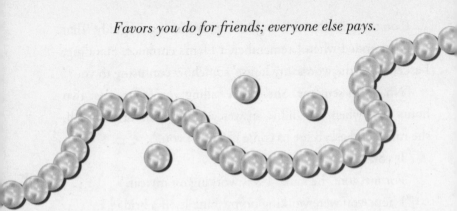

Favors you do for friends; everyone else pays.

four

I sat down and listened to the half-dozen voice mails Ellen had left on my machine. With each one, her voice sounded more irritated than concerned. "So why send Liam?" I muttered as I copied her home number onto the Lilly Pulitzer notepad I kept near the phone, along with a matching pen, of course.

Curious, I wanted to check my set-on-vibrate cell phone. So I grabbed my purse—a major score if I did say so myself. Coach. White leather with cute little tassels. Well, that wasn't exactly true. Only three of the original four tassels were still in place, which is why I paid less than thirty dollars for it in an eBay auction. My mother had cut me off from Jonathan's trust fund more than a year ago, her version of teaching me to fend for myself and be more responsible.

Jonathan and my mom married when I was still a toddler. He'd adopted me when I was three and always treated me as if I was as good as, if not better than, my sister. I'd discovered my illegitimacy and adoption when I was thirteen, after sneaking into my mother's lingerie drawer. My goal had been to check out the La Perla. Instead, I got the whole scoop on attempts to notify Misters Finley and Anderson. Eventually, my mother explained the whole story, but it was Jonathan who'd sat next to me, gently stroking my hair and my self-esteem.

At any rate, he'd left Lisa and me individual trusts but had given my mother the power to control any withdrawals. Lisa had full access while I was cut off, sending me into the nether world of discount designers and factory damage.

I was a master at it now. Not even Becky had clued in to the fact that my designer stuff was secondhand at best, gently used at worst. And I'd like to keep it that way. A girl's gotta have her secrets.

Just thinking about secrets, my mind drifts to Liam. Forget that I know virtually nothing about him. The one thing I do know is that he keeps everything close to the vest. Thankfully not literally. A guy in a vest does nothing for me. The mere thought of secrets instantly had Liam's face taunting my thought processes.

I was still fuming mad about the babysitting thing, and even angrier at myself for allowing things to go as far as they had. He thought nothing of bursting into my home without so much as knocking. For all he knew someone could be in here holding me hostage at gunpoint. And therein lay the rub. He was completely wrong for me, and yet in the past, he'd risked his personal safety for me. Did he have to be chivalrous and irritating at the same time?

I took in a deep breath, then let it out slowly as I slid the bar on my iPhone and instantly discovered I had seventeen more messages from Ellen and one from Becky. I deleted them without listening, sure they were just repeats of the "call me immediately" mantras she'd left on my landline. Dane-Lieberman owned me five days a week, and Sunday wasn't one of them.

"Lieberman."

"Ellen, this is Finley returning your—"

"So Liam finally found you."

"It's Sunday. I was at the beach, not in the witness protection plan."

"Excuse me?"

I winced. Probably not the smartest move to be a wiseass to one of my bosses. "Sorry, sunstroke," I muttered. "What do you need?"

"I've scheduled an eight o'clock meeting with Miss Egghardt. You handled the estate. The appointment is with Lenora Egghardt regarding her uncle's estate and some sort of money order she received.

"From the tenants Lenora wasn't sure existed?"

"Probably. And she now insists she has knowledge of some real property currently in the possession of those elusive tenants and thinks it is possible that they are distant cousins. Looks like you're going to have to reopen the estate, and I just want to make sure you exercised due diligence in your attempts to deal with the heirs. I want you at that meeting."

Luckily, she couldn't see me roll my eyes. "I'll be there."

"Be there at seven thirty. I want you to bring me up to speed on this before I review any real estate documents. I'll need to be sure we didn't close the estate *again,* without dotting all the 'i's and crossing all the 't's."

"I think you'll find everything was in order. I followed the law. Notices were filed in the *Palm Beach Post,*" I said, feeling a little irritated by the implication that I'd failed to do my job. While I may not be the most enthusiastic employee, I was good at what I did, especially when it came to trusts and estates. "How did this end up on your desk? Usually Vain—er, Mr. Dane handles this sort of thing."

"I'm assuming it's because of the potential contractual issues. I did meet with Mr. Egghardt once. It doesn't matter. Just be here at seven thirty. My office."

"My pleasure." I felt my nose growing. There was nothing pleasurable about being at work at seven thirty in the morning.

I speed-dialed Becky. She answered on the third ring. "Your boss just became a pain in my butt."

"Ellen? Makes sense. She seemed kinda desperate to find you. And in spite of what you think, she likes you. Thinks you have potential."

"No, she likes *you* and thinks *you* have potential. You're the teacher's pet," I teased. I then recapped everything from coming home, to the beach, to the new construction, then shared that part about Liam barging in through the door while my mother was here and finished up with the end of my phone call with Lieberman. "Can you believe that?"

"I don't know. Sounds very knight-on-white-horse-ish to me. He really just burst in?"

"I was talking about Ellen's meeting time, but yes, he did burst right in. And somehow the next thing I knew, I was telling my mother I was bringing Liam to Atlanta as my date for Lisa's wedding."

"Did she stroke out right there on the floor?"

"Practically," I said, feeling the tension drain from my shoulders. After all, the expression on her face was classic. "It did shut her up about the wedding escort. So now, when I come solo, she'll be grateful. Well played, I thought."

"Unless Tony and Liam both show up. She actually called Tony?"

"Don't remind me. I have to see him tomorrow. Not sure how I'm going to explain my mother to him."

"Mention your mother is desperate to marry you off. Most guys hear the 'm' word and run screaming from the room."

"Why didn't Ellen send you? Why send Liam?"

"Well, she did call me, but I told the truth. I had no idea where you were. I even skipped the whole brunch thing. I'm still not sure letting anyone at the firm know we're tight is in my best interests."

"I know, but that still doesn't solve my Liam conundrum."

"Ellen was probably annoyed and figured sending a Liam-O-Gram was a speedy solution."

Liam is a lot of things, but a solution isn't one of them.

◆

After a fitful night, I got up early and drank my pot of coffee while sitting on the draped chaise next to the pool. Sam was right: the cabana was perfect. The warm breeze coming off the ocean made the bug smoker unnecessary, and I watched the giant red ball of the sun rise, casting a bright golden blanket on the water. I wasn't thrilled when I had to abandon my comfy cocoon to get dressed for work.

I selected a funky Helen Berman dress I'd picked up at the thrift store for Bethesda-by-the-Sea. One of the many pluses of living in Palm Beach proper was easy access to a thrift store where I could find everything from vintage Versace to BCBG shoes, all barely to gently worn by well-heeled islanders. Twice a year, they even had blowout sales. I already had the dates circled in red on my calendar.

Because I'm only five-four, I tend to avoid empire waists with bow accents, but this dress, with its black bodice and white skirt, had been a great bargain and way too cute to pass up. Plus, it gave me an excuse to wear my black Jimmy Choo patent-leather cuff sandals with the very, *very* high heels. I'd gotten them at half price because of an imperfection in the stitching on the inside right cuff, but unless someone got down on her hands and knees for inspection, my secret was safe.

The drive to Dane-Lieberman was much quicker at o'-dark-thirty, leaving me time to swing through the Starbucks for a venti frappe. Even though I'd already downed a pot of coffee, my caffeine levels were still way too low for maximum concentration.

I parked my shiny Mercedes next to Ellen's utilitarian Volvo, grabbed my purse, and fished for the office keys as I walked toward the etched-glass doors with the names of the partners accented in gold.

Maudlin Margaret's desk was deserted, and I couldn't resist leaving a faux message on her pink pad. It read:

"Miss Egghardt arriving at eight, please send her up as soon as possible."

I wrote the date and time just to jerk her chain, then took the elevators to the second floor. It was just shy of my meeting time, so I turned on my computer and my personal coffee-maker, shoved my purse into the bottom drawer of my desk, then spun in my seat to place my briefcase—which held my study guide for tomorrow night's test—inside one of three vertical filing cabinets adorning my office.

I was still happy with my new digs. And even happier that I'd gotten them by solving not one but two murders. Well, solving may be a bit of a stretch, but I had been an integral part of unearthing the culprits, even if I did have some marginal help from Liam. Okay, so maybe marginal was a bit of a stretch, but it didn't matter. Vain Dane had given me the private office with a view of City Place to lure me back to working at the firm. He'd fired me twice in six months, and I wasn't about to return without some major perks.

With the Egghardt file and ever-ready pad and pen in hand, I took the elevator to the fourth-floor executive suite. Ellen's office was to the left of the elevator, off the circular lobby. I walked with conviction and the knowledge that five-and-a-half-inch heels were not the best walking shoes ever invented. But as my grandmother often said, "You have to suffer to be lovely."

I had just passed the conference room when Ellen called my name. Pivoting, I found her seated at the head of the long table, several boundary maps rolled out in front of her, the corners anchored by staplers.

She checked her watch. "Very good."

Very early. "Good morning," I said, refusing to allow her sarcastic tone to get under my skin. I placed my coffee and pad on the table at the spot to her left.

"Are those your notes and the estate file?" she asked as she glanced up from the map.

No, it's my grocery list. "Yes, I knew you wanted to review it before Lenora gets here. Oh, and I hear congratulations are in order."

Ellen peered up through her mascara-free lashes. "Thanks."

Thanks? You'd think she'd be a tad more excited. It wasn't like a daily thing to be named one of Florida's "Top 100 Lawyers" in the Sunday paper.

Dismissing the topic as if my comments were unimportant, Ellen read most of the pages in my file while I was left with nothing to do. Bored after seven minutes, I went to the coffeepot and refilled both our mugs. It wasn't until I placed one next to Ellen that I noticed the faint smell of sweet pea, freesia, and hyacinth, and I realized she was wearing Acqua Di Gio perfume by Armani. The designer fragrance was at odds with her brown-and-green shapeless dress and Jesus sandals. The perfume was soft and feminine, when everything else about her screamed "I don't give a shit what I look like!" She had about four inches of white-gray roots before curly red hair fell well below her shoulders. The woman is just weird. She doesn't bother to wax her brows, yet she wears a seventy-dollar-an-ounce fragrance. I'd never known her to wear perfume, but then again, this was the first time I'd seen her so early in the morning. Apparently, she didn't subscribe to the theory that perfume, like lipstick, requires reapplication during the day.

When she finished, she asked, "Why didn't you ask Liam to try to find the elusive second cousins-slash-tenants?"

"Technically, they would be third cousins, and when I handled the estate, Liam wasn't on retainer with Dane-Lieberman. Then there was the problem of Lenora not knowing any names or if they were relatives or tenants or even the location and boundaries of the land out in Indiantown."

"Did you drive out to Indiantown?"

"Yes," I practically hissed. "I went through the local property records at the library—if you can call it that—and couldn't find anything. I checked the Martin County Property Clerk's Office, and all I found was that the land was owned by Lenora's aunt and uncle and there was no record of the property being transferred after 1931. It's all right there in the abstract."

Ellen smiled. "Taking pride in your work, are you?"

If I was, it was purely by accident. "No. I just feel confident that I did everything possible at the time. It was three years ago."

"And yet you remember everything. That would serve you well if you decided to go to law school."

"Is your coffee warm enough?" I asked, not willing to beat this dead horse again. Like my mother, Ellen couldn't seem to grasp that I didn't want to further my education. I was happy with my normally nine-to-five job, and I had no intention of spending three more years in college.

"My coffee is fine. Show me exactly where the property is"— she paused to check her zillion-year-old utilitarian Timex— "then go down to the lobby and let Lenora in, since Margaret won't be here for another few—"

The sound of the intercom cut her off. "Yes?" Ellen asked as she pressed the flashing green button on the phone.

"Is Finley there?" It was Margaret. "Her client has arrived."

"Thank you, Margaret. You can send Ms. Egghardt up to my conference room."

"Where would you like me?" I asked.

"In law school." She offered a small smile with the suggestion. "Here," she said, pointing to the chair to her left. "But could you go to the elevators? Leslie-Anne doesn't get here until nine."

Leslie-Anne. So that was the name of the executive assistant who still called me Miss Tanner after eight and a half years. Then again, I still called her Mrs. Greenfelder, so I couldn't see me giving her a shout-out as Leslie-Anne any time soon.

By the time I reached the elevators, Lenora was stepping out, decked head to toe in Louis Vuitton. Her brown hair was pixie short, but it fit her small, delicate features. She was about three inches shorter than I am even without my killer heels on. When she looked up, the broad smile on her glossed lips was mirrored in her hazel eyes.

Lenora was not to the manor born but rather the great-granddaughter of a Gilded Age tycoon. The Egghardt name had some cachet, but the millions were long gone. Still, she'd married well and divorced even better.

"How are you?" I asked.

"Good. I'm glad you're still working on this mess. I thought I was done sorting through my uncle's things, and then out of the blue, I get this." She thrust a slightly rumpled envelope toward me as we walked to the conference area.

Pulling the letter out, I found a note and a money order for thirty dollars with rent scratched on the memo line, only it was spelled "rint." The note just said, "This covers the end." The signature was almost illegible.

"Ellen Lieberman, this is Lenora Egghardt," I said, then completed the introduction. As I did, I noticed Lenora's eyes fixed on Ellen. God, I hoped it wasn't the muumuu.

"Have we met?" Lenora asked as she extended her hand.

Ellen blinked rapidly. "I think we may have met once in the elevator."

Lenora was shaking her head. "No, I think it was longer ago than that. Your face looks so familiar."

Ellen shrugged, and her eyes were downcast. "I just have one of those faces."

What? I wondered. *The kind with no makeup, crying out for a facial?* How could Ellen not know that she had perfect bone structure, even more perfect, long-lashed eyes, and from what I could tell beneath the ever-present tent dress, a great shape?

"Shall we get started?" Ellen asked as she pointed to the seat opposite mine.

I passed the contents of the envelope to Ellen as Lenora explained what had transpired. We spent the next forty-five minutes looking at various maps of the area in question. Uncle Walter had died intestate in Lenora's home. His dementia was such that for his last few years on earth he spoke little more than gibberish. When he died, Lenora, as next of kin, inherited everything, including several hundred acres of primo citrus groves. Thanks to citrus canker, she was about to turn fifty acres into a state-of-the-art equestrian center, hopefully drawing clients from Payson Park, the premier racetrack in the area—until she'd received the rent payment and begun to wonder if the distant cousin Walter had once mentioned more than a decade ago had finally surfaced.

If he/she had, the only lead was the return address on the envelope, a post office box in Indiantown.

"I'm sorry for staring," Lenora said to Ellen. "I'm still trying to figure out why you look so familiar."

Ellen rolled the chair back from the table and stood. "I'm sure you're mistaking me for someone else. I'll have Finley walk you to your car, and you'll hear from us as soon as we make contact with the tenant." She turned to me. "See to Ms. Egghardt, then come back up here."

The two women shook hands, and I hurried around to the doorway to lead Lenora back downstairs. She had fine lines on her brow as she continued to concentrate. "I could swear I know that woman. I just can't place her."

I pressed the elevator button, then turned briefly to the executive assistant. "Good morning, Leslie-Anne." I left her alone with her shocked expression as Lenora and I stepped inside the empty elevator.

"Is Lieberman a married name?"

I shrugged. I'd always thought of Ellen as some sort of asexual creature. Like a worm. Lenora wasn't giving up though. She asked me question after question, and I realized I knew close to nothing about Ellen. Not even her home address. Hell, until yesterday, I hadn't even known her home phone number.

As we headed out of the lobby, I shielded my eyes from the bright sun glistening off the cars and shop windows. The heat was already stifling, creating water mirages on the pavement of the parking lot.

"I'll be in touch," I promised as I held open her door. "Take care."

"Thank you, Finley."

As I stepped away from the car, I caught a glimpse of movement over the hedge bordering the lot. When I looked in that direction, it was deserted. Obviously, the mirages weren't limited only to the blacktop.

As I headed back to my office, I walked slowly. Yes, part of it was my lack of any sense of urgency, but a huge part of my reasoning was practical—I was teetering on my heels. Well, maybe knowing Margaret was just settling behind her desk played a role as well. "Good morning," I greeted as I strolled past her, my heels clicking rhythmically until I reached the elevator.

Margaret's "Morning" was offered to my back, but I heard the resentment on every letter. She prided herself on being early to work. Normally, I was satisfied if I started being productive before ten.

I headed back up to the fourth floor. My not-so-best-friend Leslie-Anne sat stiffly behind her desk. "May I help you?" she asked.

I shook my head. "Just going back to retrieve some things from my meeting, but thanks."

Ellen wasn't in the conference room but all the paperwork was just as we'd left it. I folded what needed to be folded, then placed everything neatly back into the manila folder with EGG-HARDT typed neatly on the label. With that accomplished, I took two coffee mugs—mine and Lenora's—rinsed them, and placed them into the custom washer hidden inside one of the cabinets. I was a little surprised that Ellen still hadn't returned.

Walking over to the window, I glanced out through the darkened mirrored windows. The view faced southwest, allowing me to see some of the West Palm skyline and a sliver of the parking lot. My attention instantly went to the parking lot. Someone—a woman—stood behind Ellen's Volvo, and it looked like she was copying the license plate number. That was weird. Well, maybe not. The woman was wearing dark blue or black shorts, a short-sleeve white shirt, functional black walking shoes, and a dark baseball cap with her blond ponytail pulled through the back. She looked like a traffic enforcement officer. I smiled slowly. Apparently, one of the other things I'd never known about my boss was she either didn't pay her parking tickets or she'd left the scene of an accident.

Since I couldn't see Ellen leaving the scene, I'd already decided she was about to do penance for ignoring tickets. But I was really having a hard time believing that, either. She struck me as the type of person who followed every rule to the letter. It had to be a mistake, but at least it would inconvenience her, which was penance enough for having dragged me in at the crack of dawn.

I turned around when I heard a sound behind me. It was Ellen, two large shopping bags draped over each arm. I probably should have mentioned the thing with her car and would have if the next words out of her mouth hadn't been, "I need you to drop these off at the thrift store."

Saturday I'm a babysitter, and Monday I'm a Sherpa? Don't remember any of those being in my job description. I stared blankly.

Ellen let out a slow breath and smiled at me. "I'm not trying to be demeaning, I'm just asking a favor. I meant to get these to the St. Luke's Thrift Shop in West Palm over the weekend, but the time got away from me. The store is on your way home from work."

"But it closes at five."

"Then leave early."

I went over and relieved her of the bags. "Done."

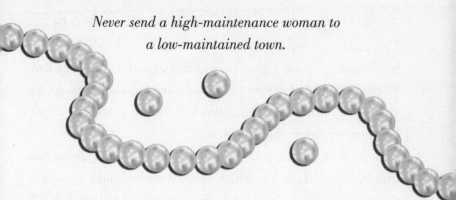

Never send a high-maintenance woman to
a low-maintained town.

five

By the time I reached my office, the weight of Ellen's bags had left red lines on my wrists and forearms. After tossing the Egghardt file on my desk, I placed the bags on the floor, then gently shoved them against the wall with my foot. In no time, my office began to smell like cedar. I knew the bags were filled with clothing and couldn't wait to secretly go through them. I don't think there's a big market for muumuus and ugly sandals at the West Palm Beach thrift store. But it would be fun to see what Ellen considered donation material.

Well, that would have to wait.

I filled a new mug with coffee, sat down, and wiggled my mouse until my computer came out of hibernation. Since I'd lost my bid on the watch face and still needed a lot of Rolex parts, I skipped checking my e-mail and went straight to eBay. I found a couple of links and a new listing for a watch face and placed bids on all of them. I could almost hear Jane's voice in my head begging me to step away from the eBid! I didn't listen. I also couldn't help checking the items Izzy was bidding on; for some strange reason I was very invested in making sure she had all the parts and pieces for her school dance ensemble. So far, so good. Well, until Tony found out his evening at the opera had cost him way more than he knew.

I sat back and sipped my coffee. "Crap," I said under my breath. I needed my job, which meant I really should say something to Tony about my eBay influence on his daughter. But if I did, I'd have to undo the invitation my mother had orchestrated at the same time. "My mommy got me a date" was so flipping humiliating.

Summoning my courage, I opened my e-mail, fully prepared to send Tony a quick message explaining things when I spotted an e-mail from Izzy. My courage-o-meter dropped. There was no way she'd know my office e-mail. Well, if she knew her dad's e-mail, maybe she had figured it out on her own. I don't remember being asked if I wanted a new buddy on my e-mail list.

Izzy's e-mail was a smart, amusing, and enthusiastic thank-you for Saturday night. Part of me was really touched, and my ego was a bit stroked by the blatant adulation from Izzy. Until I reached the third paragraph.

 . . . **am SO looking forward to Atlanta. It'll be way cool. I've never been to Six Flags, and Dad hasn't taken a vaca since before we moved here. I know it's not 100% for sure, but if we come can I wear the Betsey dress for the wedding? Will you help me with hair and stuff? —Izzy**

"Now what do I do?" I whined. Now there was no way I could uninvite Tony. Not without disappointing Izzy. It wasn't that I didn't want to go with Tony, who wouldn't? But now it was a Caprelli family affair, all thanks to my mother. I knew from experience that she would make a point of telling anyone and everyone that she'd personally selected the tall, dark, and handsome attorney for me.

"What do you do about what?" Becky asked as she sauntered in, filled her coffee mug from my personal stash, and then sat in one of the chairs across from me.

"Tony already told his daughter they might be going to the wedding."

Becky's perfect brows arched. "Well, well. Looks like you'll get that date after all."

"Date? He's bringing his daughter. It's not a date, it's coparenting." I gave her a recap of how the "date" happened and how I had "invited" Liam out of spite.

Becky's eyes glistened with humor. "So you went from no date to two dates in the span of a few seconds? Well, which one are you going to choose? You've been hot for Liam for a long time. But I know you're hot for Tony, and you said you liked the kid."

"I do."

"Then maybe you should have them draw straws or something. Or you could send each of them naked photos of yourself. First one to reply wins." Becky was enjoying this *waaaay* too much.

She sniffed the air around her. "What is that smell?"

I pointed to Ellen's four bags. "How come she didn't ask you to run her personal errands?"

"Because I went to law school," she replied with a wry grin. "I don't like you anymore."

"Sure you do. So what's your plan? Maybe you won't need one. Maybe Liam will have a *thing*."

The dreaded *thing*. "You're right. He has way too many *things*." Decision made. I'd just keep uninviting until he got it. Maybe I'll even tell him I have a *thing*.

"Good choice, given what happened last night," Becky said. I guess my confusion showed because she added, "Didn't you get an e-mail from Jane?"

I shook my head. "I haven't been through my in-box yet, why?"

Becky rose. "I think I'll leave you alone with your e-mail."

"Why? What happened?" A knot was forming in the pit of my stomach.

It was Becky's turn to shake her head. "Oh, no. You're on your own with that one. It's between you and Jane."

After Becky's swift exit, I scrolled through my e-mail until I found Jane's, then clicked to open it. It was addressed to me with a subject line reading "SOOOOO SORRY!"

I read it, then read it again, my mind spinning as I absorbed the contents. Turns out Jane went to Sunday ladies' night at the Blue Martini and was enjoying several mango martinis before the rest of the evening got a little fuzzy. The last thing she remembered was Liam stripping off most of her clothing and placing her in bed.

I felt angry and hurt. Could one of my best friends have had sex with Liam? My rational side asked, *And why not? You did announce he was free for the taking at brunch.* Which was true.

My irrational side reasoned that that didn't mean I wanted Jane jumping his bones a mere ten hours later. I had no valid reason for being angry or hurt. But I was.

In fact, I was frosted and needed to get out of the office. Stuffing the Egghardt folder in my briefcase and grabbing my purse and all of Ellen's crap, I headed downstairs.

As I breezed past Margaret, she called my name.

"What?" I snapped.

"Mr. McGarrity is on line two for you."

"Tell him I died," I said, then took two steps and added, "I'm going out to Indiantown. My cell is on."

I was so tangled with four bags, my heavy briefcase, and my purse that I had to shake and wriggle to free the fingers holding my key ring. I found my car key, hit the Unlock button, and hoisted the bags of clothing into the trunk. At least two of the bags tore, and the other two dumped their contents. Oh, and my purse tilted and my very favorite Red Envelope gift-with-purchase mirrored compact hit the ground and shattered. *Shit, shit, shit, shit, shit!*

This was turning into a seriously bad Monday, and it was only nine forty. Once I was behind the wheel, I keyed my destination into the GPS. I'd driven out to Indiantown a few times over the years, but certainly not enough to know the way by rote. I took my iPhone out of my purse and inserted it into the little auxiliary plug next to the stereo, then rested the actual phone in one of the two cup holders in the front console. Now I could talk on the phone and use a whole bunch of other nifty apps without ever taking my hands off the wheel. As I waited for the light to change on Australian, I just happened to glance out my window and saw a semi-familiar blonde. She was seated behind the wheel of a nondescript, white, two-door car. She turned her head, saw me, then quickly whipped back around into profile and was pulling her baseball cap lower when the car behind me honked its horn, startling me.

I had no choice but to drive on, but I did try looking into my mirror, hoping to get a clearer view of her face. No luck. Then again, I wasn't exactly having a rock-star kinda day. As I drove, I used only my thumbs to select a playlist on my iPhone, then hit the Play button. Indiantown was at least a thirty-minute drive. In my case, I'd have to add a few minutes so I could swing off I-95 at Palm City to grab a coffee to go from Cracker Barrel.

In no time I was walking past the trademark, for-sale Adirondack chairs, then into the kitschy restaurant-retail store, where I immediately smelled coffee, buttery biscuits, and bacon. My stomach rumbled a reminder that I had yet to eat. Unable to resist, I added an order of bacon to my large coffee, then browsed around waiting for my name to be called.

As always, the cramped space was filled with people from infant to ancient. I wasn't a collector—well, I was when it came to certain things, but hearth-and-homey things didn't do it for me. I did love the retro candies and made a point of buying Becky a box of Moon Pies. She'd be in heaven. She was a Moon Pie aficionado. I failed to see the culinary allure, but who was I to judge? I'm addicted to Lucky Charms. And I'm a purist—I think the original marshmallow shapes—pink hearts, yellow moons, orange stars, and green clovers—taste better than the ever-expanding offerings. I'm still warming up to the blue diamonds, and now they have horseshoes, balloons, shooting stars, hourglasses, and leprechauns. And don't even get me started on the magical key and door. What's the purpose of adding a marshmallow that disappears when the milk is added? Not that I use milk. I'm a right-out-of-the-box consumer.

Now I was jonesing for Lucky Charms. Instead, I had to content myself with three strips of crispy bacon and a twenty-four-ounce coffee. Just as I merged back onto the highway, my mind finally placed the face of the blond woman at the traffic light. She was the blonde who'd been copying the license plate on Ellen's Volvo.

I felt my brows pinch as a strange feeling came over me. The car she'd been driving wasn't a standard-issue traffic enforcement car. I've gotten my fair share of tickets, so I know they use smart cars and/or clearly marked and painted four-door sedans with ramming grates mounted on the grilles. The blonde's car looked more like a rental. Was I being followed?

"Am I being ridiculous?" I asked myself over the techno vocals of Lady Gaga singing "Poker Face." I couldn't fathom why anyone would be following me. The other times I'd been followed, there had been reasons for it. None of them positive, mind you.

My cell rang, and the caller ID showed it was Jane.

I hesitated for a minute, then pressed the Answer button with my thumb. I uttered a stiff, "Hello."

"Please don't be mad."

After a brief pause I said, "I have no reason to be mad."

"But you are, I can hear it in your voice."

"Sorry."

"C'mon, Finley! It wasn't like I planned anything. I was dancing and drinking fruity drinks that creep up on you. Everyone makes that mistake. *You've* made that mistake."

She was right. About everything. But she'd conveniently left out her ultimate too-much-to-drink Paolo disaster.

I, on the other hand, had unceremoniously renounced any claims on Liam, and on an occasion or two I've been known to overindulge. "I know. You didn't do anything I should be upset about."

"But you are and I'm ninety-nine percent sure nothing happened."

"Liam stripping you naked is *not* nothing."

"I wasn't naked. I still had on my bra and panties."

"I've seen your bras and panties. You might as well have been naked."

"Fin, please!" she begged. "I swear I didn't do this on purpose."

"I know. Give me a little time, and I'll get over myself." *I hope.* "What was Liam doing at ladies' night?"

"I have no idea. But he was at a table with Ashley."

Great. "Why did they get divorced? He goes out with her all the time."

"Maybe they're divorced with benefits."

"Thanks for the thought. Now I'll have that image in my head all day."

"I've got a client waiting," Jane said. "I just want everything with us to be okay. I swear I'd never do anything to intentionally hurt you. You know that, right?"

"Sure."

"Let me take you out for dinner," she said on a rush of breath.

"I've got to study."

"So I'll bring you dinner, and I'll help quiz you or something."

"Fine."

"I'll see you around six thirty?"

"Six thirty works. 'Bye."

"'Bye."

Monotonous doesn't begin to describe the drive out to Indiantown. Get a few miles away from the beach and the landscape changes drastically. Palm trees give way to pine trees, and the dense vegetation is replaced by groves, fields of crops, horse farms, and cow pastures.

Where there are cows and crops, there is the stench of manure. I switched my air-conditioning to "recycle," which cut down on the smell but didn't eradicate it completely. The odor clinging to my clothes would just top off a seriously lousy morning.

The homes I passed were paradoxical, running the gamut from large, two-story custom houses to shabby, dilapidated trailers. The only thing they had in common was land. These people traded quick access to the beach for acreage. I never understood the concept of owning land, especially in Florida. Controlled burns were a regular event since the climate encouraged fast and thick regrowth. Plus, there was the whole snake thing. I don't care if they play an important part in the food chain, the only way I like snakes is in the form of a wallet, purse, or shoes.

The closer I got to my destination, the more developed the

home sites. Don't get me wrong, the place was still rural, but once 710 turns into Warfield Boulevard, the historic aspects of the northwestern part of Martin County are immediately recognizable. Especially the Seminole Inn. It was built in the 1920s and serves as both a B and B and a Sunday-brunch destination.

I ate there one time, and while it was fun looking at the photos of all the celebrities who've visited over the years, it has a buffet, and I'm not big on sneeze guards.

I groaned when I saw the inn. Not because of the sneeze-guard memory but because I'd missed the turn to the library. If I hadn't dashed out of the office so quickly, I would have filled out and printed the form to have the USPS release the name of the box holder so I could search for the elusive tenants. But now I was stuck with the library.

The Indiantown library was a relatively new addition and very state of the art. After I parked next to one of only three cars in the parking lot, I grabbed my bag and the Egghardt file and headed toward the spotlessly clean walkway. The smell of freshly cut grass swirled around me as I was rendered deaf due to the roar of mowers circling the building.

Inside, I immediately felt two sets of eyes on me. I went to the service desk, introduced myself, and asked about the availability of a computer and printer.

"Follow me," the elderly woman said as she came out from behind the desk.

We weaved through the maze of stacks, ending up in a narrow room with a total of ten computer stations and a fancy, megasize laser printer. The walls were littered with signs warning against using the machines for chat groups, the mandatory time limits, and the schedule for the computer lab and what to do in case of a computer or printer glitch.

"Do you need any assistance?" she asked as she leaned over one of the keyboards and typed in some sort of pass code.

"No, thank you."

"Then fill out this form and please return it to the desk when you're finished." She left a trail of heavy perfume I didn't recognize. That was weird. I could normally name a fragrance in one note. Probably some drugstore knockoff.

I glanced at the sheet of paper, and it required my name, address, driver's license number—if applicable—and what Web sites—if any—I'd visited. It took me less than a minute to download the USPS form and maybe three to fill it out and print it. While I waited for the printer to spool, I completed the library form and placed it on top of my file.

With that accomplished, I grabbed up my things and was about to leave when I spotted a shelf along the back wall with a series of city telephone directories. Too bad I didn't know the name of the PO box holder yet.

As I left, I thanked the librarian and turned in my computer usage form. The short drive to the post office took me maybe two minutes. Again I parked in a nearly deserted lot. Unlike the library, the post office could use a little updating.

File in one hand and purse dangling from my wrist, I walked into the post office and went directly to the first of two windows. After about thirty seconds, I cleared my throat.

No one came out.

I waited another thirty seconds and called out, "Hello?"

A large, masculine woman waddled out from the back. She

was dressed in a uniform that I guessed, based on the strain on the buttons, was about two sizes too small. Her rubber-soled shoes squeaked as she walked, and her scowl pinched her face and two of her three bonus chins.

"Help you?" she asked with a partially masticated bit of food in her pudgy cheeks.

I sure as hell wasn't in Kansas anymore. I introduced myself, pulled out my ID, then handed her the form and said, "I need to know the name and address of the box holder."

Her washed-out green eyes narrowed. "Got a subpoena?"

"No, ma'am." I placed my file on the counter and flipped to the notarized Letters of Administration authorizing me to obtain any information regarding the estate of Walter Egghardt. "I'm trying to find the person who sent this." I paused and pulled out the envelope and money order. "There's a possibility this individual is an heir."

She looked at the document while she finished chewing, then swallowed. "I'll have to get clearance from Frankie on this."

I reached over and tapped the court-assigned case number. "This is a legal document. I've routinely gotten post office information in the past."

"Not from me, you haven't."

"How long will it take for Frankie to review this?" I asked, careful to hide my annoyance. I knew from experience that small towns aren't the place for sarcasm.

"To review it?" she repeated. "I imagine he'll take care of it quickly."

"Great."

"He won't be in until noon, though."

I took a deep breath and gritted my teeth after checking my watch. "What time would you like me to come back?"

She shrugged her broad shoulders. "One, one thirty."

I had at least an hour and a half to kill. So I reclaimed my file—minus the form—and, after she'd made a copy of my Letter of Administration, I went out to my car. There wasn't a lot to do in Indiantown, so I decided to head up to the Vero Beach outlets.

Never go to the grocery store hungry—or, in my case, to an outlet when you're in a crummy mood. I found some super-cute watches at the Liz Claiborne store as well as purses at both Coach and Dooney & Bourke. But my find of the day was a stunning black silk taffeta dress with front and back V necklines and a darling grosgrain belt with chiffon accents. It retailed for two fifteen but I got the dress at the bargain price of one hundred because of a lipstick smudge along the neckline. Not a problem for my killer dry cleaner. Now I could stop stressing over the rehearsal dinner.

It was close to three thirty by the time I returned to the post office. The parking lot was empty, which was great since I wanted the information in a hurry.

Again I took my file and walked up to the door, pulled on the handle, only to find it locked. Creating a tunnel with my cupped hands, I looked through the glass door for signs of life. It was dark. Then I looked around and found the sign: HOURS OF OPERATION 8–3.

My entire vocabulary of curse words swirled in my head. The last thing I wanted to do was come back tomorrow. The only way I could avoid a second trip was almost worse than actually making the trip.

I walked back to my car with the enthusiasm of walking to the guillotine. As a PI, Liam had access to the Post Office Box Break. All he would have to do is hit the database and almost instantly, he'd have a reverse post office box listing. Too bad I didn't know any other PIs.

Disconnecting my phone, I tapped Favorites, which so was not true at this juncture, then touched Liam's name.

On the third ring, he answered, "Hi, Finley. How are things in Indiantown?"

"How did you know—never mind. I need you to give me a reverse post box listing."

"Someone got up on the wrong side of her coffee cup. I'm guessing this has something to do with Jane?"

"Don't flatter yourself. I can't think of a reason why I'd care two shakes about your going home with one of my best friends."

"I'm sure Jane told you that's all I did."

"Of course, right after she told me how you'd undressed her."

"For someone who isn't interested in me, you sure sound pissed."

Arrogant snot. I sighed loudly. "Can I please have the information I need?"

"What's in it for me?"

God, I hated that his voice was so sexy. "A payment from Dane-Lieberman."

"Not good enough."

"Could you stop being a jerk and just do it?"

"Can I wear a black suit, or do I need to wear a tux to the wedding?"

"You're not going to the wedding."

"You invited me."

"So now I'm uninviting you."

"That's very poor etiquette."

"Yeah, well, I'll consult Emily Post later. Right now I need a name and address."

"Be happy to. But not until you answer my question. Suit or tux?"

"It doesn't matter since you won't be at the wedding. Tony is my escort."

"Your mother arranged that, so it doesn't count. You, on the other hand, personally invited me."

Frustrated, I pounded my phone on the cushioned driver's seat. "And we both know that was purely designed to frost my mother's cookies. Which also means I can *un*invite you. Can we get back to the reason I called?"

"In a minute. I have no problem with Tony going as a guest. We're friends. But he's already got someone to escort."

"Who?"

"His daughter."

"You're an ass."

"I love it when you talk dirty."

"I'm hanging up now."

"Don't be childish."

"Me? You're the one being annoying."

"I'm also the one who knows you're looking for information on Donald and Wanda Jean Bollan."

"How can you know that when I haven't even given you the post office box?"

"I'm very perceptive."

"No, you're a freak of nature."

"I'm a freak who knows they live at 101 Collier Lane."

"Thanks," I snapped, then instantly pressed End.

I spent the next fifteen minutes trying to convince my GPS that Collier Lane was a road in or around Indiantown. After the irritating conversation with Liam, I was not in the mood for the GPS to cop an attitude. I decided to go to the closest gas station to ask for directions.

I got a lot of looks when I got out of the car in my five-inch heels, walked around a tractor with its hood raised, past the pumps where three men with tricked out pickups openly ogled me, before I finally reached the entryway to the garage bay. "Excuse me!"

A lanky teenager with more acne than skin and a middle-aged man with a protruding belly came out from the back. The pencil-necked kid stared at my boobs while the older man wiped grease onto his sweaty, possibly-was-once-white T-shirt.

"Ma'am," he greeted.

"I'm trying to find Collier Lane."

The two men looked at each other. "You know where it is, boy?"

"Back down 710, I think. Yeah, yeah. It's just after the trailer park. The Bollan place is out there."

"Right, right. Sleepy's place," he said nodding.

Sleepy? What was he? One of the freaking seven dwarfs? The older of the two gave me vague directions. "Thank you."

Doing the best I could to follow instructions like "look for the live oak with the two stumps next to it on the left," I kept driving deeper into the groves and sugarcane fields. After passing the rodeo and the trailer park, I slowed until I saw a crudely fashioned street sign.

Collier Lane was nothing more than a dirt road marked by a slanted mailbox with plastic spinners and red reflector dots on the leaning post. At the base of the post was a faded ceramic planter with a man in a sombrero pulling a cart filled with plastic flowers. Not exactly PC. I made the right and slowly crept up the road, driving in slalom fashion to avoid the deep potholes. It took about three minutes before a structure came into view.

Calling it a home was a stretch. It was a trailer with a curled and dented aluminum skirt. Twelve dogs came rushing toward my car, some barking, some growling, all scary. There were two cars on the side of the house. Both had weeds jutting up through them. On the opposite side was an older-model truck with as much rust as paint under a crudely constructed carport. Well, it wasn't a carport so much as it was four metal poles with a worn and torn tarp across the top. There was a kiddy pool in the front yard, flanked by two Barcaloungers, both with springs popping through the fabric. The same was true of the sofa on the porch. As I slowed my car to a stop, Cujo and company continued to bark and growl. When the screen door opened, I was hoping it was the owner. It was, but he wasn't alone. His companion was a really large shotgun.

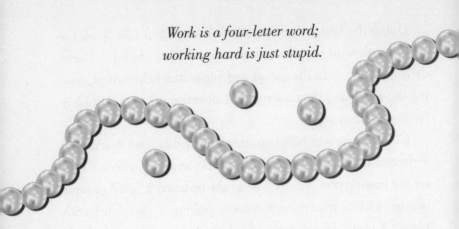

Work is a four-letter word;
working hard is just stupid.

six

Needless to say, I wasn't feeling wrapped in the warmth of his welcome. Like the man at the gas station, the armed bozo wore a stained wife-beater and had that pregnant-man physique going on. What little hair he had was swept over to one side. It was gray and as dull as his washed-out brown eyes.

The dogs continued their attack on my car while the man on the porch cradled the gun like an infant. I could hear more dogs in the distance and wondered if they were the understudies for the Hounds of the Baskervilles. Great. Dogs with a side order of more dogs.

Just behind armed guy I could make out a shape in the shadows of the tattered screen door. I wanted to slam my car into reverse and head back the way I'd come when he placed his thumb and forefinger in his mouth and whistled loud enough to be heard over the hum of my car engine.

The pack of matted, mangy dogs instantly raced toward him.

The unseen pack in the distance still barked and snarled, but even after a scan of my surroundings—such as they were—I couldn't seem to locate them. With the visible dogs heeled, I felt comfortable enough to depress the button, opening my window little more than a crack. "Mr. Bollan?" I asked politely.

He nodded as the ears on two of the hounds lifted alertly.

"Who's asking?"

I had to tilt my head to one side so my lips were closer to the narrow space I'd created. I gave him a quick explanation. He rested the gun against the aluminum home and started walking toward me. A woman stepped out from inside the trailer and followed closely on his heels. She appeared far friendlier, quite a feat given that what I could see of her gray hair was up in pink foam curlers and her attire consisted of a faded paisley house-dress and slippers that scuffed the dusty ground with each step.

I so didn't want to leave the relative safety of my car. Reluc-tantly, I opened the door, my eyes fixed on the six dogs watch-ing my every move. I have a history with dogs, and it isn't good.

Mr. and—I assumed—Mrs. Bollan walked past the garden of fake flowers and weathered lawn ornaments until we met on neutral ground.

"Nice to meet you," he said, offering me a sun-leathered hand with dirt and God only knew what else crusted beneath his nails.

I quelled the urge to reach for the Purell in my purse after we briefly shook hands.

"Call me Sleepy and this here is the wife, Wanda Jean."

"Miss," she said as she reached around her husband's girth. "Did I hear correctly? Mr. Walter passed?" she asked.

"Three years ago," I answered as I felt the first trickle of perspiration slithering down my back.

"We didn't know." Wanda spoke for both of them.

Fine with me since I was in no hurry to get a second glance at Sleepy's three yellowed teeth. I reached back and pulled out my briefcase, dug out the money order, and said, "My firm represents Lenora Egghardt, and until she received this"—I paused and passed Sleepy the money order—"she had no idea anyone was living on the property."

I think Sleepy scowled. Hard to tell since a serious overbite made him look like a perplexed beaver. Then he explained, "We've been here for near on thirty-five years. Used to tend the groves until the canker came a few years back. Now we farm sugarcane and run a few head of cattle."

"Sleepy," Wanda interrupted with a smidge of irritation, "let's go inside where we'll all be more comfortable."

I didn't have high hopes for that option, but I followed along and pretended I didn't smell the stench of sweaty dog and grease.

The smell of the cooking grease was stronger in the trailer, and once I spied the pots on the stove, I figured I'd taken Wanda away from preparing the evening meal. Two flies zipped around the room, occasionally stopping long enough to visit the flour-dusted chicken thighs sitting out on the chipped Formica counter. Some sort of greens that looked more like they belonged on the shoulder of I-95 sat in a colander near the sink. A thick, yellowish cloud of smoke hung in the air.

"Have a seat," Wanda said, pointing to an animal-hair-covered chair near the window air-conditioning unit that had dripped condensation down the wall. "Let me get you some iced tea."

Just to be polite, I said thank you even though I would have preferred coffee. At least with a hot beverage I had the possibility of boiling off some cooties. I perched myself on the very edge of the dirty chair and began taking all the documentation for Walter Egghardt's estate out of my briefcase.

After handing me a plastic cup of tea, Wanda and Sleepy sat down, swiveling their seats away from the small television balanced on an old orange crate. A cable box teetered atop the machine. Grabbing a remote off the armrest, Sleepy muted *Judge Judy*.

"I need to get some information," I began. "And I'll need to see your lease."

"We don't have no lease," Sleepy said, his tone defensive. "Walter and me was in 'Nam together. That's when he offered to let me live on this land. We got pinned down in Dak To in '67. Walter got hit, and after I carried him to the aid station, we, well, we was friends from then on."

"And you came to live on this property because . . . ?"

Sleepy shrugged and scratched his sizable belly as he took a long pull on a can of generic beer. "We was as different as night and day. Me? My kin ain't rich like Walter was, so once we were back stateside, he said I could live here. Came back once with some hot redhead in his car. That's when he gave me a letter that lets me live on this land for life."

Not good. Not at all good. "So you're not related to Walter? But you do have a letter or know the name of the woman who was with him?"

"Got the letter someplace. He even had it notaried and all official. The redhead just sat in his car. Never knew her name."

I checked the urge to correct "notaried" to notarized. Hopefully the letter wasn't legally binding on Walter's heir.

"There may not have been no blood bond," Wanda added. "Mr. Walter's always been good to us. She reached behind her on the windowsill and took a framed photograph down and handed it to me. "Raised all eight of our children right here."

I tried to imagine the trailer holding ten people.

"This is L.D., short for Little Donald."

I glanced at the picture, and "little" would have been the last adjective I'd use to describe the rotund, balding man in the back row.

Wanda continued, "Then Walt, after Walter. Next is Homer—he works as a firefighter in Montana. Lorraine, she's a nurse. Mary-Claire is raising her own family. This pretty one," Wanda stopped and stroked the cheek of the girl in the shot, "that's my Penny." Wanda's eyes seemed to inexplicably mist over. "Got us five grandbabies so far. Duane is in the navy, and last is Mitzi. She's the baby, and we're real proud of her. Mitzi just finished her third year at the community college."

"You have a lovely family," I fudged as I returned the photo. "I'm not sure how to explain this, but Walter dying has changed things."

"How?" Sleepy asked, his eyes narrowed to beads.

"Well, Mr. Egghardt died without a will, so his niece inherited all of his estate, including this parcel of land."

Wanda looked at me with bulging, alienesque eyes while Walter just looked really pissed. Red blotches rose from his neck to his face, and I was very, *very* glad the shotgun was out on the porch.

"Me and Walter had an agreement," Sleepy insisted. "I don't see how him dying changes that."

Now I could hear a stereo chorus of barking and growling dogs. Acoustically, I realized some were in the backyard and others were mere feet away with their snouts pressed against the screen door. Obviously, they'd picked up on their master's displeasure. I was growing uneasy, wondering if the animals were plotting to attack.

Again Sleepy whistled, and the porch hounds fell silent. The backyard dogs just kept on yelping, growling, and barking. It was hard for me to concentrate, especially when a cat came out of nowhere and snaked its way through my ankles. It had harsh, brittle hair and a jagged scar down its face, leaving it with only one eye and part of one ear.

Wanda made a clicking sound with her tongue. "Come here Lucky," she coaxed.

"Lucky?" I asked as I watched the cat cross the three or four feet separating us. The thing had more scars on its body, and its tail was little more than a calico nub.

Wanda smiled. "She was a stray. A few years back she got into the kennels. Of course, we hurried out and got her when we heard the ruckus"

"Of course," I murmured, as Lucky, now occupying Wanda's lap, gave me a cycloptic glare.

"We fixed her up best we could but didn't think she would make it. But she's tough," Wanda said, scratching the cat between the ear and a half. "That's why we call her Lucky."

I'd been there too long because the explanation made perfect sense. It fit that these people wouldn't do vets. From the decor—early 1970s greens, browns, and avocados—and the antiquated appliances—who doesn't have a microwave?—and all the other knickknacks, I guessed the Bollans had little if any income.

"What happens with the proceeds from our sugarcane?" Sleepy asked. "We've lived here since the late sixties. Raised all them kids here. You trying to tell me some woman we've never met can toss us out? Just like that?"

"It would help if you could find any documentation you have from Mr. Egghardt. And I can assure you," I began as I rose and started for the door, "we'll do everything possible to bring this to an amicable resolution."

"Sound like a load of crap to me," Sleepy grumbled, not moving an inch as I walked past him.

"Sleepy, mind yourself. This young lady is only doing her job."

I reluctantly stepped onto the porch, fully prepared to pick up the shotgun and start picking off the herd of vicious dogs. I was spared that unpleasant task by Wanda Jean, who also had perfected the two-fingered, piercing whistle.

The dogs chased me halfway back to the main road. It wasn't until I saw them in my rearview mirror that I let out the breath I hadn't even realized I was holding.

Glancing at the dashboard clock, I decided to call Ellen and give her the update. It was four fifty, so there was no way I was going to go back to the office. I pressed the preprogrammed number for the firm.

"Dane, Lieberman, Zarnowski and Caprelli. How may I direct your call?" Margaret greeted in a much friendlier voice than when she normally spoke to me.

"This is Finley calling for Ellen."

"Oh." Now I got the tone. "I'm afraid she's gone for the day. May I connect you to her voice mail?"

"Yes." I intentionally waited for Margaret to transfer the call, knowing full well I wasn't going to leave a message. Childishly, I just wanted to force her to take that extra step.

It took me just under a half hour to get back to my place. The sun was still hanging in the sky, and the humidity had picked up considerably. Even though I'd worked up a sweat, I was dying to go through Ellen's donation bags.

My trunk smelled like cedar, but I smelled like stale tobacco and wet dog, so I had to give that one to the trunk. With some effort, I was able to move all the stuff from the trunk to my house without dropping anything.

After depositing the four bags in the center of the great room, I went back out to the car to retrieve my cell phone. I pressed the little icon for voice mail as I returned to the cottage.

The first was from Jane. She'd forgotten an appointment and hoped I wouldn't mind pushing dinner back to seven thirty. I texted her back to say that since she was supplying the moo shu, she could name her terms.

A small trickle of hurt mixed with anger slithered along my spine. I know it was stupid, but I still wasn't over the whole Liam-took-me-home-and-tucked-me-in scenario. That said, I also knew it was important for me to move past it. My friendship with Jane would last long enough that in a few years, we probably wouldn't even remember Liam's name.

Only right now I did remember his name. And the hooded sensuality in his gaze. And the chiseled outline of a tanned, sculpted six-pack that made LL Cool J look like a slacker.

I gave myself a mental smack. No lust, no problem.

Not a chance in hell.

As I walked toward my bedroom, I used one hand to brace myself against the wall as I slipped off my shoes. They were cute as sin but the very definition of "killer heels." I stopped long enough to massage my insteps, then changed into an ankle-length, fuchsia halter sundress with tiny white flowers embroidered on the straps and at the hemline.

Leaving my sore feet bare, I went back into the kitchen and poured myself a glass of red wine as the second message played. It was from my mother, hence the need for the wine chaser.

"Since you haven't bothered to make your plane reservations, I've had to take that on as well." I raised my glass to her martyrdom as she continued her voice-mail lashing. "Your flight leaves at ten a.m. on Thursday; that will get you into Atlanta at—"

I groaned. "I don't have Thursday off," I argued over the rest of the message. I travel a lot like I shop—bargain hunting. It wasn't like I didn't know I had to be in Atlanta on Friday afternoon; I did. I even had a fare watcher on Travelocity.com with the trip specifics. Now, thanks to Controlling Cassidy, again I was faced with choosing between bad and worse. I could call her and tell her to change the flight, which would surely result in ugly and prolonged tension. Or I could go to Vain Dane and grovel for an additional personal day off from work. So I could lose my mind or lose a day's pay.

"Hands down, take the day without pay." I drained my wineglass, then refilled it.

I had almost an hour and a half before Jane was due, so I decided to entertain myself by going through Ellen's bags-o-muumuus.

Hiking up the hem of my dress, I knelt down and opened the shopping bag closest to me. Since I'd basically shoved the tattered garbage bag and its contents into the shopping bag to get it out of the trunk, this was my first real look at what was inside.

My suspicions were confirmed as I unrolled a wad of material. Only it turned out not to be an emerald paisley muumuu, but a vintage Von Furstenberg wrap dress. I stared at it for several seconds, trying to imagine Ellen Lieberman in a real dress. Not just any dress, but a classic.

In eight years, I'd never seen her wear anything that clung to any part of her body. Yet each item I pulled from the bag completely contradicted all I knew about her. And there was something else. All the items were vintage: late eighties, early nineties. Oh, and everything was a size two or four, and I'd bet my last dollar—no pun intended—that under her current love of tent dressing, Ellen was still a svelte single digit.

There were several pairs of barely worn Nina shoes—size six—as well as three pairs of boots and four coats. I decided I should make an inventory list for the thrift store, then I could copy it for Ellen so she could get the tax deduction.

"Ouch," I muttered as I stood on cramped legs. My laptop was in my bedroom, so I got it, and, almost as an afterthought,

I also picked up my study guide. At some point, I had to continue studying for my exam.

I began to organize the items, creating a spreadsheet of everything by size, color, and style. As I did so, I carefully folded each item. I'd been at it long enough that I'd become numb to the smell of cedar. My guess was that Ellen had stored all this stuff in cedar trunks and/or a cedar-lined closet. *But why?*

Taking a quick break before logging the shoes and coats, I sipped my wine and admired the neat stacks of clothing I'd created from four green trash bags. Going to the pantry, I took out a half-dozen shopping bags from high-end stores. Placing my wineglass next to my computer, I then placed a bag with each pile of sorted items.

When I reached down for a suede coat with what I was pretty sure was a coyote collar, I felt a hard bulge in one pocket. It took me a minute to feel my way around the chocolate-colored coat until I found the opening to the pocket. Slipping my hand inside, I let out a sharp squeal of pain.

"Dammit!" I yanked my hand back just as a small flow of blood made a bubble on my forefinger. So it wasn't reason to call an ambulance—the pinprick still hurt.

As I stuck my finger in my mouth I asked, "Does this qualify as a worker's comp case?"

I was much more methodical and careful in my second attempt. I turned the coat upside down and just shook it until a small wad of tissue tumbled out and wobbled around until it came to rest against the leg of the coffee table.

As I went to pick it up, I tripped over my hem and sent myself flying, face-first, toward the tile. I hit hard. I hurt my pride and my head.

Standing, I went to the bathroom and grimaced when I saw the small gash at my hairline. Dabbing it with a Kleenex went only so far. In another blow to my self-esteem, I had to place a Band-Aid on my forehead—at least I had the clear kind—and as I did, I felt the beginnings of a goose egg.

My first thought was, what would my mother do if I showed up at the wedding looking one scintilla shy of perfect? My second thought was wondering why I'd had the first thought.

"Whoever said bringing back the maxi-dress was a good idea?" I was still irritated as I returned to the great room. I took a sip of wine—hey, it was good enough for the ancient Greeks—then gingerly bent down to retrieve the tissue-wrapped package. It'd better be worth it. The frigging thing had already cost me two personal injuries.

Gently, I peeled away the wrappings. Inside were a bracelet, a pair of drop earrings, and four brooches, including the one that had pricked my finger.

"So what the hell is Ellen doing hiding jewelry inside a coat pocket? Especially *this* jewelry." I held one of the brooches up to the light. Just as expected, they were costume but not cheap. No, these had a maker's marks and brilliant craftsmanship. One-of-a-kind sort of thing. And if Ellen wasn't hiding it, why did she have it in the first place? I just couldn't see her wearing frilly, large accessories. No more than I could picture her wearing the acid-washed jeans in stack number five.

Bad decisions make good stories.

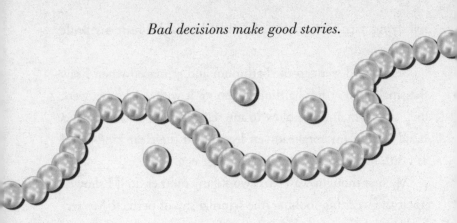

seven

I spread the jewelry out on the coffee table. There was a theme to the pieces. The earrings were freshwater pearls with a tiny crown fashioned from silver and what I thought might be cubic zirconia stones attaching them to the shepherd's hook. The bracelet had tiny crowns—also silver with possible CZ mountings—placed inside circles. All together, the bracelet had five rings of crowns.

The brooches were another story. At least I thought so. I went over to the kitchen junk drawer—yeah, I know, new house, no junk, but that's not how I roll—and retrieved the jeweler's loupe Becky had given me. Sounds like a strange gift, but it was actually the lead-up to the real gift, a pretty pink sapphire ring to commemorate my twenty-fifth birthday. Returning to the table, I picked up the first brooch, the smaller of the four, and peered at it through the loupe. The ten-times monocular lens confirmed my suspicions. Though expertly made, the pin was not diamond-encrusted. As on the earrings, the crown motif was repeated. Turning it over, I had to search for a few seconds before finding L.S. & Co. stamped just below the clasp. I wasn't familiar with the company, but that didn't mean much. A lot of jewelers placed maker's marks in their higher-end pieces.

Since I had the loupe out anyway, I checked the earrings. Again I found the same marking but no .925 stamped into the piece. Given the overall quality, my guess was that the silver had a rhodium finish, which explained the luster and replicated the look of platinum.

Turning my attention back to the stones, I examined them closely. Thanks in part to my job in trusts and estates, I'd gotten fairly good at defining CZ. Like natural diamonds, cubic zirconia was graded according to four criteria: carat weight, clarity, color, and cut. These were top-of-the-line stones and better quality than the typical quality preferred by jewelers. I'd still want a jeweler to appraise them, but I was guessing I was seeing at least five carats of brilliant cut C AAAAA.

"Weird," I mumbled.

I repeated the process on the rest of the brooches. All but one shared the characteristics of the first. The fourth one immediately had my full attention.

It was three inches in diameter and sorta resembled the jewels at the midpoint of Elizabeth II's official crown. Sad that I knew my crowns, since it revealed my childhood fantasy of becoming a princess. "Mom would have loved that," I commented sarcastically. She'd value a title above all else. No more taunts about being an underachiever by choice, no more talk of law school, reinstated access to my trust fund. And just possibly a reason to like me. And vice versa. My mother and I were stuck in that place where on some level we loved each other, but on every other level we just irritated each other.

I sighed deeply and went back to the task at hand. This brooch was diamond-encrusted platinum. At least I thought so. Mentally, I added it to my list of items to have the jeweler appraise.

The doorbell startled me, and I called out, "Just a minute!" For the sake of safety, I scooped up the jewelry—again getting pricked in the process—and my loupe and put them in the junk drawer.

The instant I opened the door, I smelled moo shu, and my stomach gurgled.

"Hey there," Jane greeted.

There was some tension around her mouth and eyes. Or maybe it was guilt.

Or maybe I was just funneling everything through my residual annoyance. Which was childish. And silly. And above all else, wrong.

Jane placed the box of food on the counter, then asked to use the powder room. In the few minutes she was gone, I set the counter up with place mats, chopsticks, napkins, and another wineglass. I retrieved my glass from the coffee table, and my nose pinched at the scent of cedar competing with the Chinese food.

Jane reemerged a different person. Gone were the form-fitting red dress, stunning silver pumps, and assorted silver accessories. Instead, she'd put on her clinging yoga clothing. I wondered if she was ever going to get saddlebags or cellulite.

Probably not.

"What's that smell?" she asked as she took the glass of wine I offered.

"Cedar. Give me a sec."

"And what did you do to your head?"

"Nothing major," I assured her as I carried the bags out to the lanai and closed the sliding glass door. "Better?"

"Much. Please tell me you didn't go on a five-bag spending binge." She frowned.

I made a cross over my heart while saying, "Nope. That's all Ellen's crap. I'm taking it to the thrift store in the morning."

"Ellen the lesbian?"

"She's not gay," I said. "I think she's just asexual."

"Does the asexual manual state that you have to work hard on looking like a thin version of Cass Elliott? And by the way, did you know there's an official Web site for her fans?"

"Can you have fans when you've been dead since 1974?" I began opening the cartons to inspect the contents. "You were obviously hungry when you went into Mi Lang's. What'd you do, get one of everything on the menu?"

"So you'll have a bunch of leftovers."

"No, you should take it home; you paid for it."

"You forget, I know every dime you have to your name. I know it barely makes a dent in what you spent on the babysitting outfit, so every penny counts."

My guess was now wasn't a good time to mention that I'd already shopped the Vero Beach outlets and purchased another little black dress. It wasn't like I could wear the ultra-expensive one since both Liam and Tony had seen me in it.

We each pulled up a bar stool, leaving one between us for better-shared access to the food. I topped off our wineglasses. "Want me to open another bottle?"

"No, I'm driving."

So why didn't you have that epiphany when you were at the Blue Martini? Then Liam wouldn't have ended up in your apartment. Stripping you nearly naked and God only knows what else.

I took a dumpling out of the container, dipped it in the accompanying sauce, then bit off half of it. "Yum," I said, holding my hand over my mouth so I could compliment with my mouth full. I tried the beef with snow peas first. Another winner. On my next trip down the buffet line, I took a small portion of Hunan shrimp. "Spicy. But in a good way," I told Jane. Passing on both the fried and sticky white rice, I went right for the moo shu pork. Taking a flour pancake, I began to build my entrée. Pork, egg, mushrooms, all in a ginger/sesame sauce. Folding it like a pro—which I am, since I moo shu at least once a week—I brought it to my mouth. As always, it was stellar.

"There's an elephant in the room, and his name is Liam," Jane said as she downed what was left in her wineglass.

Placing my chopsticks on my plate, I swiveled in my seat and looked at her. "There shouldn't be. We've been friends for years, and the first rule of girlfriends is that men come and go, but we women stick together."

"Nice sentiment," she said, her eyes sad. "But I know I hurt you, and I'm truly sorry."

I waved my hand. "Let's just forget it. The truth is, Liam and I have no future. Meaning I have no right to care what he does and with whom."

Jane sucked in a breath, then exhaled as if she was doing a yoga warm-up. Maybe it was the outfit. That's why I don't own any workout clothes.

"He didn't do anything with me except keep me from making yet another mistake," Jane insisted.

"Paolo was more than just a mistake," I reminded her.

I watched as Jane shivered. "Tell me about it. I bought an entire new bedroom suite. I couldn't sleep on furniture where I'd found a dead guy. Isn't that why you had the closets redone here?"

"Partly. But mostly because I wanted a walk-in with lots and lots of storage space."

Jane smiled. "That's because you never throw anything out or donate stuff to charity. That is a great tax deduction. You should consider it."

"I get to deduct what I paid. Yeah."

"Up to five hundred dollars."

I frowned. "That's like one pair of shoes and maybe a purse."

"As long as no single item is valued at more than five hundred, you can get the tax relief."

"I wonder if that's why Ellen decided to donate stuff out of the blue."

"The cedar-stinky bags?" Jane asked.

"Yep. Most of the stuff covers from the Whitney years to Paula Abdul. There are a few things in there that might be donation-worthy, but not a lot." I thought about the jewelry and for some reason decided to keep that tidbit to myself. No point in bringing it up until after I got it appraised.

"How come you got that job? Aren't there assistants or other people lower on the food chain for this kind of thing?"

"Of course. Ellen just has this passive-aggressive need to give me jobs that she wouldn't give a fellow attorney."

Jane nodded her head. "I get it. Can we get back to the Liam thing?"

"Not really anything to get back to."

Jane rolled her eyes. "I think it's time you faced facts. You're hot for the guy."

Couldn't deny that. "Could he be any more wrong for me? And let us not forget that he's a liar and still boffs his ex."

"First," Jane began as she ticked off her fingers, "how is he a liar? And second, what makes you think he's still got benefits with Ashley?"

"He knew about Patrick, but he didn't say anything to me. In my book, that's a lie of omission."

Jane tilted her head to one side. "Maybe he thought you knew. Maybe he felt like it wasn't his place to say anything. There could be a dozen reasonable explanations why he didn't say anything."

I suddenly came to the realization that I might be wrong. Still, I continued to argue my case. "Once he found out, he could have at least apologized for being complicit."

Jane massaged the back of her neck. "As for the Ashley thing, I just don't get that vibe."

"Then why are they always out together? Or in. I called Liam once, and she answered the phone."

"Maybe they both like the same bars. Maybe she was at his house returning something she'd borrowed or that he was awarded in the divorce. Again, dozens of reasons."

Oh yeah, I was wrong. "None of that matters. He's never asked me out on a proper date. It's like he's just stringing me along. Only I don't know where the string ends."

"So take him to the wedding."

I grimaced. "Izzy is looking to forward to it."

"So? She's a kid. She'll get over it."

"And you don't see a problem with uninviting my boss?"

"Nope. Actually, you don't even have to uninvite him. Technically speaking, your mother invited him and his kid. He's nothing more than an invited guest."

"But my mother will expect to see me dangling off his arm for photographs and the reception and the rehearsal dinner and—"

"Liam isn't exactly an eyesore," Jane said.

"Neither is Tony. Oh God! I've got to log in to eBay to see if Izzy is still the top bidder on the sweater."

I opened my Vostro 3000 and powered it up. It took me a matter of seconds to reach my target. Izzy was still the top bidder with an hour left to go. I prayed she remembered my instructions about how to swoop in at ten seconds remaining to outbid anyone hiding in the wings. If there was competition, hopefully she'd up the bid enough to knock out his or her highest bid.

"Aren't we supposed to be studying?" Jane asked. "I mean, you've been attending these classes for four hours a week for the last six weeks. You don't want to blow it now."

"Give me a second." I went to my own pending auctions, only to find I'd been outbid on the first of four extra links. I entered a higher bid, but the minute I did, I was outbid again. "Shit."

"You're on eBay, aren't you?" Jane asked. Technically, it was an accusation.

"Don't worry, I'm not winning anything."

"You need an intervention."

"No, I need a huge infusion of cash."

"Speaking of cash. If Dane-Lieberman was actually paying you overtime to attend the classes, how much would they have to pay you?"

"I'm not eligible for overtime. A little something Vain Dane decided *after* I came back."

"How much?"

"They bill my time at one-seventy-five an hour, so that would be—"

"Four thousand two hundred."

"Geez." I remembered that Ellen had me come in early, and that wasn't the first time. I did a few calculations in my head. "Add another six hundred or so."

"Did they at least kiss you before they screwed you?"

I closed my laptop, forcing it into sleep mode. "Not even a brush on the cheek. Let's study."

Jane stood very still. "Are we okay?"

I nodded. "Yes. And you were right about Liam. Maybe if we have wild sex, I can get him out of my system."

"Sounds like a plan. Where's your stuff?"

I handed her the study guide.

Jane thumbed through it, obviously planning on giving me random questions. She kept her pinky on the last section; that way she could quickly check my answers. "Okay. Are the police required to give the Miranda warning to everyone?"

"No, only if the person is in custody and they want to question the person and use their answers at trial."

Jane flipped to the back of the guide. "That's right. Seriously? Then why do they do it that way on TV?"

"Because it's TV. Next question?"

"How long can the police hold an inmate without charging him?"

"Seventy-two hours."

"Right again."

We went on like that for forty-five minutes. My confidence was boosted. I didn't miss a single question. Jane and I both got up to stretch when my cell phone rang. I went over to the counter and looked at the display. Blocked caller. Intrigued, I answered in the same way I answered all anonymous callers. "Albright Messaging, how may we assist you?"

"I'm sorry. I dialed wrong."

"Izzy?"

"Finley?"

"Yes."

"Albright whatever? What was that like all about?"

"Never mind. What do you need?"

"Will you hang on with me so I don't screw up the auction?"

"Give me a second." I glanced over at Jane, who looked tired enough to call it a day. Covering the microphone, I asked, "Are you as tired as you look?"

She nodded. "And I still need to hit the gym."

I shook my head. "Can't you just skip tonight?"

"Bikram yoga tonight. Wanna come?"

"Thanks, but I'd rather stick a pencil in my eye. Doing yoga is bad enough, but doing it in a steam room is just crazy."

"Finley? Are you still there?"

"I'm here. Hang on."

Jane gave me a hug. "Glad we talked. I'll see you soon."

"Thanks for all the food."

"My pleasure."

After she collected her gym bag I walked her to the door. "Thanks again."

"Last chance to get in on Bikram."

I closed the door while she was still chuckling.

"Sorry about that, Izzy. I had a friend over."

"Like a guy?"

"*Like* no," I teased.

"There's less than a minute until the auction ends. So far I'm the top bid— Oh crap, someone just outbid me!"

"Calm down and put in what you're really willing to pay. Use one-click bidding."

"I'm going up to three fifty."

"You go, girl," I said as I went over and started closing up the containers so I could place the generous leftovers in my fridge.

"I won!" she squealed so loudly that I had to hold the phone away from my ear.

I heard a man's voice in the distance—Tony, but I couldn't quite make out the words.

"Gotta go. I'm not allowed to be on my cell this late."

I was smiling as I filled my near-empty fridge. I had enough food to last for a week. I was still on a high from my Q&A with Jane, so I went to my computer and started to surf eBay for Rolex parts. I found a couple of new listings, but I didn't place a bid. I was going to employ a new strategy. I wouldn't bid until the last minute of the auction. Maybe I could fool my competition into thinking they had a lock on the item.

Remembering the brooches, I typed "L.S. & Co." into my search engine and discovered that the "L.S." stood for Lucy Shaw.

According to the home page, she designed jewelry from the early 1950s until the early 1990s. She died in '92 at the age of sixty-three. Her Detroit store was, and is, a highly regarded landmark.

I clicked over to the "items" page, only to discover that Lucy was most famous for designing one-of-a-kind pins for several first ladies, as well as celebrities, the military, and several beauty pageants. So how did Ellen come to have several custom pieces of Lucy Shaw jewelry? Inheritance? Gift? *Theft?*

I switched to my e-mail program and logged in to the Dane-Lieberman system. Remembering how the firm had shafted me with the course work and all of the early meetings, my fingertips hovered over the keyboard. I wasn't going to lie, but I didn't mind being vague.

Addressing the e-mail to Ellen, I typed:

> **Found what I think is costume jewelry in pocket of one coat.**
> **Do you want it back?**

A few seconds later my in-box pinged. Ellen replied:

> **No. I'm not big on jewelry. You're into accessories, you keep it.**

I replied:

> **Don't you want to see it first?**

Ellen's reply:

> **No. You keep them.**

My reply:

> **Thanks. I've made a detailed list of items for your taxes.**

Ellen's reply:

Not necessary. Just make the donation. See you tomorrow.

My reply:

Yes. I have a lot to tell you about the Egghardt estate.

◆

Tuesday was a warm September day. West Palm was not yet bursting with extra residents. Season, as it's called when we get the influx of snowbirds, lasts from October to April. Personally, I think there should be an extra tax on snowbirds. An inconvenience tax. In another month I'd have to add extra time to my commute just because a bunch of gray heads could no longer stand the winters in New York or Ontario.

My first-thing-in-the-morning meeting with Ellen had been strange. No digs about law school. No new mundane chores. In fact, I felt as if I didn't have her complete attention. Her eyes kept darting to an envelope clipped to her keyboard. Reading upside down I caught only part of the return address . . . "N . . . a Dept. of Corrections." At the end of the meeting, my guilt made me say, "I've got the jewelry from your coat in my purse downstairs. Would you like me to get it for you so you can make sure you don't want it?"

"I'm sure I don't," Ellen said as she stood. "Good work on the Egghardt thing. Research the laws relative to conversion of real property versus tenancy. I want to make sure we either throw them off the land or come up with some sort of quitclaim."

"Got it."

"Good luck tonight," she said as an afterthought as she was leaving the conference room.

Afterthought or not, I couldn't remember the last time Ellen had given me a compliment. In fact, I was fairly certain she'd never given me one.

I was using my lunch break to take the jewelry to Barton's up in Stuart for an appraisal. I didn't want to use the jeweler Dane-Lieberman used for our estate appraisals. As always, the entire staff of Barton's greeted me by name.

"Finally here to buy that bracelet you've been eyeing forever, Finley?"

"Sadly, no. I'd like to get an appraisal on these items." I carefully took the velvet pouch out of my purse and laid it on the counter. "Can you tell me how long it will take?"

"Tomorrow soon enough?"

"That would be great." I filled out the paperwork required, then left Stuart to head back to my office.

Because I'd used a jeweler up near Tony's house, my lunch hour was more like a lunch hour and a half. I parked between Ellen's Volvo and Vain Dane's Hummer. What a dweeb. Who needs a Hummer in the flattest state in the union?

As I locked my car, I got that tingly sensation that I was being watched. I looked around, but no one stood out. A postal worker. A couple of businessmen walking up Australian. A blond woman sitting with her back to me on a bench who looked a lot like my friendly neighborhood traffic enforcement officer. Maybe I was just paranoid because of the jewelry.

Even though I could justify taking it as partial payment for the extra hours I'd been working, I was still riddled with guilt.

No sooner had I walked in the door than Margaret said, "You're late."

"I had an errand."

"I wasn't told by Mr. Dane that you had permission to take personal time."

"Because it wasn't personal. I was here at seven thirty yesterday, so let's just call it even."

"That isn't how it works."

"It does in my world."

As soon as I reached my office, my world changed dramatically. Tony was placing a beautiful vase of red velvet roses on my desk. The smell was amazing. I stood watching him, filled with a sense of vindication. May have taken him a couple of days, but he finally got that his offer of payment for babysitting Izzy was an insult. And nothing says I'm sorry better than a spray of guilt flowers.

I cleared my throat to let him know I was in the doorway.

He smiled. "So much for an anonymous gift."

"They're beautiful," I said, moving close so I could smell one of the blooms. Inhaling the fragrance also meant moving close to Tony. Big mistake. "What are they for?" I wanted him to have to say he was sorry, too.

"Because tonight is your final class, and I wanted you to know how proud we are that you accomplished so much in such a short time. And with perfect scores."

Was he kidding? Did he really not get that he'd humiliated me on Saturday? First by insinuating we were going on a date and then by trying to slip me seventy dollars? God, men are clueless!

"What happened to your forehead?" he asked as he reached out and carefully moved my hair out of the way.

Luckily, I'd iced it all night, so the expected goose egg was barely noticeable. In fact, the only thing calling attention to my injury was the Band-Aid. "I, um, fell." It was hard to put a sentence together when I could feel the warmth of his touch all the way down to my toes. "At, um, home." Apparently, I was able to be pissed and turned-on simultaneously.

His palm slipped down until he was cupping the side of my cheek. I could smell his cologne, and it momentarily rendered me incapable of rational thought. His head dipped. Closer, until his minty breath washed over my upturned face.

I was almost shaking with anticipation. My breath hitched as a lump the size of the Hope Diamond lodged in my throat.

And then the buzzer sounded, and we jumped apart like two teenagers caught by their parents.

"Good luck tonight," Tony said as he quickly left my office.

I felt drained and cheated. Then the intercom buzzed again. I snapped up the receiver. "What?"

In a cheery tone, Margaret announced, "Mr. Dane wants you in his office. Now."

Tattletale.

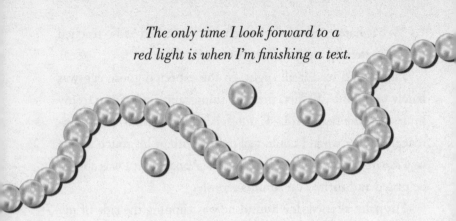

The only time I look forward to a red light is when I'm finishing a text.

eight

Approaching his office, I breathed deeply and evenly, something I'd learned in the only yoga class I'd managed to attend, even though I'd paid for a full year of sessions. Apparently, a single class wasn't enough to convince your heart to stop pounding against your rib cage when summoned to meet with the senior partner.

Crap, I should have brought a pad. Vain Dane got off on people taking notes. It made him feel powerful.

Which he was, since his ultra-conservative butt had the power to fire me.

Walking past the pin-neat, unoccupied desk of Dane's executive secretary, I slowly crept down the corridor toward the impressively carved mahogany door to Dane's office. Catching a whiff of Burberry cologne was slightly soothing. The signature scent reminded me of Jonathan Tanner. Even though my stepdad had been gone for more than a decade, I missed him every time I smelled that cologne.

The door was ajar, but I knocked and waited to be granted entrance.

"Come," Dane's voice boomed from inside.

Victor Dane's office was very posh, very masculine, and very, very self-congratulatory. Lining the walls were various diplomas, awards, and community service acknowledgments. The custom shelving held professionally framed photographs of Vain Dane with various celebrities, politicians, and dignitaries, including a nearly twenty-plus-year-old photo of Dane dancing with the Princess of Wales at the Palm Beach Polo Club.

Dane sat at the edge of his desk, arms folded, expression hard.

The wall behind Dane's desk wasn't a wall. It was a floor-to-ceiling window with breathtaking views of the Intracoastal, Palm Beach proper, and the Atlantic Ocean in the distance.

The silence dragged on so long that I contemplated throwing myself through said window. Not a good plan since I had to pass my test tonight. The alternative carried two penalties. One, I'd have to reimburse the firm for the cost of the class; and two, I wouldn't get to work with Tony on criminal cases. Besides, I knew the glass was impact-resistant and hurricane-proof, so my hundred-and-seven-pound body would just bounce off.

Dane reached behind him, grabbed the phone, and pressed the button. "She's here, Margaret, thank you."

Yep, I'm here, you traitor.

Dane was the picture of coiffed and polished. He was dressed in a handsome navy suit, monogrammed gunmetal polished cotton shirt, red-and-navy silk tie, and Bruno Magli loafers. He wasn't tall like Liam, but he had presence. A commanding presence that managed to ball my stomach into knots. He was the male version of a nun. Every time I was in his office, I half expected him to crack my knuckles with a ruler.

His dark hair was overly gelled and styled, but it went nicely with his shiny, buffed nails. His eyes were also dark, and expressionless. Like a shark about to roll in for the kill. Whatever was on his mind didn't show on his face. Nope. I sure as hell would not want to play poker with this person.

"Sit," he said as he rounded his desk.

Come. Sit. Beg. It was like I was in frigging PetSmart getting obedience training! "Thank you."

He slid a time sheet across the handcrafted mahogany desk. "It's been brought to my attention that you took a long lunch today?"

Caught, I had to scramble for a minute. "Yes, sir. I fell and hit my head and woke up this morning with a terrible headache." I paused to show him the Band-Aid, punctuating it with a taut grimace. "I thought it prudent to see a doctor." Okay, so some of that was true, and there was nothing wrong with a little bit of creative thinking. After all Jane did have a PhD in mathematics, so technically speaking, she was a doctor.

Dane's shoulders relaxed a bit as he split his attention between me and the greenish-blue shadow from his computer screen. Lacing my fingers, I placed my hands in my lap while Vain Dane was busy typing away. Attention still fixed on the computer screen, he asked, "You need to let someone know if you've got a medical emergency."

I'm fine, thanks for asking.

He continued. "I also understand that there is a major problem with the Egghardt estate?"

"Not major, but I'll have to petition to have the case re-opened."

Suddenly, his full attention was on me. "The Egghardt name carried a lot of weight in this town."

"I'm aware of that."

"How did this happen?"

I met his gaze full on. "Lenora—um, Ms. Egghardt—received a money order. That was the first we knew about the real property. Everything was done correctly, including placing ads in the paper to draw out any heirs or potential heirs to the estate.

"I've tracked down the people who've been living on the land. They claim they have a letter that serves as a lease. I'm giving them a few days to find it."

Dane nodded. "Sounds as if you're on top of it. Keep me in the loop."

How about the loop part of a noose?

"Will do."

"Your last exam is tonight?" he asked as he again swiveled slightly in his supple leather chair.

"Yes."

"Well, good luck, and don't forget you'll need a copy of the attendance records to prove you complied with the terms we agreed on."

"Thank you, and I'll make sure to provide you with everything you need." *You cheap bastard.*

"Still have a headache?"

You. "Yes, but it's not a big deal."

"Take the rest of the day so you can relax before your exam."

"That's very nice of you, Mr. Dane."

"Practical. This firm has a lot invested in you."

I was so not feeling the love. I waited about thirty seconds, and when he didn't say anything, I knew I was dismissed.

After I left, I went back to my office to collect my things. Becky was waiting for me.

"Cute dress. Is that new?"

I nodded. "Don't tell Jane. She'll freak if she knows I spent a penny."

"New shoes, too?" Becky asked through a smile.

They were cute. Platform pumps in a beige tone with my new favorite style, the peep toe. Because of the platform, the four-and-a-half-inch heel felt more like three and a half. Totally doable.

They were perfect for my new Suzi Xhin Maggy Boutique dress. It had a watercolor print in various shades of pinks and purples, as well as pleating at the cap sleeve and the waist. Hey, I needed something new to wear for my final test.

My turn. "New jewelry?"

Becky ran her fingers across the large, polished amber chunks that made up the thirty-inch necklace. When she did, I noticed the huge amber ring on her finger. It took up more than half her finger. "Guilty."

She was seated in one of the two chairs opposite my desk. She passed me her empty coffee mug, which I filled from the coffeemaker behind and just to the left of my chair.

"What happened to your head?"

I explained the injury for the third time, only this time I added the good news that Vain Dane had given me the rest of the day off. "What are you doing down here?" I asked.

"Not very welcoming, are you?"

"I didn't mean it that way," I insisted. "It's just that it was your idea that we downplay our friendship here at work."

"That's only because I'd get in hot water if the partners knew about all the times we've shared long lunches. I just don't want to jeopardize my—"

"Stop. I wasn't complaining. I just wondered why you were spending so much time here. Aren't you worried that Ellen will notice?"

"She isn't here."

My eyebrows pulled together. "She's always here."

Becky shrugged. "Something personal, apparently. Happened so quickly that all she had time to do was send me a text."

"Wow," I said before taking a sip from my mug. "She has a personal life?"

"Seems so." Becky leaned forward, and her necklace clinked against my desk as she stood; she drained her mug in the process. "Is the Egghardt thing on track?"

"On it. I just have to do some more research."

"Well, then, good luck tonight."

"I wonder when they'll devise a test for criminal procedure that requires you to pee on a stick."

♦

Once I arrived home, I kicked off my shoes and decided it wouldn't kill me to go over the study guide one last time. I grabbed a bottle of water and was about to go out to the cabana when my cell phone rang.

"Hello?"

"Hi, Finley. This is Ginger from Barton's. Your appraisals are ready."

"So soon?" I asked, glancing down at my watch. It wasn't the watch of my dreams, but it was a perfectly acceptable Full-Blooded rose-tone Swatch that complemented my dress.

"Yes."

"I'll be there in thirty minutes."

Just in case anyone from Dane-Lieberman wanted to reach me, I had calls from my landline forwarded to my cell. Twenty-three minutes later I was pulling my Mercedes into the parking lot. Barton's took up one half of the bottom floor of a two-story building just off Federal Highway.

I stepped out of the car at the same instant a sharp crack of thunder boomed in the near distance. Great, all I needed was to get rained on. It's a fairly common occurrence during the summer months; that's why I keep a few umbrellas in my car. I reached inside and grabbed a four-inch umbrella that fit nicely in my white Coach bag. Lightning flashed, and another boom of thunder. Luckily no rain. Yet.

Going into the store, I was greeted again by Mary. She went into the glassed-in area, where the owner checked mountings and settings, did repairs, and appraised items. He was a large man, balding, and I'd never seen him without a jeweler's light strapped on his head. To my embarrassment, I couldn't remember his name and couldn't summon the nerve to ask for the fifth time.

He draped a dark blue velvet cloth over the counter and lined all the pieces up. "You've got quite a collection here."

"Is it all costume?"

"All but this one," he said as he picked up the large crown brooch. "Platinum, four carats of brilliant cut stones. The diamonds at VS1, color between an E and a D. Worth in the neighborhood of twenty-five hundred to three thousand."

My guilt side told me I should let Ellen know immediately. The rationalization side reminded me that I'd already asked Ellen and she'd relinquished the jewelry to me. Plus, there was the whole issue of my working roughly five thousand dollars' worth of overtime with no compensation. "And the others?"

"The other three pins, maybe eight to nine hundred. The bracelet and earrings, roughly two hundred each. You know what you have here?"

"Lucy Shaw and Company pieces?"

"Very good," he said. "I looked on the Internet, and I'm fairly sure these are pageant pieces."

"As in beauty pageants?"

He nodded. "Got some years on 'em, too. I sent pictures of the serial numbers to the company in Detroit, and they'll do a search of their records."

"Thank you."

"I told them to call you when they had the information."

"Thanks," I said as I shook his hand. "What do I owe you?"

"Two fifty will cover it. I'll mail you a written report before the end of the week."

Luckily, my credit card cleared. I would have been humiliated if Visa had outed me as a pauper. Jane was right: I needed to start living within my means. And once I sold the costume stuff on eBay, I could recoup what I'd paid for the appraisals.

I still had more than an hour before I had to leave for class, so I decided to go home. Abandoning the idea of studying, I got my digital camera out and photographed each piece of the costume jewelry as well as taking one group shot. I took the platinum brooch to my bedroom and placed it in the tampon box I used to hide all my good jewelry. I figured any thief wouldn't think or want to look there.

Opening my laptop, I logged in to my secondary eBay account and began uploading the pictures of the items. Much to my surprise, eBay actually had a category for pageant items. *Who knew?*

I wrote a brief description, including that the pieces were vintage, that I could provide an appraisal, and that they all had maker's marks. I decided I would let the auction go until the Friday before Lisa's wedding. Hopefully, someone out there in the pageant world would be all over the stuff, bidding it up over value with so much time to bid.

But it still begged a question. Why would Estrogenless Ellen have beauty pageant jewelry?

I didn't have time to ponder that conundrum. Time for me to head up to the Jupiter campus of Florida Atlantic University. Slipping my shoes back on, I took the forward off my phone. The professor had a very strict take on cell phones in the classroom.

My key was in the ignition when my cell rang. A blocked caller. I started the car, then slid the bar and switched the phone to the cool hands-free device I'd gotten through Hammacher Schlemmer.

"Hello?"

"Hi, Finley. It's Izzy. Am I bothering you?"

"Nope. On my way to take a final exam."

"Yuck. Mine start in three weeks. Right after the dance."

"Sorry."

"The dress came today."

"Did your father see it?" I asked when I heard the subdued tone in her voice.

"No, but I can't wear it."

"Why?"

"I think it needs like a special bra or something."

I smiled. "How about dinner tomorrow night? We can hit P.F. Chang's in the Gardens Mall, then make a swing through Victoria's Secret."

"Really?"

Her enthusiasm was contagious. "Yes, really. I'll pick you up at five thirty. Okay?"

"This is way cool. Do I bring the dress?"

"Yes."

"My dad never gets home before like seven thirty. Can we make it by then? I want to have the dress in my closet before he gets a chance to see it and like go all nut job on me."

"Consider it done." *If she thought Tony was going to get pissed over the dress, wait until he sees it. It'll happen eventually. My guess is during a dry run for the wedding. Another reason to uninvite him.*

"Thanks, Finley. Good luck on your exam."

"I'll see you tomorrow."

"Finley?"

"Yes?"

"Just so you know, I'd be totally cool with you dating my dad."

Using my thumbs, I was able to disconnect the cell without taking my hands off the wheel. I felt a kind of panic making it difficult to breathe. I had the Izzy seal of approval? What does that mean? Had Tony run the idea past her? Lord knew it hadn't happened to me. Unless I counted those few seconds in my office. Why did all this have to be so freaking complicated?

I allowed my mind to wander. I felt for Izzy. It had to be uncomfortable being raised by a single dad. Tony probably had no clue that the girl needed proper lingerie. I wondered how he'd feel when all the bills started rolling in. Most likely, he'd lose interest in me the second he discovered I'd turned his kid into a shopaholic.

Well, that would have to wait. I'd reached my destination—the Starbucks just a little way away from the campus—got a venti latte, and was soon pulling into the school's parking lot. The sky was still threatening rain, so I left the tiny umbrella in my purse. It was time for me to think only of police procedure. My heels clicked rhythmically as I walked down the hallway, went into my classroom, and joined the other twenty-eight people in the class. As always, I took the second seat in the first row.

It wasn't like we had assigned seats, just more of a pattern we'd gotten into over the course of the class. I took a long pull on my coffee, then pulled a pen out of my purse. In no time, a blue exam book was passed to me.

♦

While there are many positives to living alone, the one negative is when you have great news but no one to share it with. At least when I had the condo, I could run upstairs and force Sam to listen to my successes and failures.

Don't get me wrong, I love being an Islander. I mean, where else can you live that has trash pickup seven days a week?

I'd foolishly left the porch light off, but, thanks to Sam's brilliant forethought, as soon as I started toward the house, a motion sensing flood lamp blinked on.

I slipped my key into the door, then entered, only to find the faint scent of cedar still hung in the air. Maybe it was the Ghost of Jewelry Past. Maybe it was karma.

"Maybe it's just me being an ass. Ellen said I could have the stuff. Stop obsessing," I mumbled as I placed my purse on the chair, kicked my shoes off, and then went to the freezer and took out a bottle of Grey Goose. From a lower cabinet, I retrieved the cosmo mix. So it wasn't as good as the real thing. It was close enough to use to toast the end of all those continuing-ed classes.

Lifting my glass to self-on-self toast my success, I was about to take a well-deserved sip when the doorbell chimed. I put my drink down, then went to the door and opened it. I let out a long breath that sounded a little like a groan. "What do you want?" I moved my head around. "I didn't hear that piece of junk you call a car."

Liam smiled down at me, and I couldn't help but notice how his eyes sparkled in the porch light. I made a mental note for Sam—adjust the location of the sensors. Obviously, Liam knew the blind spots. I'd have to make sure Sam did it when Liam wasn't looking so his car couldn't sneak up on me anymore.

His hand swung out from behind him, and he presented me with a box the size of a shirt box, only this one felt like it was full of gravel. No, too light for gravel.

"This is for you," he said. "Congratulations, well done, and thank you."

"Thank you for what?"

"Making me fifty bucks. Ellen bet me that you wouldn't make it through all the extra work and the classes."

"Nice to know someone had faith." I took the box and began to close the door.

"Invite me in."

Intelligent Finley screamed, *No! No!* But Dry-Spell Finley yanked the door as wide as the hinges allowed.

"Okay, you're in." I returned to my drink and took a huge sip.

Liam straddled the bar stool across the counter from me. His unbuttoned Caribbean Joe shirt teased me with a little preview of his muscled body.

Lord, I had to have sex. This dry spell wasn't working for me.

"Don't you want to know?"

"Kn . . . know what?" I asked. He always seemed to know what I was thinking. Did he telepathically know I wanted to ravage him right here and right now?

"What's in the box. Got any beer?"

I went to the fridge and pulled one from the veggie bin. Until Harold started working for me, I never had beer in my fridge. I placed the long-necked bottle in front of Liam and didn't bother with a mug. I started checking drawers, looking for an opener. Unnecessary. Liam did something, and the cap popped right off.

"That can't be good for my counter. What if you'd chipped it or something?"

"I'd put in another one. How's your head?"

I took another fortifying sip of my cosmo. "Fine. Barely a scratch. Is this an apology gift or a congratulatory gift?"

"What am I apologizing for?"

My head tilted to one side as I got the first whiff of his subtle cologne. It was as appealing as the Breitling Chronograph around his wrist. I still wondered how a PI could afford a nine-thousand-dollar watch. "You really don't know?"

"No. But if you want me to say I'm sorry, fine. I'm sorry." He rolled his eyes. "Is this about the Jane thing?"

"No," I replied. "It's about you whoring me out as a babysitter."

His grin was slow, sexy, and reached all the way to his eyes. "Tony asked for my recommendation."

"And you thought of me?"

"I thought Izzy would like you."

"So you orchestrated that just to please a thirteen-year-old?"

"That was just a side benefit. I gave you a chance to see what it would be like if you dated Tony."

I felt a blush creep up my neck. "We aren't dating. He's my boss."

"He and Izzy come as a package deal. And then there's his thing."

"What's his thing?"

Liam shook his head. "Not my place to say." He took a pull on the bottle. "I pointed out to Tony that it was more complicated to do an interoffice thing. I think he took that to heart."

"So what? The two of you got together and decided my future?"

Liam laughed. "No, it wasn't like that. We were just working out that part of the guy code."

"Which part of the code?"

"The part that says friends shouldn't make a play for the same woman at the same time."

"So this is some sort of noncompetition competition?"

He stroked the shadow of dark stubble on his chin. "It sounds kind of weird when you put it like that."

I longed to reach out and brush the black hair off his forehead. But I didn't dare touch him. I knew that would be a fatal mistake.

"C'mon, open your present."

As soon as I tore the paper, I made some sort of girly-happy-squeally sound. "You bought me Lucky Charms?"

"I heard you were a fan."

"From whom?"

"Doesn't matter. Do you like your gift?"

"It's absolutely the best under-five-dollar gift I've ever received."

"That was a little backhanded."

I felt badly. "I didn't mean it *that* way."

"You can make it up to me. Come here."

Stay, stay, and stay as if your feet were nail-gunned to the floor. Be strong. You can do it.

Screw that.

As soon as I came around the counter, he pulled me into the circle of his arms. His parted thighs created a close, tight place for me to stand. Heat radiated from his body. His hand slipped up my back until his fingers entwined in my hair. Gently, he tugged my head back. His eyes were fixed on my mouth, but he made no move. "This is definitely one of my wishes," he said in a rough, sexy tone that I heard all the way down to my toes.

"Still holding me to that whole three wishes for saving my life?"

"You bet. Especially since the other night. I like the way you feel against me, Finley."

"How do I know this isn't another one of your head games?"

"Trust. My third wish."

His mouth covered mine. There was nothing tentative or cautious about the kiss. I grabbed fistfuls of his shirt. The way his tongue sparred with mine was just throwing fuel on an already-blazing fire.

Why couldn't I stay mad at him? Life would be easier if I stayed in a constant state of annoyance. But no. I have to torture myself into thinking I can steer this ship. Shit, my boat doesn't even have a rudder. And yet Liam was knocking the wind right out of my sails.

Unlike our previous encounter, this was urgent, but somehow softer and slower. He explored my throat, my earlobes, and pretty much every part of my head and neck with hot kisses.

I slipped my hands under his shirt, and he did the same. Well, almost the same, his fingers rested on my ribs, just below the swell of my breasts. When I couldn't stand it any longer, I started to reach for the buttons of his shirt. He pulled back.

"Not yet."

I blinked. "We've already been halfway there," I argued. Recalling that he'd wanted me to ask for a kiss, I guessed he wanted the same treatment. "I want you. I know you want me, so stay."

He offered a weak smile. "You have a few things to work out before we take this to the next level."

"What things?"

"You're a smart lady. You'll figure it out."

There are good touches and bad touches.
It just depends on whom you're dating.

nine

When my alarm went off, the first thing I did was touch my lips. After Liam's searing kiss, I half expected to be lipless. I wasn't, but I was spineless. I banged my head into my pillow. "What the hell was I thinking?" I grumbled to myself. Memories of last night came back like a boulder racing downhill, with me standing at the bottom of the hill.

As I tossed off the comforter, I felt myself blush all over again. Going into the bathroom, I stared at my reflection. Like Macaulay Culkin, I placed my palms against my cheeks. I rubbed vigorously. "You practically begged." *Loser.*

It was hard to look at myself, so I went to the kitchen to turn on the coffee. My secret hope that last night had been a dream or hallucination was dashed when I saw the half-full bottle of beer and the empty cocktail glass. Oh yes, it was real. "And amazing," I said as I turned and leaned in backward. I leaned so that my hands and the small of my back were against the counter and I watched the pot brew.

I grabbed up my cell phone and sent three urgent text messages that all said the same thing:

Did more than just talk to Liam
Lunch @ Saito's. 911

I dressed for work, mindful of my dinner with Izzy. I needed shoes that could go all day and all night. That meant only one thing—wedges.

My solution was a Donna Ricco peplum dress, purchased at a deep discount because of a tear at the peplum. I paired it with my Michael Kors Cassie wedges and switched handbags to my Coach hobo bag; the black leather worked perfectly, and if I held it correctly, no one would know about the small imperfection at the side seam. Dressing on a budget is really taxing. I miss the days when I could just walk into a store and buy *whatever* without counting pennies.

Before I went to work, I hopped on to my laptop and called up my eBay listing. I was surprised that the bidding on the pins had already neared their appraised value. The bracelet was doing okay, but the earrings had yet to get a nibble. Ah, well, I could always relist them if they don't sell. Or I could just keep them. The tiny crowns were kinda cute. I held back on the platinum pin, still concerned that Ellen would realize her mistake and want it back. Just to assuage my conscience, I sent her an e-mail reaffirming that she wanted me to have all the pieces. I avoided mentioning the appraisal from Barton's.

♦

The morning flew by, mainly because I'd spent much of my time researching the potential problems with the Bollans living on Egghardt land without a lease or other type of agreement. I couldn't imagine having eight kids, let alone raising them in such a tight place.

Having said that, Lenora Egghardt would never want for anything ever again if she could turn the land into an equestrian center. I still hadn't heard from the Bollans. Without any type of written agreement, Ellen would have to advise the client to evict the tenants.

As prearranged, Becky left the office five minutes before me so no one at the office would know how close we were. I caught up with her at the base of the MuviCo steps.

"Well?" she pressed.

"Wait till everyone is here so I don't have to keep repeating myself."

"C'mon, do you have any idea how hard it was for me *not* to go to your office for a preview?"

"And I appreciate that. There's Jane and Liv now," I said, pointing toward the cigar shop. Once we were all assembled, we went up to the second floor, all the while complimenting one another's clothing and/or accessories.

We came to Saito's often enough that the kimono-clad hostess greeted us with a warm smile. "Follow me, Miss Garrett," she said to Liv.

"Don't you just feel invisible?" Jane whispered in my ear.

I nodded. Even women got a girl crush when Liv was in the vicinity.

The hostess showed us to a quiet corner of the restaurant. I wondered if she could sense I was in crisis mode. Once the waiter had taken our orders, Liv leaned in and asked, "How's your head?"

My fingers reflexively went to the small scab at my hairline. "Don't even need a Band-Aid."

"Great. Now spill. You had sex?" Liv pressed.

"You had *great* sex?" Jane asked.

Becky sighed. "You had crappy sex?"

"I had no sex." My three friends looked as if I'd just told them they had to donate all their clothes to the homeless.

"So why the urgent text?" Becky asked as she took her cell out and placed it next to her chopsticks.

"I tried to have sex."

"Oh, honey," Liv breathed. "Are you telling us that Little Liam couldn't rise to the occasion?"

"Seriously?" Becky asked as she leaned forward. "The general wouldn't stand at attention?" Humor danced in her eyes.

Liv and Jane chuckled.

"Glad my life crisis is fodder for your amusement."

Jane patted my hand. "We're sorry. It's just that, well . . . we're talking Liam here. He's the last guy any of us would think couldn't . . . close the deal."

"That's what I'm trying to tell you. There was no deal."

"You lost me," Becky said, leaning back in her seat while she absently played with her amber pendant so the waiter could serve our uninteresting round of iced tea.

I waited for the staff to place steaming bowls of miso soup in front of each of us, then said, "He came to my place to give me a present and—"

"What did he get you?" Jane asked, her spoon hovering above her soup.

"A box of Lucky Charms."

"That's really sweet."

"Can we get past the cereal?" Becky asked.

"So I open the present. I gave him grief for setting me up as Tony's babysitter. Then the next thing I know, we're kissing."

"Polite good night?" Liv asked. "Or rock my world?"

"Rock my *universe*," I answered on an expelled breath. Even now, just thinking about it made heat pool in the pit of my stomach. "And then it happened."

"What was *it*?" Becky demanded her tone short.

Becky was never one for protracted storytelling, but I just shot her an I'm-telling-this look.

"We're hot. We're heavy. We're pressed together, and my legs were turning to mush."

"I need to call my garage-boy squeeze for a hookup," Liv said under her breath.

I wasn't into discussing the fact that Liv had a boy-toy who lived above his parents' garage. "Anyway," I paused when the waiter came over to ask me if everything was all right. "I've just been talking," I assured him. Then out of politeness, I put a spoonful of soup in my mouth.

"You're kissing . . . ?" Jane prompted.

"Oh my God, the man has magic lips. And a body—"

"You went skin to skin?" Becky asked?

"I went skin. I slipped my hands under his shirt. Molded, hard muscle."

"What was he doing?" Becky asked.

"Just holding me. Other than that, nothing. Absolutely nothing," I said, presenting my hands, then letting them slap back down on the tabletop. "No touchy feely. He didn't touch a thing but my hair, and that was only so he could move it out of the way. He nuzzled my earlobes and then traced a line of kisses down my throat."

"This is better than a sexy romance novel," Jane insisted. "Keep going."

"Glad I'm entertaining all of you. So all I can think about is getting him into the bedroom. He's nibbling my ear and his breath is heating my skin, and so I said, 'Stay the night,' and boom. Done. Over. Finished."

Jane looked horrified. "He did not!"

"He did. And then he set me off to one side and said some bullshit about how sleeping with me was one of his three wishes."

"Three wishes?" Liv asked.

"Remember that horrible time on the yacht a few months ago? Well, afterward I kinda promised him three wishes for saving my life. Mr. Opportunistic is gonna hold me to it. I meant it as a joke!"

"Guess the joke was on you," Becky grunted.

We stopped talking as the waiter cleared our soups and set a platter of freshly made sushi in the center of the table. He dealt each of us a plate and told us to enjoy.

"I'll never enjoy anything ever again," I mumbled after he left.

"The three-wishes thing was all the explanation you got?" Becky asked.

"I think he said something about me having to work through something. Only I don't have a clue what he meant. But apparently actually sleeping with me is moving too fast for him."

"Too fast!" Jane dropped her sushi. "You've known him a year."

"And this isn't the 1950s," Jane added. "God, that would be rich. A prudish guy."

"A *hot*, prudish guy," Becky corrected. "So how did it end?"

"Well, you'd think I'd know that no means no, but you'd be wrong. I reached out, took his hand, and said, 'Please.' Do you believe it? I actually begged."

Liv said, "I don't think that's begging. Begging would be, 'Please, please, please!'"

I shot her a look. "I did everything short of grabbing onto his pant leg so he couldn't leave." I rested my head in my hands. "He must think I'm totally desperate."

"I'm sure he doesn't," Becky said.

"Then you tell me why he put the brakes on. Correction. He didn't just put the brakes on, he threw the car in reverse."

"Maybe he had on torn underwear," Liv suggested.

Becky added, "Or maybe he'd already had sex last night and isn't the kind of guy who does a twofer."

"That's gross," Jane said.

"So now the question is, what do I do from here?"

"Go sleep with his best friend?" Jane suggested.

"Pretend it never happened," Liv offered.

"Pretend you don't give a shit that it happened. His loss." Becky said with authority. "In fact, turn the tables on him.

Get him all hot and bothered, and next time you slam on the brakes. Send him on his way with the mother of all erections."

♦

My day was almost over. Or rather my *work*day. I still had dinner with Izzy, but I didn't think of that as work. At four thirty, Tony knocked on my open door. "Got a minute?"

"Sure," I pointed to the two empty chairs opposite my desk. Of course I had time, I'd spent the last hour surfing the Internet and/or logged on to eBay.

"Izzy is very fond of you," he said after he took a seat.

"I like her," I said, tension knotting my shoulders. Tony's demeanor was different, and I wasn't sure why. And he'd closed the door behind him. Very out of character. I could only pray it wasn't because Liam told him I'd invited him to spend the night.

Tony nervously rubbed his palms together, then smiled and let out a kind of short half laugh. "This is a little awkward. I'd be lying if I said I wasn't interested in you."

I wasn't sure if I should thank him or admit that I, too, was curious, so I remained mute.

"Um, I don't know what went on Saturday night, but Izzy really looks up to you. She hasn't bonded with anyone since we moved from New York.

"She's at a tough age. I've got to be careful when it comes to my personal decisions. Then there's the issue of my being your boss. But honestly, that doesn't bother me as much as how dating you would impact Izzy."

Oh my God. I was about to get the single daddy brush-off.

"Right now I'm leaning toward avoiding a sticky situation. I just can't date someone my daughter likes so much. If that happened and things went sour, you wouldn't be part of her life, and I won't do that to her. I know I'm supposed to escort you to your sister's wedding, but—"

"Yeah, I've been meaning to talk to you about that. My mother corralled you before I had the chance to tell her that I'd already arranged for an escort."

I watched his broad shoulders relax. "Okay, then. I'll just call your mother and—"

"You should still go," I insisted. "Izzy is looking forward to going to Six Flags with you. Plus, when was the last time the two of you took a long weekend?"

He stroked his chin. "I honestly can't remember. When we lived in New York, her maternal grandparents tended to be the ones who took her to museums and zoos. I was usually working."

"I was raised for a short time by a single parent, Tony. Trust me when I tell you it's very important for you to set aside time for Izzy that doesn't include you on a laptop, answering e-mail, text messaging, or any other diversion."

"She's the queen of texting. Which reminds me: she wanted me to ask if it was okay for her to text you."

"Sure. Do you know I'm taking her shopping tonight?"

"You? I thought it was some friend from school." Tony stood up and headed for the door. "I wonder why she lied."

"She's not trying to lie, Tony. She was just embarrassed."

He stopped and turned. "Embarrassed by what?"

God, this was a surreal conversation to have with a boss. "She needs some new undergarments, and, well . . ."

"She couldn't ask me?"

"You want to take her to the bra fitter?"

Tony's neck turned pink just above the collar of his white shirt. He looked exceedingly handsome today. There was something about his dark coloring and a white shirt that just made him hot. Or maybe I was just feeling residual hot from last night. *To hell with Liam, I'd already given him too much thought.*

"I see what you mean," he said as he reached into his pocket and took out some neatly folded bills. "Let me pay for dinner. A way to thank you for—"

"Would you stop insulting me by offering to pay me for everything I do?"

He blinked. "I wasn't trying to insult you. I just wanted to thank you for helping Izzy."

"Then stop treating me like your hired help."

"I'm sorry, Finley."

"Thank you. Now, I've got to get going so I'm not late."

"You don't have to pick her up. I'll just call the housekeeper and have her run Izzy down to the mall. Saves you from driving all the way up to Martin County when the mall is what? Fifteen minutes from here?"

"That would be a help. I'll bring her home, though. I'm not sure how long we'll be."

"Okay."

Tony was just at the threshold of my office when he stopped with his back to me. "Hey, Finley?"

"Yeah?"

"If it wasn't for Izzy, I'd ask you out in a New York minute."

"O-okay."

As soon as he left, I rolled my eyes. "Okay?" I repeated. "That's the best you could come up with, Finley?"

So now I had a guy who wanted to date me but wouldn't and a guy who made my knees weak who wanted to kiss me but didn't want to sleep with me. "What kind of karmic bullshit is this?"

My mood wasn't a whole lot better when I reached the mall and valet parked in the row next to the giant horses guarding the entrance to P.F. Chang's. Izzy was seated on the fountain, a small shopping bag dangling from her wrist, and she glared at me as I walked toward her.

"You told my dad," she whined when I was still a good five feet away.

"Nice to see you again, too."

"Did you tell him about the dress, too?"

I placed my hand in the middle of her back and steered her over next to one of the equine statues. "Of course I didn't. But you've got to understand that your dad is my boss, and he came into my office as I was getting ready to leave. I can't just lie to him."

"Swear you didn't say anything about the dress?"

"Swear. Now, should we start over?"

"I'm sorry," she said. "I just didn't want him to be mad, but I also don't want to hurt his feelings."

"You won't."

"How do I get back home with this?" she asked as she lifted the small Bloomingdale's shopping bag and swung it back and forth.

"I told your dad we were going bra shopping. Trust me, he won't ask to see what you bought, and he sure as hel—*heck* won't look in the bag."

"That was wicked smart," Izzy said, all of her earlier anger dissipated.

Since I'd talked my way through lunch, the smell of food wafting out the restaurant door had me salivating. "Ready to eat?"

"Yep. Lunch, as always, sucked."

I laughed softly. Cafeteria food had never been my thing, either.

Once we were shown to a table, I asked, "Do you have any homework?"

"Some dumb reading, but I can get that done in twenty minutes."

I picked up my menu and asked, "Do you like the lettuce wraps?"

"Love them."

"Great. I'm going for the crispy honey chicken. How about you?"

"Wok-charred beef."

"Excellent."

The server came over and asked if we'd ever dined at a Chang's before. Since we had, he went directly into taking drink orders and creating our sauce mixture.

"What's in a mojito?"

"Rum, sugar, lime, water, and mint. How was school?"

"Great. Lindsey Hetzler tripped in B hall and fell on the floor."

I touched my forehead and felt a kinship to Lindsey. "That's mean to be glad she's hurt."

"She didn't get hurt," Izzy insisted. "Mr. Canahan said the only thing she hurt was her pride."

"Eighth grade is brutal."

As we ate, Izzy filled me in on the players at St. John's Academy. By the time the waiter brought our check, I knew who all the hot guys were, who all the slutty girls were, and who was smoking weed. If I were paying upward of twenty grand a year, I'd make damned sure my kid wasn't one of them.

My kid. I shivered. My biological clock hadn't gone off yet. In fact, it wasn't even ticking. I was only twenty-nine, and besides, even if I did want the whole family thing, I'd have to find Mr. Right sometime soon. And that didn't look promising.

Once Izzy had all the proper lingerie, I drove her up to Martin County to drop her off. Tony came out to the driveway.

He looked deliciously different in casual clothing, doing justice to a pair of jeans and a polo shirt. Where Liam looked just-out-of-bed sexy in jeans, Tony seemed almost preppy, but in a good way. Like he'd be right at home strolling down Worth Avenue or the boardwalk outside the Breakers.

"Everything go okay?" he asked Izzy as she bounced out of my car.

I turned down the radio. No sense letting Tony know that Izzy and I shared the same taste in music and had blasted 95.5 FM all the way from Palm Beach Gardens.

"Great! Thanks, Finley," she said as she got out of the car, kissed Tony's cheek, and went inside the house.

I tried to capture my hair and twist it into something a little less wild since we'd done I-95 with the top down. "Here," I said as I unhooked my seat belt, reached down to the floor of the passenger's side, and picked up the Chang's bag. "This is Izzy's, and don't worry about it being out too long. We had the restaurant keep it in the fridge until we finished shopping."

"I never would have thought of that," he admitted. "You must be a frequent shopper."

"I do what I can," I joked.

There was an awkward few seconds when Tony's eyes roamed over my body, lingering on where my dress had hiked up to reveal a generous amount of thigh. I remembered the daddy speech and immediately reached for the gearshift.

"I'll see you in the morning," I said.

Tony stood and said, "Sure thing."

As I was driving back to the gate, my cell rang. "Hello?"

"Fin, you won't believe what just happened," Becky said so quickly I almost had to make her repeat herself.

"What?"

"I just got a text from Ellen."

Nothing new, except that it meant Becky was still working at nine fifteen at night. "What?"

"Ellen quit."

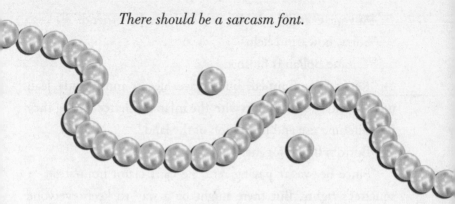

There should be a sarcasm font.

ten

"You look like hell," I said days later when Becky came in and practically collapsed into a chair.

"I feel like hell. No, what's worse than hell?"

Her green eyes were bloodshot, and her auburn hair was mussed as if she'd been pulling it out at the roots.

"Ellen's been gone only a week." That still bothered me. Ellen just didn't seem the type to up and quit without notice of any kind.

"It feels like an eternity. Especially since she won't return my calls, or e-mails, or texts. I swear, you'd think she took the last shuttle to the space station."

"I'm pretty sure we can talk to the space station."

Becky shot me a glare. "Don't be literal. Be my friend. Please tell me you've finished with the Bollan thing. Victor is all over me."

I arched one brow. "Calling him Victor these days, eh? Movin' on up, are you?"

"Anyone ever tell you that you suck as a best friend?"

"Sorry, how can I help?"

"Tell me Bollan is finished."

"Research is finished, but I gave Sleepy and Wanda Jean until Monday to come up with the infamous letter stating they have lifetime use and possession of the land."

"Bottom line it for me."

"Since he wasn't paying rent, he can't claim homestead or squatter's rights. But there might be a way to keep everyone happy."

"How?"

I reached for the giant three-ring binder off to one side of my desk and flipped through the indexed tabs. I removed the plat I'd gotten from the tax collector's office and spread it out, holding it down with a glass Tiffany paperweight my mother had given me for college graduation. I'd wanted a trip to Paris. Instead, I got a fancy glass ball that cost more than a trip to Paris.

"We move Sleepy and Wanda Jean's trailer here," I paused to point at the far southwestern corner of the property. "Then we give them eighty acres for soy beans so they have some cash. Their cattle can graze around the equestrian center. It's a win-win."

Becky looked relieved. "Think Lenora will go for it?"

I nodded. "She's reasonable. It's the Bollans I have doubts about."

"Why?"

"They swear there was a witness when Egghardt delivered the letter eight years ago, but all they had was some story about a hot redhead in a car. Plus, they're very . . . *committed* to their home."

"They can be committed, or they can take the deal."

"Or they can litigate." I checked my watch. "I've got about an hour before I have to go home, finish packing, and get to the airport for Lisa's wedding."

"Liam on the same flight?" Becky asked with a devilish smile.

"You suck as a best friend, too. And no, he's on his own. As far as I know my mother only booked a flight for me."

"Have the two of you talked since the *incident*?"

I shook my head. "I sent him a text about what to wear and gave him the info for the Ritz-Carlton in Atlanta."

"Are you going to give him the silent treatment all weekend?"

"I prefer to think of it as not cluttering his mind with superficial chitchat."

"And Tony?"

"He and Izzy are flying in tonight. That way they can spend tomorrow at Six Flags."

"Brushing up against all those sweaty tourists?" Becky shuddered. "Pass, thanks. Remember when our sorority took a trip there? Worst day of my higher-education life."

"No, the worst day of your college life was when you got dumped by Brian Hastings."

"I was in *luv*," Becky joked.

"I wonder what ever happened to him."

"Last I heard he'd gotten his MBA and is some sort of sports agent."

Tilting my head to the side and letting out a long sigh, I said, "So you both negotiate for a living. Wow, you were soul mates."

On that note, Becky dragged herself out of the chair. "I hope you have fun at the wedding. Tell your mom I said hi."

"I will."

"And don't forget to bring me back some Moon Pies."

"You can buy Moon Pies at Publix."

"Not the same as the ones from Georgia. It's closer to Tennessee. And some RC Cola. You can't eat Moon Pies without RC Cola. Too bad you can't bring me an order of onion rings from the Varsity Grill."

"Are you planning on eating your way through Ellen's sudden meltdown?"

Becky gripped the chair back. "Does this make *any* sense to you?"

"No. I never would have pegged Ellen as the type to have a midlife crisis. And the whole out-of-touch thing is just too weird. Has anyone gone over to her condo? Maybe corner her in person."

"I did. No one answered the door, but I heard motion inside."

"Did you peek in the windows or anything?"

"That'd be tough; she lives on the third floor."

"Oh. So she isn't even talking to Vain Dane?"

Becky shook her head. "No, and I know he thinks I knew this was coming and just kept my mouth shut."

"And you didn't get a tiny hint?" I asked.

Becky breathed in and out. "Maybe she was a little distracted that last day, but I just assumed she was stressing over a financing deal about to close."

I thought back to my last encounter with Ellen before she pulled her Houdini. "Yeah, the last time I met with her she seemed distracted, too. She had an envelope on her clipboard. Something from a Department of Corrections."

"Ellen?" Becky asked as her brows pulled together and she frowned. "Other than briefly helping Jane, I don't think she's ever done criminal work."

"So why would she be getting prisoner mail?"

Becky twisted her hair into a messy updo, securing it with one of the Dane-Lieberman pens from a holder on my desk.

Guess the firm's name would have to change now. "Did you find the letter or the envelope in her office?"

"I didn't know to look for it," Becky said.

"Want me to come help?"

"If you have time. Finish up what you're doing and then come up."

"See you in a few."

I put the plat back in the binder and did a few other minor things. My last task was to check my in-box one last time.

I found an urgent message forwarded through eBay from Tiara64. Scary thing about that was it meant there were probably sixty-three other people who wanted "tiara" in their name. At any rate, she was the high bidder on all the pageant jewelry, but she had a rather strange request. My seller profile listed me as living in Palm Beach County; she said since she was in nearby Lake Worth, she'd like to pick the items up personally when the auction ended on Sunday.

I thought about it for a minute, then decided it made things easier for me, so why not? I replied to her and received an instant response. She didn't want to wait for me; she wanted the items at the moment the auction ended at noon. Only problem with that? I wouldn't be back from Atlanta, so I sent her another e-mail letting her know that wasn't possible.

Then this pageant junkie tells me she'll pay an additional one hundred dollars per item if I get them to her by one p.m. That's five hundred extra dollars. That's a pair of Manolo Blahniks, and not from Nordy's Rack, either. We're talking walk into the store and select that perfect shoe. No way was I going to turn down this gift horse.

I couldn't be in two places at once, but I had a solution. Carrying my super-cute pink bowling bag-style purse with me, I headed for the elevator. The purse was, if I did say so myself, a stunning replica of a classic zip-top Chanel bag. The white lamb's wool morphed from white to black at the bottom, but unless you inspected it up close and personal, you'd never notice the uneven stitching.

I'd picked it up at a flea market for under a hundred dollars about a month before the man with the stand was arrested for selling counterfeit goods.

It went nicely with my Muse houndstooth ponte knit sheath dress. The dress normally retailed for about one sixty, but I'd gotten it half off because the back zipper was broken. An easy twenty-dollar repair for my trusty dry cleaner. I wasn't so sure I loved the faux-leather belt with the oversized studs, but it did give the dress an edgy, trendy look. I'd completed my ensemble with a darling pair of Betsey Johnson stilettos that were a mix of patent leather and pleated satin. The four-inch heel would make traversing airports a bit of a pain—literally—but achieving the overall look made it all worth it. Besides, my mother would be at the other end of the flight, so the last thing I wanted to do was show up looking like something a cat spewed on a carpet.

My heels clicked as I passed the executive sentry, who seemed quite discombobulated when I failed to follow protocol and announce myself.

I found Becky seated in Ellen's red leather chair, an empty wastebasket perched in her lap.

"Any luck?" I asked.

"Cleaning people," she explained. "I've been through this office with a fine-tooth comb."

"Desk and credenza?" I asked.

"All but the two locked drawers."

Reaching into my purse, I retrieved a nail file as I came around the desk.

"What do you think you're doing?" Becky asked.

"Do you have the key?"

"No."

"Then can you think of another way to get inside here?"

"This desk is private property."

I glared at my friend. "Isn't there some sort of law that addresses abandoned property? You've made a few zillion attempts to get in touch with her. Who knows? Could be there's some pressing Dane-Lieberman stuff in these drawers."

"Or Ellen just keeps a few private items in her desk," Becky countered skeptically.

It took me three tries, but I managed to jimmy the lock. A

neat row of hanging folders held labels for such mundane things as STORAGE, BANKING, HEALTH INSURANCE, VEHICLE INSURANCE, etc. "How boring," I mumbled. "Move," I told Becky, then replaced her in Ellen's chair.

The lock on the thin top drawer was a little more difficult to open. While I finally managed to twist the lock, in doing so, I also chipped a big hunk out of my favorite Barton's nail file with the cute Swarovski crystal flower on the end. "Damn."

The nail file did not die in vain. There, sitting on top of a set of unmarked keys, was the envelope I'd seen a week ago. "Got it!" I quickly blew into the folds of the paper, only to discover the contents missing. Flipping it over, I read the partial address. " . . . tment of Corrections." The rest of the address had been obliterated by a Sharpie. "There was more the other day."

"More what?" Becky asked as I handed her the envelope.

"More to the address. A few letters of the actual name of the department."

"So you remember it?"

I closed my eyes, hoping I could focus on the memory. "All I can remember is N-A."

"Can we do an Internet search with that?" Becky asked. "I mean, how many departments of correction can there be?"

"One for each state and one for each county."

Becky frowned. "How many counties are there, do you think?"

"Three thousand one hundred forty," I answered. Becky looked at me as if I'd just recited the Bible by rote. "It was one of the questions when Izzy and I played Trivial Pursuit."

"I guess that makes an Internet search kinda tough."

"Yeah, it's not like hangman." I glanced at my watch. "Sorry, but I have to go. By the way, would you mind doing me a favor on Sunday?"

"Sure, what?"

"There's a lady coming to my place to pick up some items I sold on eBay." I considered telling Becky where I'd gotten them but decided now wasn't a good time. "I'll send you a text with the amount she owes."

"You want me to meet some loon from an online auction? What if she's some sort of mass murderer?"

I laughed. "With a screen name like 'Tiara64'? I think you'll be safe from a beauty pageant junkie."

"What time?"

"One o'clock. I'll leave the stuff on the counter. All you have to do is take her cash and give her five items I'll put in a velvet jewelry bag."

"Can I do the transaction on the porch, or do I have to let her in?"

"Do it in the street for all I care."

Becky met my eyes. "Are you that hard up for money? I can—"

"I'm fine," I insisted. "This is a sale of opportunity, not necessity."

She hugged me. "Have a great time in Atlanta."

I cringed. "That's kinda like telling me to enjoy my own execution."

◆

It took me two suitcases to fly to Atlanta for a long weekend. In my defense, I had to pack my maid-of-honor gown, and that alone took up half of the first bag. Then I had the substitute little black dress, plus three casual outfits and my return-flight ensemble. I'm a firm believer that if you dress well to fly, you get better service.

The second bag was smaller, and it was full of hair, makeup, shoes, purses, and other accessories. That I blamed on the strict TSA rules regarding liquids. Okay, that wasn't exactly true. I'd never been one for lugging my own bag onto a plane and forcing it into the overhead compartment. When I traveled, I wanted my own stuff, not those complimentary bottles, even if they were from one of the best hotels in the world.

Carrying only my purse and a tote with my laptop, I cleared security and went directly to the Starbucks at the entrance to the gate area. Taking a seat near my departure area, I took a sip of my frappe, and then dug the cloisonné compact Jane had given me for my birthday out of my bag. There was still a little redness around the injury at my hairline but nothing I couldn't tackle with some concealer. I wouldn't have to worry about how it would look for the wedding. There would be stylists available who could easily make it invisible.

My cell rang, and when I glanced at the caller ID, I smiled. Right on time.

"Hello, Mom."

"Are you at the airport?"

"Of course."

"Don't sound so impressed with yourself," she warned. "Remember Great-aunt Mary's funeral."

Even though a decade had passed, I was still doing penance for missing my flight and the viewing. I think it was a subconscious thing. I was nineteen and didn't want to view a dead body. "I remember, and I also recall apologizing a few zillion times."

"Yes, but it still reflected badly on me."

"I'm sorry I was late for Great-aunt Mary's funeral."

"Did you pack your dress?"

"Yes, though asking me now might not have been the best plan."

"No, the poor planning was your decision not to ship it to the hotel so it could be properly steamed."

"I'm sure the Ritz can properly steam my dress between tonight and Saturday."

"Well, worrying about your dress is one more headache Lisa doesn't need."

I doubted my sister was stressing about the dress. She was probably still trying to remember how to walk in heels. But when it came to Cassidy Presley Tanner Rossi Browning, I picked my battles. Not that I ever won any of them, but placating her was the safest route. "I'll apologize to her as soon as I see her."

"So now you want her to stop tending to details to listen to you say you're sorry?"

No, now I wanted to stick a pencil in my eye. "I'll send her a text."

"Really, Finley. Electronic apologies do not replace an appropriately sincere note."

I wasn't going to win this one. Not even close. "Mom, I hate to cut you off, but I need to step into the powder room before they call my flight."

"Fine. I'll see you for dinner at eight o'clock. The Atlanta Grille. Do try to be on time."

I downed my frappe and went to the ladies' room to fix my lipstick. While I was there, I brushed my hair and touched up my blush as well. The flight to Atlanta was less than two hours, but I still wanted to log in to the airport Wi-Fi to check my eBay auctions.

As I expected, Tiara64 was the high bidder on the pins, the bracelet, and the earrings. I couldn't help but smile, knowing I'd be getting the auction price plus an additional five hundred dollars. I couldn't imagine anyone wanting costume jewelry so badly. I sent her an e-mail, telling her that I would contact her with my address at the end of the auction and that she could pick up the items around one.

She instantly zinged back a positive response. "Do you live on eBay?" I wondered aloud.

My flight was called, and I powered down my laptop and placed it in my tote. Because I was flying business class, I was allowed to board before the masses.

I settled into the window seat in the second row, stowing my purse and tote under the seat. As the plane filled, I glanced out the window, watching suitcases being tossed onto a conveyor belt. It wasn't a gentle process, and I almost wished I could open the window and chastise them. Then again, the brief chat with my mother had taken all the fight out of me.

As the flight attendants began marching down the aisle, slamming overhead bins, I settled into my seat, glad the one to my right was unoccupied. I'd be spared the possibility of snoring and drooling or incessant talking, allowing me to relax before what promised to be a taxing weekend. I was happy for Lisa, but I wasn't exactly looking forward to spending time with Liam. Or Tony. Izzy was going to be the only bright light during the next three and a half days.

A pretty brunette in a navy uniform took the microphone and began the seat-belt-and-safety drill when she was interrupted by a late arrival.

The next thing I knew Liam was standing at the entrance to my row, shoving a duffel bag into the overhead.

"Shouldn't you be in coach?" I asked in my most sarcastic tone.

"Then I wouldn't get to sit next to you."

I speak Italian . . .
Prada! Dolce & Gabbana!

eleven

"*There's a seat across* the aisle that's open," I suggested as the plane began to taxi down the runway. "In fact," I paused to look around the compartment, "we're the only ones in business class, so there's no need for you to crowd me."

"I'm not crowding you," Liam said between gritted teeth as he pried one hand off the armrest long enough to yank tightly on his seat belt.

Leaning to one side, I looked him up and down. I could see the rapid, uneven rise and fall of his chest beneath his rumpled shirt as he choked in breaths. His thigh muscles were taut, his feet braced firmly on the floor. As the plane bounced slightly upon takeoff, the color drained from his face.

I laughed. "You're afraid of flying."

"No, I'm afraid of crashing."

His knuckles were snow white. I reminded him, "You know you're more likely to wreck your car than to die in a plane crash."

"Yes, but if I wreck my car I don't fall thirty thousand feet."

As the plane leveled off slightly, Liam seemed to relax. Well, it was either the leveling off of the plane or the knowledge that the flight attendant was about to get him a beer.

The roughness of his denim jeans rubbed distractingly against my leg as he continued to fidget in his seat. And I wasn't the only one distracted, either. The tall, lanky flight attendant with her perfectly made-up face and manicured nails must have checked on him three times before we even reached cruising altitude, while practically making me go self-serve.

"Here you are, sir," she said, in what I could only classify as a coo. "Are you sure I can't get you something else?"

"Thanks," Liam said, his voice less tense.

I glanced around him. "A pinot grigio would be nice, though."

"Of course," she answered, in a tone that made me wonder if I'd be drinking it or wearing it.

As soon as she'd stepped into the galley, I said, "If you two need some private time . . ."

"Jealous?"

"No. I just have better things to do than beg for a drink. I have a command performance in"—I checked my Liz Claiborne watch from the Vero Beach outlets—"less than three hours. Drinking for fortification is an essential part of the perfor-mance."

"Is this our dinner with your family?"

Our? When did that happen? "No, it's my dinner with my family. You can sit in your room and watch anything from car-toons to porn. Whatever floats your boat."

Reaching into the pocket of his very Florida, faded-palm-tree-motif shirt, he pulled out a folded slip of paper. Before he had the thing completely open, I knew it was the e-mail I'd sent. Since I'd copied it directly from my schedule, it did include the Thursday-night Tanner family gathering. Well, Tanner family plus one. Two if Liam showed. This was supposed to be my time to get to know the groom a little bit better. Which sounded a lot like getting to know a dust tumbleweed, but hey, I wasn't dealing with options. I felt guilt wash over me. I was being catty when it came to David, but that was my jealousy rearing its ugly head.

I thought about the duffel he'd so unceremoniously shoved in the bin, and said, "Dinner is dressy."

"You want me to wear a dress?"

Between the heat of his body being in such close proximity, the scent of his cologne caressing my senses, and the incessant rub of his leg against mine, I was fast running out of patience. "I mean, tie and jacket, which I doubt you crammed into your . . . *luggage*." I made the last word sound like an STD.

"I might surprise you," he said as he accepted an array of snacks from the devoted flight attendant.

I, on the other hand, was practically tossed a bag of pretzels with my wine. Maybe she was hoping I was one of those peanut allergy people and might die of anaphylactic shock so she could have Liam all to herself. Not that I had him. No, that much he'd made perfectly clear with the whole not-wanting-to-sleep-with-me speech.

"How are things at work?" he asked casually. Half the bottle of beer was gone, and the color had returned to his knuckles.

"Busy because of the Ellen situation. How weird is that?"

"Don't know," he answered with a shrug.

Of course, it was a shrug that caused us to rub shoulders. I'd had only a few sips of wine, but I took a hefty gulp, hoping it would douse the heat in my belly.

"I don't know Ellen well, but Tony thinks it might have been her reaction to Dane bringing him in as an equity partner. That cuts into her profits," Liam said.

I hadn't thought of that, though I felt a kinship with Ellen. There was nothing I hated more than getting screwed on a paycheck. "I thought Tony was supposed to be some hotshot rainmaker."

"He is." Liam agreed, pressing his head back into the pillow so his brilliant blue eyes locked with mine.

As usual, a lock of jet-black hair had fallen haphazardly onto his forehead, and it took all my strength not to reach out and brush it back into place. One thing I knew about Liam was that it was in my best interests to stay hands-off.

"Maybe she had a midlife meltdown." Or just caught a glimpse of her hideous shoes and went into hiding.

"Maybe," he agreed as he stroked the not-yet-five-o'clock shadow on his chin.

Suddenly Liam went silent. It was the noisiest quiet I'd ever endured. Part of me was grateful, but another part of me missed the civilized conversation. It was a side of Liam I'd never seen, and I liked it. I more than liked it.

I am an idiot.

"Are we ever going to talk about the other night?" he asked.

Correction, I am an über idiot. "No."

"I think we should."

"Did you know your seat cushion can be used as a flotation device in the case of an emergency landing over water?" His grip tightened on his bottle of beer. "Not that I've heard of many people floating away from a plane crash."

"Nice distraction, but I still want to know why you've been so frosty. It's Thursday, and on Tuesday you were practically begging me to—"

"Can we *please* not go there? Just chalk it up to having a great night, followed by your very thoughtful gift. I just got swept up in the moment."

"In a moment of Lucky Charms?"

I glared at him. "I was on a high because I knew I'd aced my exam and you . . . well . . . just happened to be there."

"You're so full of crap."

"Yeah, well, you aren't much better. You set me up as a babysitter." I wiggled my finger a few inches from his face. "And don't tell me it was some esoteric way of your giving me insight into Tony's world. Then you have the audacity to think you and Tony can flip a coin and decide just whom I might be interested in. You put one of my best friends to bed naked, and what else? You insisted on coming to this wedding after I explicitly told you to stay home. Oh yeah, and let's not forget that you humiliated me a scant forty-eight hours ago with your dumb-ass three-wishes bullshit."

The bastard smiled.

"You are so hot when you're pissed." He laughed softly.

I reached under the seat and grabbed my purse and tote. "Excuse me."

Liam reluctantly released the death grip of his seat belt to graciously allow me to exit the row. He laughed harder when I moved back one row and squished myself against the window. The only minor satisfaction I got was watching him battle his phobia as the plane landed at Hartsfield-Jackson in Atlanta. As soon as the flight attendants opened the hatch, Liam zoomed out of the place.

I dallied, hoping he'd get the hint and not linger around the gate, thinking we'd share a cab or something.

My girlish fantasies came true. When I deplaned, Liam was nowhere to be seen.

After taking the plane, a rolling walkway, a train, and hiking up some stairs, I was finally in the baggage claim area. I noticed two things right off. My luggage was slipping back outside on the conveyor belt, and a gentleman dressed in a suit, tie, and hat was holding a sign with my name printed on it. There were times when my mother's attention to etiquette paid off. Sending a car for me was an unexpected pleasure.

"I'm Miss Tanner," I greeted him.

"Simon, ma'am," he returned in a thick southern accent. "May I take that?" he asked, pointing to my tote.

"I'm fine with it, thanks."

He just smiled, a display of white teeth against chocolate-colored skin.

"I have two pieces of luggage. But they just went into the twilight zone."

Simon laughed. "We're in no hurry."

"You can't miss them. My luggage is Barbie pink."

As Simon went over to stand sentry at the carousel, I dug in my bag, making sure I had the cash for a generous tip. I guessed he was somewhere in his late forties, maybe early fifties, and I also figured he wasn't raking it in as a livery driver. As an underling myself, I felt a kinship for him and wanted to make sure I showed my appreciation properly.

Once Simon had my bags on his handcart, I followed him out into the thick, humid air I remembered less than fondly from my college days. Yes, Florida is hot, but I have an ocean breeze and the temperatures rarely climb to the hundred-degree mark. Conversely, breathing in Atlanta was a lot like standing outside and sucking in dryer exhaust.

Simon had been kind enough to leave the engine running, so when he opened the door, I was greeted by a rush of fresh air scented with a spicy oriental blend with undertones of orange blossom and cedar wood. A true blend of sensuality and masculinity. Dolce & Gabbana's The One for Men. Liam's cologne of choice.

"Took you long enough."

"What are you doing in *my* car?" I shot back.

Simon cleared his throat, drawing my attention. "Mr. McGarrity made the reservation, ma'am."

"Hey, if you'd rather wait around for a taxi or take one of those SuperShuttle things, then—"

"Fine," I snapped as I got in, carefully dumping my tote and purse between us like a barrier.

"Now is when you say, 'Thank you, Liam.'"

"Screw you, Liam."

"We can revisit that issue later."

◆

"We can revisit that issue later," I mocked as I unpacked my second bag. "In your dreams."

I'd already called the hotel laundry and arranged to have the maid-of-honor dress picked up and steamed. They promised to have it back by late Friday morning, which should get me off the hook with my mother.

My room wasn't a room. It was a one-bedroom suite with stunning views of Buckhead and the downtown skyline. Lucky for me Lisa and her groom were footing the bill. If not, I'd be down in the basement next to a janitor's closet. Rooms at the Ritz didn't come cheap. Obviously, neither did this wedding. Other than the outrageous price of my gown and some shoes I still had yet to see, I was out only fifteen hundred and change. More than I would have liked, especially since the dress had no rewearability. I was dreading the whole shoe thing, though I had a small glimmer of hope because Lisa had instructed me to allow for four-inch heels.

There was a knock at the door, so with my bare feet, I jogged through the eight-hundred-square-foot suite and got on my tiptoes to check the peephole.

No one.

There was another knock. Only then did I realize that it was coming from the door on the side of the dining area. I walked over, placed my ear against the cool wood, and yelled. "Yes?"

"Open the door."

I unlatched the deadbolt and found Liam standing on the opposite side of the double doors. With the door open, the suites could be combined into a spacious three-bedroom. "What are you doing up here?"

"Your sister took care of it."

"You hit my sister up for a room?" I asked, kinda stunned. Especially since his suite had two bedrooms and mine had only one.

"No, this room was booked for your escort. I explained that Tony wasn't coming, and she spoke to the hotel. I tried to convince her that this was not my style, but she insisted. And before you decide I took advantage of your little sister, I made sure the hotel will bill my credit card."

"It's going to run you close to—"

"Six grand per," he finished. "I'll live." He reached onto the table and pulled a chilled bottle of champagne from the bucket, then grabbed two flutes as he casually brushed by me and entered my room.

With my shoes off, he towered over me, so I quickly corrected that by retrieving them and slipping them back on. "I don't remember inviting you in."

"You said you needed liquor to get through dinner. I'm just being a good escort."

"Wait. Tony's not coming?"

"He said he tried to call you, but you must still have your phone off from the flight." He popped the cork on the champagne. "Don't look so disappointed. You'll just have to make do with me."

"I'm disappointed for Izzy."

"So is Tony. Apparently, she's locked herself in her room and refuses to talk to him."

"I should call her." But first I'd have to take my iPhone off airplane mode.

When I went to turn, Liam gently took hold of my upper arm and passed me a flute of perfectly poured, sparkling champagne. Cristal at that. "You sure are living large," I teased.

"Actually, your family is. Or the Huntington . . ."

"Huntington-St. John. A combo of two old, *old* Atlanta families. David sent you champagne?"

He pointed to the stunning pink roses on the counter and the gigantic basket of gourmet coffees and a new top-of-the-line Cuisinart coffeemaker. "Is that what they sent you?"

"Yes, but I'm family."

"Apparently, I'm being welcomed by your family."

I took a sip and let it tickle my mouth and nose before swallowing. "Why isn't Tony coming?"

He frowned. At least I think he did. "Does it matter?"

"Yes."

"One of his clients got arrested. Some big hedge-fund guy."

I silently hoped I wouldn't have to use my newly acquired criminal skills on that case. Ponzi schemes and math weren't two of my favorite things to tackle.

Liam picked up the bottle and headed back to his room. "See you for dinner."

"That's it? You just interrupted me for nothing?"

"No. I interrupted you because I could."

If it hadn't been Cristal, I would have thrown it at the door. But even Liam wasn't worth wasting a stellar glass of sparkling wine.

The next time there was a knock on my door, it was the front door. I flung it open and gave my sister a big hug. Despite the fact that my mother liked to pit us against each other, Lisa and I had never shared any animosity. We weren't close like the Brady sisters, but each of us genuinely cared about the other.

Unlike me, Lisa favored our mother. She was dark-haired, with the same aqua-blue eyes. Lisa's hair was pixie short, and the style was flattering with her small frame. Though she is an inch taller that I am, she's tiny-boned, making her appear much smaller. I'd say frail, except that her latest passion is doing triathlons with David, so she was quite buff in her simple white sheath dress.

"Thank you for this," I said, spraying my arm in an arc around the living room. "I feel like a princess."

With just a slightly strained gait, Lisa walked over to the sofa and placed a gift bag on the coffee table. "Mind if I get a water from the fridge?"

"Let me get it, you're the bride. Sit down."

I grabbed two bottles of water from the fridge, snapped up the special napkin, and then joined my sister on the sofa. I tried to remember the last time we had been in the same room and decided it was about two years earlier when I'd brought Patrick up for New Year's. Of course, now I understood why he hadn't been able to travel on Christmas. And that it had *nothing* to do with his job at FedEx.

"This is for you," I said as I handed her the water and the napkin from AirTran.

"Why did you write 'I'm sorry' on a cocktail napkin?" she asked.

"Mom says I owe you an apology for not shipping my dress up ahead of time."

Lisa smiled patiently. That was one of the major differences between us. She had the patience of the proverbial saint. "I'll make sure to tell her you fulfilled your obligations."

"Thank you."

"And this is for you," she said as she nudged the gift bag closer to me.

"You've already been overly generous. Thanks for the coffee stuff. You know me well."

"I also know enough to tell you that your body needs more than caffeine to function."

"I had a muffin this morning."

"Finley, you eat like a teenager."

I patted her knee. "You've got healthy covered for both of us."

"Open it," she said with giddish excitement.

All I had to do was pull out the tissue and my heart stopped. Inside were not one but two Jimmy Choo boxes. I dove for the shoe box first. Inside was the most stunning pair of sling-back pumps in a glittering champagne color. "Oh, Lisa, these are amazing." I already had one out of the box and was removing the rib and paper so I could slip it on. It fit like a Jimmy Choo glove. I quickly unwrapped its mate and then took them for a test drive. They had a really cute peep toe and a two-inch plat-form, so the three-inch heel was deceptively comfy. I had to go into the bedroom to admire them in the mirror.

Lisa followed me much the way she had done when we were kids and I was prepping for a date. "These are beautiful, but you really shouldn't have."

"I wanted you to have something special, and I'm wearing the same shoes. The rest of the girls have similar shoes, just not the real thing."

I hugged her. "Thank you so much."

"We're not done yet," she said, dragging me back into the living room and pulling the smaller box out of the bag.

Inside was a shimmering fabric clutch that matched the shoes. I almost wept. It was small, maybe four inches by five inches, but I didn't care. It would hold lipstick, a compact, and a credit card. What else do I need?

"This is too much, seriously."

"I know you," Lisa countered. "My sister wears only the best."

If she only knew. Then it dawned on me: Why didn't she know? Lord knew I'd borrowed money from her often enough. I was suddenly awash in guilt. "Lisa, I really shouldn't accept this," I said as I slipped off the shoes and reluctantly began to lovingly rewrap them. "I probably still owe you more than you spent on all my fabulous gifts combined. Especially counting this room."

"Open the clutch."

I did. Inside I found a prescription sheet that simply read:

All debts forgiven and see me at the chapel.

My eyes welled with tears. "Now I know you've gone way overboard."

Lisa hugged me. "Those are doctor's orders. You have to follow them."

"Does Mom know you're doing all this for me? She must be hemorrhaging money."

"David's family is picking up most of the expense since this is really their show. David and I would have been happy going off to Cumberland Island with a Justice of the Peace. Between Mom and the Huntington-St. Johns, this has exploded into the stratosphere. I make a good living, Finley. Stop thanking me and just accept the gifts in the spirit in which they were given."

I felt like a real schmuck since all I'd gotten them was a set of candlesticks off their registry. Well, that and the gift I had made for Lisa.

"Since we're doing this now," I said, "hang on." I went into the bedroom and took the small package out of my dresser. Bringing it back and handing it to my sister, I said, "I hear you need something old for this whole wedding day thing."

Lisa opened the gift with the same precision I imagined she used when removing a tumor. Inside, she peeled back the tissue and immediately began to tear up.

"The lady said that chain should wrap around the stem of your bouquet. So don't go throwing it out into the crowd."

She laughed. "I hate to tell you this, Fin, but these days you buy a separate bouquet to toss. The real one gets preserved. You had this made especially for Dad. Are you sure you want to give it away? I can just borrow it and—"

"You keep it." I didn't have the heart to tell her the recent history of the medal, namely that it had been stolen only to turn up in the hand of a mummified skeleton. I'd had it cleaned and strung on a delicate chain. "You're Jonathan's daughter. You deserve to have something that was his. He was so proud of winning that polo match, it only seemed fitting for you to have it on your special day. Besides, I bought the cottage on Palm Beach."

Lisa dabbed her eyes and laughed. "Mom said you'd, um, redone the place."

Oh, I had no doubt my mother had conveyed her opinion of my decor. "It's really fabulous. I'll send you pictures. Look at the time! We'd better get downstairs." I slipped on my pink Betsey Johnsons and grabbed my purse to hunt down my lipstick. "Mom'll kill us if we're late."

"So when are we going to talk about *him*?"

We stepped out into the hallway and turned toward the elevators. "Him who?"

"Your date. Finley, he is really cute, but nothing like the guys you normally date. Tell me about him." She nearly stumbled on the carpet. "God, I don't know how you walk in these things."

"Balance on the balls of your feet. Weight more toward your toes."

"Forget my toes. Tell me about Liam."

"Not much to tell."

"Does he work at your firm?"

"On and off."

"What does that mean?"

"It means he's not a staff attorney. He's a private investigator. Used to be a detective."

Lisa locked arms with me. Probably to keep her balance as we walked the long hallway. "That sounds sexy. Does he carry a gun?"

"Aren't you a healer?"

"Yes, but I grew up watching reruns of *Miami Vice*."

"Yes, I've seen him with a gun."

"What college did he go to?"

"I don't know."

"Where is he from?"

"Don't know."

"What *do* you know?"

"He makes my spine melt."

A deep voice behind me said, "That's good to know."

The more I'm with men, the more
I think I'll end up alone . . . with a cat.

twelve

My head whipped around, and I could feel the heat of total mortification spreading up my neck. Only then did I get the scent of Liam's cologne. *Ohgod ohgod ohgod!*

The transformation was amazing. Gone was the funky, faded beach look, replaced by a tempered elegance I would never have expected from Liam. He was wearing a dark gray suit, white shirt, and—the only homage to his real self—a Jerry Garcia tie. He was clean-shaven, but his hair was still quintessentially Liam tussled. Liam looked just like James Bond. Post sex.

"You might want to push the Down button," he suggested.

I closed my gaping mouth as if it was the first time I'd ever attempted to cure a dropping jaw. Affianced Lisa was on the verge of drooling too, which should have made me feel better, only it didn't. Nothing seemed to stem the waves of embarrassment crashing inside me. I willed it away, which as it turns out was a bad idea. Once we were inside the elevator and I'd banished my mortification, a serious case of the oh-man-do-you-have-the-best-eyes-ever bore through me like a precision drill, a direct hit on my overtaxed and underused libido.

"I didn't mean to interrupt you ladies," he said casually, shifting his weight to one foot.

He had on actual shoes. Not flip-flops or deck shoes, but honest-to-God Italian leather loafers. I knew quality, and Lord knew I also knew seconds, and his ensemble was definitely quality. Where and why would Liam McGarrity have such incredible clothing? I couldn't see him sitting in a pew on Sunday mornings, so what was the deal? I knew he didn't dress for success at work, so either he was a professional wedding crasher or some sort of closet funeral junkie. The more I got to know Liam I realized how little I actually knew about him.

" . . . doesn't he, Finley?"

"Sorry," I said to Lisa as my hot-guy brain freeze melted. "Doesn't he what?"

"Look handsome tonight?"

I couldn't meet his eyes. "Yes."

Lisa exited first, and as I went to leave the elevator, Liam's lips brushed against my ear as he asked, "Spine-meltingly handsome?"

"Asshole," I whispered back.

"What?" Lisa asked.

"A-atlanta Grille," I lied. "Do you know where it is?"

"At this point, I think I know every inch of this hotel."

She was walking way too fast for her shoes. Even the best shoes aren't meant to be jogged in. "Slow down," I urged.

"Sorry. I'm not used to taking leisurely strolls."

"Are you nervous?" Liam asked as he stepped forward so that he was walking between the two of us.

"Not really. I'm just not accustomed to so much pageantry."

Speaking of pageantry, and, by association, pageant jewelry, I reached into my purse and pulled out my phone. Lisa instantly slapped my phone. "Mom and David are straight ahead. Want to greet them with a phone in your hand?"

I glanced ahead and saw my mother, coiffed head to beautifully clad toe in an aqua raw silk suit with a pale coral shell beneath the fitted jacket. Her recent plastic surgery touch-up had settled, since her lips no longer looked like suction cups.

I could feel my cells starting to cement from tension as soon as I saw her eyes lock on Liam. However, no one from the outside would notice the subtle slip in her smile. I did. She was not happy. There was no way I was coming out of this dinner smelling like a rose, not when my mother already had steam building in her ears.

Conversely, David was one tall, lanky smile. He had a runner's shape, so his navy suit coat hung loosely from his shoulders, making his neck appear unnaturally long. Like my sister, he was dark-haired, and, like her, he was an oncologist. But tonight, at least for a short while, he was just the perfect guy about to marry my perfect little sister.

"My baby," Mom said to Lisa, grabbing her and giving her a double-cheek kiss, then dabbing away the impression of her coral lipstick from Lisa's face. She handed her off to David and leaned forward to send some air kisses in my general direction. "Finley."

"Mom. You remember Liam."

She extended her arm, locking it at the elbow to make sure she kept as much distance as possible. "Yes. Mr., um."

"Liam is fine," he said amiably as he took her hand for a mere second.

"Shall we go in?" she asked.

We followed a smartly attired maître d' to a small anteroom with a round table set for six. As my mother was assisted to her seat, David saw to Lisa. Liam pulled out my chair, but I waved off any further assistance.

"I hope you don't mind . . . ," my mother began.

This was clearly rhetorical, since I was fairly sure she didn't give a hoot if we minded.

"I've taken the liberty of designing a menu with Lisa in mind."

I was sensing green beans in my future. I hate green beans.

A waiter arrived on our heels and asked, "Are we waiting on one more?"

"I thought we'd have a young lady joining us, but apparently Finley didn't let me know otherwise, so, thank you, but you can clear that setting."

"I believe Tony contacted you directly," I said, practically shoving my glass at the third server, who was busy filling our water goblets and wineglasses.

"I was under the impression that he was attending."

"He had a client emergency," Liam said. "So I told him I would send along his apologies. So," Liam lifted his wineglass, "apologies."

"Fine then. Well, David, I know how busy you and Lisa are, and I really wanted you to have an opportunity to spend more than a few minutes with Finley. For sisters, they're very different, as I'm sure Lisa has mentioned."

"She hasn't said," David replied, and then looked across the table at me. "She just says the two of you don't get to see each other enough."

"We don't," I agreed. The last time I'd been to visit Lisa, David had been off at some medical seminar on tropical diseases. I wondered if it was too late to come down with a case of dengue fever.

"As you can tell, Finley has to work very hard at her job. I don't even think she had an opportunity to change clothes after her long flight."

Strike one.

"Sorry, Dave, but—"

"I prefer David."

"Forgot, David. I did have to leave directly from work, so if I look less than appropriate, my apologies."

"I think you look lovely," he said. "What about you—Liam, is it?"

"Yes. Liam McGarrity. For the record, I did change before dinner," he joked.

Four of the five of us laughed. My mother simply smiled tightly.

"No, I mean what do you do at Finley's firm?"

"At Finley's firm." Liam paused and turned those ice-blue eyes on me. "I'm an independent contractor; a PI."

David asked, "So you two work together?"

"Yes."

"No," I answered just as quickly. "I mean, sometimes we do. It depends on the case."

As an amuse-bouche was presented to each of us, my mother asked, "So if you need an errand done, he does it?"

Strike two.

I savored the single bite of spicy ahi tuna. It was a nice contrast with the dry wine.

"A lot like that," Liam said.

Still, he wasn't rising to a single caustic Cassidy moment. For that he earned my admiration.

Dinner went about as well as could be expected. During the meal I was treated to David's long, boring history of his life to date. Okay, so it wasn't actually boring, but I was still trying to find some chink in his armor. I didn't catch all of his comments, sometimes zoning out when Liam's leg brushed mine or when his arm draped casually against the back of my chair.

Normally, I would have found the distraction annoying, but by the time the dinner plates were cleared, I was thrilled for the diversion. Well, that wasn't completely true. I was also thrilled on another level. If I thought Liam was hot in his normal clothes, it was nothing compared to how I felt when he was in a suit.

My mother seemed placated playing matriarch, especially when the waiter asked if she and her "sisters" would like coffee with dessert. I thought she'd beam right out of her chair.

Of course he thought we were sisters. My mother was only fifty-one, but thanks to aestheticians and plastic surgeons, she could easily pass for forty.

"Well, hello," came a proper, cheerful female voice from the doorway. I turned in my chair, while Liam and David got to their feet. A lovely couple stood in the entranceway. The man looked dapper, and the woman was a dead ringer for the American actress Dina Merrill in her heyday. I'd seen the actress around Palm Beach in the 1970s and 1980s, and she always had a friendly and cultured air about her.

"I'm Tenley Huntington-St. John, and this is my husband, David. Though he goes by Tripp. Short for triple, as in 'the third.' David, bless his heart, didn't end up with a nickname. I do hope we're not intruding. I was just dying to meet Finley. And her gentleman friend, of course. I couldn't wait for the dinner tomorrow night. Not to meet family, that is."

My mother waved her hand. "We need seats for our friends, please."

In no time the staff had cleared and redesigned the table for eight, making it look effortless. While they did that, the Huntington-St.Johns made a circle of the room, hugging and kissing their way through the lineup.

They seemed nice enough, and it was good to have a distraction. Tenley declined dessert, but among the rest of us, I think we ordered one of everything on the dessert cart. I was already on my second cup of coffee when Tenley turned her attention to me.

"So, Finley, your mother tells me you work at a law firm in Palm Beach?"

"Well," my mother said quickly before I could respond, "I said she works in West Palm. She lives on Palm Beach."

"How lovely for you," Tenley said. "We've visited friends there, and it is a spectacular place."

"Yes, it is."

"Are you from Palm Beach as well, Mr. McGarrity?"

"Lake Worth area," he said.

"Lake Worth is the waterway that separates Palm Beach from West Palm Beach," my mother explained.

"Yes," Liam agreed. "Only it isn't a lake, it's actually part of the Intracoastal. Just for the record, I live in the town of Lake Worth. On the mainland."

"You should visit there," I suggested. "They have a cute little Old Town that's on the Historic Registry."

Tripp steepled his fingers. "We may just do that, Finley. The wife and I do love history. Did you know the chapel David and Lisa are getting married in on Saturday is on the same land where every member of my family has been married since my family first came over with Mr. James Oglethorpe on *The Ann*. The chapel was built in 1750, and generations of Huntingtons and St. Johns are buried in the small plot adjacent to the chapel.

"Alley of Oaks, our ancestral home, was burned during the Battle of Atlanta. My forefathers tried to rebuild, but it was never the same. My great-granddaddy donated most of the land to the city. It's now part of St. John Park off East Paces Ferry Road."

"Now, Tripp," Tenley said as she squeezed her husband's arm. "Let's not bore these fine people with rehashing the effects of the War of Northern Aggression."

"It's fascinating," my mother insisted. I knew she was lying. She hated history, unless she was the central character. I didn't care; it kept me out of the line of fire.

We finished dessert, and after some more polite conversation, the evening broke up a little before one.

As Liam and I walked back to the elevator, I said, "Sorry about my mother and her digs. However, on the positive side, she only got in a couple. Must be distracted by the wedding."

"I'm a big boy," Liam replied as he held the door open for me. Once inside he turned and braced a hand on either side of my head, trapping me as the elevator slowly rose toward the top of the tower.

"So what happens now?" he asked.

"Now?" My voice was unnaturally high.

"Uh-huh." Liam's lips brushed against the sensitive skin just below my earlobe. The feel of his featherlight kisses drew my stomach into a knot. Closing my eyes, I concentrated on the glorious sensations. His grip tightened as his tongue traced a path up to my ear. My breath caught when Liam teasingly nibbled the edge of my lobe.

His hands traveled up and rested against my side, just shy of my breasts. I swallowed the moan rumbling in my throat. I was aware of everything—his fingers, the feel of his solid body molded against mine, the magical kisses.

"You smell wonderful," he said against my super-heated skin.

"Liam," I whispered his name. It was the best I could muster over the lump of desire clogging my throat. "I don't think this is such a good idea."

His mouth stilled and his hand slipped to grip my waist. "Why?"

"Well," I said as the elevator door slid open on our floor, "sex in an elevator isn't one of my three wishes. Night."

◆

"I did it!" I crowed into the phone.

"It?" Becky asked excitedly.

"Not that *it*," I corrected. "I did what you told me to do. I revved Liam up and calmly walked away."

"How'd he," she yawned. "How'd he take it?"

"Better than me, I hope. Oh my God, Bec. He had on a suit and looked positively luscious. I could have jumped him right there in the hallway."

"Why are you whispering?"

"He's in the next room."

"You have adjoining rooms?"

"Long story. Tony isn't coming."

"I know, I saw him at the office, and I have a feeling we'll be seeing a lot of him on the evening news for a while. Not that I'll be seeing it. I'm still knee deep sorting out Ellen's cases."

"Don't you have some vacation time coming?" I joked.

"Dane would have a fit. There's stuff Ellen was doing that I didn't even have a clue about."

"Do you need time? I can put the woman off on Sunday?"

"God, no," Becky said. "I need to get away from the office for some downtime. Taking Sunday afternoon off isn't going to change the world."

"Hang on." *Who was beeping in on my phone at one thirty in the morning?* "Izzy is on the other line. Can I call you back?"

"No. I'd like to sleep. Call me tomorrow, and keep up the good work with Liam. Make him want and make him wait."

Great advice, if only I could apply it to myself as well. I clicked the Answer button on my phone. "Izzy, what are you doing up this late?"

"Wishing my dad wasn't such a total jerk."

"He's just doing his job."

"I know, but I'm supposed to be his job, too. Instead, I get a quickie trip to Universal."

"Islands of Adventure can be really fun," I insisted. "The Harry Potter thing is awesome."

"It's not the same."

"Right, but if you play your cards right, you can work this to your advantage."

"How?" she grumbled.

"You act all grateful for the Universal trip, just keep telling him how happy you are to get just one day with him. Hammer that home, then when the time is right, you hit him up for something you really want while reminding him how nice you were about missing the whole Atlanta trip."

"That's excellent. How'd you learn all this stuff?"

"I was raised by a master manipulator."

"Is Liam there with you?"

"Not with me, but he's here."

"Ewww, I didn't mean, like, *with* you. That would be gross."

Not so much. "I know. I just meant he wasn't in this room. Are you ready for the dance next week?"

"Except for knowing how to do hair and makeup and stuff."

"I said I'd help you."

"What if something comes up?"

"My life's not that interesting," I said honestly. "I've got it marked on my calendar. I'll be at your place by six. You'll be ready no later than seven. The dance starts at seven thirty, and—"

"Dad's coming."

The line went dead. I listened to the nothingness for a while, then started scrolling through the messages I'd neglected by accidentally leaving my phone off. Liv and Jane were begging for updates, and there was a text from Izzy that pretty much summed up our conversation except in her text she said Tony sucked as a dad.

I couldn't imagine a steady diet of all that teen drama, but it felt pretty good to swoop in as the voice of reason and then exit gracefully.

◆

The next day zipped by, thanks to a bridesmaid's luncheon and a few more stolen moments with my sister. The rehearsal was pretty straightforward. Walk in, stand here, move there, and walk there. Done.

If the traditions of marriage were an education, I'd have a PhD by now. This would be my seventh stint as a bridesmaid, albeit my first as a maid of honor. I think I was supposed to like the honor part the best, but I really did love my new shoes and clutch more.

Once we had done a couple of dry runs, we were released until four the next afternoon, when we would all begin to assemble for the five o'clock service. We took the twenty-minute trip back to the hotel in the limo and met up with the other rehearsal dinner invitees.

The Donna Karan knockoff I'd gotten at the Vero Beach outlets might have been my second choice, but judging by the response it got from Liam, it wasn't such a bad substitution. His eyes instantly went to the front of the deep V, then down over the tonal belts wrapping the nipped-in waist. The sleeveless stretch taffeta with the elegant asymmetrical ruffle hemline was a little on the revealing side. Especially when seen from the back, where the V was cut even deeper.

I added a splash of color with a pair of Stuart Weitzman studded pumps I'd gotten for nearly nothing because one shoe had several studs missing. I'd taken a quick trip to a craft store and replicated the look perfectly, well *almost* perfectly. At any rate, they added a modern touch to my ensemble.

"You look nice," he said as he joined me.

He was wearing the same suit as the night before, only this time he'd paired it with a monochrome shirt and tie. He was holding an empty beer bottle, which he deposited on a passing waiter's tray.

Unlike a traditional rehearsal dinner, this was a fifty-plus-person affair. Including me, there were a dozen attendants on each side with their spouses and/or dates, a ring bearer and a flower girl, and assorted family members who were participating in the service. With Jonathan dead, my mother was going to walk Lisa down the aisle. Nontraditional but completely acceptable, and it did accomplish the task of giving my mother a moment in the spotlight. David's family included aunts, uncles, and cousins who would be reading scripture or singing or both. Even the pastor and his wife were there, ready to partake in the lavish spread put on by the Huntington-St. Johns.

It was an interesting combination of new American cuisine mixed with some very traditional southern favorites. I had to admit the fried everything looked really good to me. If only they had fried chocolate, my life would be whole.

I lost Liam several times during the evening, but I could usually find him again by listening for a silly, high-pitched giggle from one of his many female admirers. I rolled my eyes. Could he be in a room with single women and not flirt?

And why not? my conscience challenged. It wasn't like I had anything to say about it.

After grabbing a fresh glass of wine, I went to the hors d'oeuvres and decided to give the stuffed jalapeños a try. Immediately, it became me versus an obstinate string of jack cheese. I fought gallantly, finally getting some sort of separation from the pepper.

"You have cheese on your face," Liam said as he appeared and placed his palm against my cheek.

Involuntarily, my lips parted as he ran his thumb roughly across my bottom lip. I watched as his gaze dropped to my mouth, following the movement of his thumb. The pressure of his hand against my face increased as his range expanded to include my upper lip. It was gentle at first, then building. Liam's thumb worked magic against my lips more sensual than any kiss. My breath stilled in my throat. My pulse was quick, uneven, and racing. Heat from his touch seemed to reach every cell in my body.

"I think I got it," Liam said. "Would you like more?"

As if I'd answer that one.

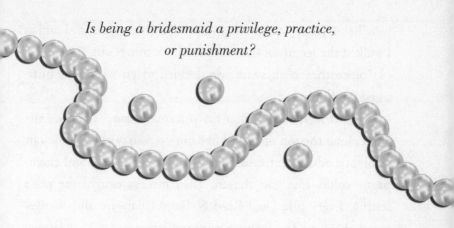

*Is being a bridesmaid a privilege, practice,
or punishment?*

thirteen

The morning of the wedding I'd offered to go down to the ball-room to see how the transformation was going. The Ritz was opening all three adjoining ballrooms into one enormous room to accommodate the nearly five hundred guests, two dance floors, sitting area, and assorted other spaces that had my head ringing *ka-ching*.

Lisa's wedding planner hurried over, one hand on the Blue-tooth in his ear, the other clutching an iPad.

"Miss Tanner," he greeted. He was wearing a smartly cut suit, a tie, and leather loafers. He looked more like a wedding guest than the wedding planner, but I guess that's what you get when you pay fifty grand for planning. Except that he wasn't a planner. Jeffrey preferred "wedding consultant," and everyone acquiesced to his desire.

"Hello, Jeffrey. I can't believe what you're doing in here." I was dumbstruck. At the far right end, the finishing touches were being put on the seventy tables. "This is amazing," I said as I walked the length of the room to check things out.

"Since they both swim, we decided to go with a sophisticated sand theme."

I didn't have a clue what that meant. "Okay." I rubbed my hand along the top of one of five hundred sixty chairs. The raw silk fabric added texture as well as repeated the latte and champagne colors Lisa had chosen. Then my eye caught the place setting. Every place had Reed & Barton flatware and Wedgewood chargers. The flatware was monogrammed. "They let you engrave rentals?" I asked Jeffrey.

He smiled. "These aren't rentals. Except for the centerpieces, everything on the tables belongs to the Huntington-St. John family."

Geez, other than Palm Beach functions, I'd never seen so much privately owned stuff in my life. "Who has this much flatware?" I asked as I straightened a knife.

"Back in the day, the family patriarch gave each of his six children service for one hundred. They pool their respective resources for large functions."

"Oh. These are pretty," I said of the plates. "The pale blue mixed with the beige stuff reminds me of the beach." The centerpieces were glass vases with river stones in the bottom and also sprinkled around the outer base, around a half-dozen votives. In one corner of the room, a group of ten women were cutting and trimming pale tropical orchids, which I assumed would fill the glass vases.

Waterford crystal stood at attention as well. I guessed the Huntington-St. Johns also cornered the market on drinking vessels.

I turned and pointed. "What's that?"

"In that corner"—Jeffrey gestured with his iPad-holding hand—"we'll have a harpist. On the opposite side, a flutist. Center right will be the seventeen-piece swing band with clamshell, and we're building a dance floor in the center area. Crystals will hang from the chandeliers."

"They're replacing the chandeliers?" I asked, truly stunned by the extravagance.

"Of course. The drop crystals will look better with the lighting scheme."

"Which is?"

He held out his iPad to show me a color mock-up, complete with 360 degree views of the room. Some of the areas were brightly lit, while others had soft, subdued lighting. In the center of the dance floor, a custom flood would highlight a monogram of a D and an L. The sand and beach motif was repeated by using huge panels of white silk, on which different images would be projected during the night. The lives of David and Lisa on handmade Trinitrons.

"We'll also be showing the video of the service," Jeffrey said.

"Why?" I asked.

"The chapel holds only one hundred, so four hundred guests will have to watch via digital upstream while sipping champagne and sampling caviar from around the world. We'll be moving in chairs for the wedding video and closing off the dining area until I call to let them know the bride and groom are on their way."

"Very high tech."

Jeffrey leaned in closer to me. "Truth be told, I would have preferred they marry at a venue that could handle all the invitees. It would have saved me a step."

I touched his arm. "I'll let Lisa know that everything is coming along perfectly. You've created an elegant ocean in the middle of Atlanta."

"Thank you," he said, and then reached into his breast pocket. "Here," he said as he handed me his card.

"I'm from out of state," I explained when I made no move to take the offering.

"I travel," he said with a smile.

Out of politeness, I took the card. If I ever did marry Li— Oh God! Did that thought really creep into my brain? If I married anyone, I'd have Liv do the event.

I headed back upstairs, knowing it was about my time to be coiffed and polished by the team of stylists hired to make me— and everyone else—look fantastic.

Faster than I imagined, I was being spirited out the back of the hotel into the waiting Bentley limo. Other limos were lined up behind us, waiting to load the rest of the ladies in the bridal party.

"Lisa!" my mother exclaimed as she instantly grabbed for a hanky from her small purse. "You look like royalty."

"Thank you," Lisa said nervously. It was the first time I could remember ever hearing my little sister sound anything other than completely confident.

Lisa had selected a Vera Wang ivory tissue organza ballroom gown with zibeline trim, a front bow, and a back bustle. Well, Lisa probably hadn't selected the gown herself. Too girly and too froufrou. Left to her own devices, she'd most likely have preferred to get married in white scrubs. My dress was a strapless satin ball gown in latte with a pickup and a champagne sash.

The other bridesmaids had the same dress, though theirs were all champagne.

My mother had gone, predictably, with Chanel. Her silk gown was the exact color of my own, though it had cap sleeves and a bead-encrusted bodice. "Finley," she acknowledged as she looked me up and down. "Do you have any bronzer?"

"No, why?"

"You're just so washed out in that dress. Oh well, too late now. You should have gotten some sun. Something to put color on your skin."

"And let's not forget the potential for developing melanoma," I muttered.

"I think she looks perfect," Lisa insisted, some of her jitters calmed by mediating our mother and me.

I was sitting across from my sister, legs crossed so I could peek at my Jimmy Choos for the short trip. I mean, I was glad she was getting married, but that came a close second to my new shoes.

The small family chapel was a lovely stone building with pretty stained glass and beautifully milled woodwork framing the art.

I could hear the organist playing subdued music as we were sent into an anteroom. Jeffrey was there, as well as the videographer. Well, he was more than a videographer, and he wasn't alone. It felt like being filmed for a Hollywood blockbuster. One guy held a big boom mike over the crowd, and another aimed a bright light wherever instructed by the guy with the gigantic camera. Oh, and there was a regular photographer clicking away, capturing my sister lifting her bouquet of specially flown-in orchids and magnolia leaves; another one of the two of us looking at each other. The special moment when Lisa pinned the orchid corsage to my mother's dress. Which, as it turned out, was just for the purpose of the photograph. Jeffrey didn't like the placement, so he repinned it a bit higher on her shoulder.

As if he was a master sergeant and we were his minions, Jeffrey inspected each of us, often telling a stylist to touch up some makeup or lacquer uncooperative hairs. I got away with a one-word critique. "Fantastic." I glanced at my mother, making sure she'd heard the praise. She'd never back down, but I derived great pleasure just knowing she'd had to sit in silence as a pro complimented me.

For some reason I had butterflies in my stomach. It made no sense. This was my seventh—no, my *eighth*—time as a bridesmaid. True, it was my first stint as maid of honor, but it wasn't like that job came along with daunting duties. I think the butterflies had something to do with knowing Liam was in the audience. There was something freakishly odd about having a guy you were hot for watching you walk down the aisle.

"Get Liam off your brain," I chastised softly.

"Pardon me?" my mother asked.

"I said Lisa's dress has a pretty train." It was true. The custom-made gown included a ten-foot train that had the same D and L monogram I'd seen on the dance floor.

Once we all passed Jeffrey's inspection, we lined up and, via cordless microphone, Jeffrey cued the organist. Wagner's Bridal Chorus, aka "Here Comes the Bride," vibrated through the centuries-old church. At the last second, I was handed a bouquet of magnolia blossoms.

"Elbows bent, flowers at the waist, please!" Jeffrey instructed. "And go," he told the first bridesmaid.

It took a while for my turn to come around. I was ready. Or at least I thought I was until I saw Liam in the back row. He didn't just look at me. He stared with an intensity that made my blood boil. The sensation didn't last long. Only until I saw the pretty brunette sitting pressed up against him.

He'd been the toast of the rehearsal dinner, and now he was probably arranging for a hookup while I was trapped in a sea of satin.

Once I had taken my place at the altar, my mother and sister appeared at the double doors, and the entire audience got to its feet. I half expected my mother to do that screwing-in-a-lightbulb, Queen of England wave at the audience. Even I had to admit that she looked radiant as she escorted a now-veiled Lisa.

On the other hand, Lisa looked as if she was struggling to walk in a straight line. Perhaps she should have spent more time practicing the fine art of walking in killer heels instead of running triathlons. Anyone can bike, run, and swim, but it takes talent to get the pitch and balance of a new pair of stilettos.

The tux-clad video guys and the photographer moved discreetly along the walls of the church, while Jeffrey stood in the back grinning broadly. He should be pleased with himself. The chapel was stunning. The lighting was subdued everywhere except in the small area occupied by David, Lisa, and the pastor. After I'd adjusted Lisa's gown and taken her bouquet, I sorta zoned out. I was standing on a diagonal, so I could see Liam in my peripheral vision. If the brunette got any closer, she'd be in his lap. If he noticed, it didn't show on his face.

I was so distracted that I almost missed my cue to hand Lisa's bouquet back for her joyous walk through the on-their-feet-applauding crowd. I looped arms with the best man and tried to smile as naturally as possible. After all, my mother wanted perfect pictures, and I didn't want the headache of being caught with my smile down.

My mother alternated between dabbing her eyes and clutching her hanky to her heart. You'd think it was the first wedding she'd attended. Hardly. She'd made the same walk five times and was actively looking for number six.

After shaking ninety-nine hands, I saw Liam bring up the rear of the receiving line. He smelled as good as he looked. No wonder the brunette had been campaigning so hard. I wouldn't have minded nuzzling his neck.

I decided that was because he was in a tux. Most men look better in formal wear. Very James Bondy, and totally sexy—Liam even more so because of that lock of hair that always fell to his forehead. I really wanted to rake my fingers through his hair. Who was I kidding? I wanted him, period.

The next thirty minutes was spent on photographs. The poor photographer was getting it from both sides. My mother was giving him direction, as was Tenley Huntington-St. John. Since the guy's portfolio included stars and professional athletes, I'm sure he was accustomed to all the instruction. I could just tell he was tired of it.

David and Lisa kept sharing little kisses between group shots. It would have been kind of sweet except that David kissed like an angelfish. I didn't know a guy could pucker so long or so hard. Lisa could probably stand a foot away from him and those nasty lips still would have reached her.

It was time to return to the Ritz. Liam was nowhere to be seen, possibly in the company of the brunette, so I was relegated to sharing a limo with best man Mitchell something, as well as two other groomsmen and two of the other bridesmaids. Everyone seemed giddy and chatty on the way to the reception. It wasn't that I was trying to be standoffish. I wasn't. I just didn't have much to add to conversations about medical procedures. One of the women, Brandi, Candi—something like that—was also an oncologist. The other woman was a surgical nurse. The best man and both groomsmen had been close to David since elementary school, and both had gone on to medical school. The one who wasn't the best man had also earned a J.D. Guess that came in handy if he wanted to sue himself for malpractice.

"Your mother mentioned you worked for a law firm in Palm Beach?" Mitchell inquired politely.

Knowing my mother would kill me if I outed myself, I simply said, "West Palm Beach, actually. I specialize in trusts and estates and some litigation work." True enough, but I felt kinda sleazy lying about my perfectly good job.

We made appropriate chitchat until we reached the hotel and I was freed from medical personnel hell. Yet again Jeffrey gathered us together and coordinated the way in which we would enter the ballroom. And yet again, I was next to last, looped arm in arm with Mitchell Who-Gives-a-Shit.

The bandleader announced us as if we were game-show contestants. "And here we have maid of honor and sister of the bride, Finley Tanner. She's being escorted by Mitchell Helner, David's close friend and best man."

I almost expected parting gifts when Mitchell and I reached the dining area. Liam was already seated at a large circular table and had risen along with the rest of the attendees to greet Lisa and David. I joined in the applause as my sister beamed when she walked through the door. I don't even think she noticed that the bandleader called her Mrs. David Huntington-St. John IV. No recognition that she was a doctor. I glanced across the table and read the pinched expression on my mother's face. As much as she didn't want me to tell a soul what I actually did for a living, it was nothing compared to how strongly she needed people to know that her other daughter was a successful physician.

I saw the brunette one table over and would easily have laid odds on her switching out her place card to be closer to Liam. If he noticed, it didn't show as he pulled out my chair for me.

I liked that Lisa and David had forgone the traditional head table and opted instead to seat the wedding party up front, but at tables where they had friends or family. Lisa and David had a small table to themselves right near the edge of the dance floor.

If I thought the ballroom was incredible in the morning, it was nothing compared to how magical it looked all pulled together. The color scheme really did remind you of the beach. All we needed was an Ocean Breeze Yankee Candle to make it complete.

Wait staff in crisp, black uniforms poured champagne and passed trays of appetizers. There were shrimp, dates wrapped in bacon, caviar on tiny blinis with crème fraîche, prosciutto wrapped around melon, and sumptuous pâté de fois gras on toast points. The choices seemed endless, and I decided to pace myself since I knew a dinner of surf and turf was soon to follow. The champagne, on the other hand . . . I was all for having my glass topped off a few times before Liam leaned over and asked, "Don't you have to give a toast?"

"In a couple of hours," I answered more curtly than I'd intended. It was just that the brunette was leaning back in her chair listening to our exchange.

"Finley?" My mother spoke from her place on the opposite side of the table. "Remember your responsibilities."

I shielded my mouth with my hand. "She reads lips when she isn't flying around on her broomstick."

Liam smiled. "Mrs. Rossi, would you care to dance?"

My mother looked as if he'd just asked her for a kidney. "I believe I will wait until after the traditional first dance by the bride and groom."

If her condescension bothered Liam, he certainly didn't show it. Instead, he called the waiter over and asked for a beer rather than the champagne. I thought my mother would get the vapors, whatever the hell vapors are. The only thing that would make it worse was if he drank it straight from the bottle. And given his choice, I'm sure Liam would have preferred that over the fancy glass the waiter placed in front of him.

"Is she always like this?"

"Only when she's awake."

I spent the next forty minutes sipping my drink and accepting the kind words of strangers. Most of them pointed out that Lisa and I looked nothing alike. I was sorely tempted to say, "That's because my mother got knocked up by one of two men she was boffing at the time." But I didn't. The risk was far greater than the reward.

Liam couldn't take a breath to please her. My mother began

sharing her complaints with Great-aunt Susan—for whom my mother was named before she legally had her name changed from Susan to Cassidy. Because Great-aunt Susan is close to ninety, my mother had to yell to be heard. That gave her a nice excuse to point out that Liam's handkerchief was not properly folded, that Liam was slouching in his chair like he was attending some sort of sporting event, that Liam had embarrassed her last night by flirting with other women at the rehearsal gala—which wasn't true, they had been flirting with him. She finished by promising Great-aunt Susan that Liam and I weren't seriously involved. In fact, she continued, in the world according to Cassidy, Liam and I barely knew each other. Her constant sniping made dinner seem to last an eternity. Then the bandleader called Mitchell up to the microphone to give his speech. I swear, it was longer than the State of the Union address. He started with his first meeting with David and ended with a more current recollection. When it was my turn, I went up, took the microphone, and said, "It can be hard to share your sister with someone else, but I am thrilled to share Lisa with David. The love you show for and to each other is inspiring and beautiful, and I look forward to seeing it continue to grow. I am honored to be able to raise a toast to my wonderful sister and her new husband. To Lisa and David!"

Took me all of ten seconds, which judging by the applause, was appreciated after Mitchell's seven-minute blathering.

I had just about reached my seat when the bandleader announced it was time for Lisa and David's first dance. I knew from speaking to Lisa that Tenley Huntington-St. John had arranged for private lessons with a choreographer so the waltz would be perfect. It paid off. Other than a few missteps because of her shoes, Lisa got through the first part of the song without falling face-first into the six-tier cake.

Then came the whole will-the-rest-of-the-wedding-party-please-join-our-couple invitation. I waited by my chair for Mitchell to join me. As soon as he held out his hand, I awkwardly took to the dance floor. If the weasel stepped on my Jimmy Choos, I'd probably knee him in the testicles.

We'd been dancing for maybe ten seconds when I realized Liam was tapping Mitchell on the shoulder. Suddenly, I was passed off. Liam pulled me close. Not just bodies touching but pressed together. Hard.

A slight murmur went through the guests as Liam spun me around and pulled my hand against his body. "What are you doing?" I asked.

"Pissing your mother off. A little payback for the way she treats you."

I glanced over his shoulder and smiled. "It's working."

His hand dropped lower until it rested just below the small of my back. "I'm liking it myself. Great toast, by the way. I wouldn't have pegged you as the sentimental type."

"I'm not. I got it off IDoWeddingToasts.com."

Liam's hand dipped lower still, pressing our bodies even closer. "Well played."

"You, too. You're managing to frost my mother and break the heart of your brunette girlfriend all with one dance."

"Jealous?"

No, I was hot. Really hot. "The song is ending."

"So it is," Liam agreed as he waited for total silence before releasing me.

My knees felt weak, and I wasn't sure I still had a fully functional spine. I got an express ride back to reality when I turned and saw my mother's red face. She was hot too, only in a different way.

"What were you thinking, Finley?" she asked as soon as we returned to the table. "That was inappropriate and disgusting."

"Thought you said it wasn't serious," Great-aunt Susan remarked. "Looked mighty serious from here."

"Really, Finley. And you," she paused to glare at Liam. She let her narrowed gaze complete the thought.

The next few hours were a bit painful. My mother and Liam had both drawn their lines in the sand. The brunette had asked Liam to dance twice. Both times he accepted, though he didn't grind her the way he had me. Just to irritate her, he asked my mother to dance. She declined, but Great-aunt Susan was all over her invitation. She probably hadn't danced since the Reagan administration, so she and her artificial hip went for it.

Then we had cake—chocolate with champagne buttercream—and then . . . it happened. The most humbling experience at any wedding is the dreaded tossing of the bouquet. Normally, I make sure to time a trip to the ladies' room to avoid participating, but that wouldn't work in this situation. The leader of the full orchestra had already introduced me to the wedding guests, so my absence would be conspicuous. Not to mention my mother would have a fit if I wasn't one hundred percent into the festivities.

But a bouquet toss? Standing huddled in a lump of desperate, single women holding on to the myth that the lone catcher will be the next one down the aisle held zero appeal for me. It was a spectacle. Not to mention that it often turned physical. Some women were so eager to get their hands on the silk-flower prize that they actually hip-checked you out of the way. Worse still, the whole thing was set to music. In this case, it was an instrumental version of "It's Raining Men."

"Get up there," my mother said with a clenched smile.

Dutifully, I rose and began weaving my way through the tables. "Good luck!" Liam called after me.

Good luck? Hardly. Getting into position was not an easy task, given that my dress had some volume and my heels were too high for bouquet hockey. What if I broke a heel? The mere thought of harm coming to my Jimmy Choos gave me chills.

Joining the throng of about thirty-five bachelorettes, I stayed toward the back of the pack, in what I like to think of as the safe zone. Seven of my sister bridesmaids were clumped in the crowd of hopefuls.

As Lisa took her place on a chair in the front of the banquet room, I fiddled with the double-strand pearl necklace that she'd given all her attendants. We also received a matching bracelet and drop pearl earrings, so I was accessorized to the gills.

When the wedding guests began a countdown, Lisa swung her arm in unison to the cheers.

"Two . . . one!"

The next thing I knew I was holding a silk replica of Lisa's bouquet. I received a rousing round of applause that made my cheeks warm as embarrassment crept up from my neck. Maneuvering back to the table, I tried to ignore the condescending smile on Liam's face.

I actually added that to my list of things to ignore about

Liam. Seeing him in a tux was still a distraction. Then there was the whole didn't-actually-kiss-me-at-the-rehearsal-dinner thing. Having him around was proving to be a test, one I wasn't so sure I was passing. But my situation was about to change. David and Lisa were getting ready to leave, which meant I could go up to my room and relax. Well, as much as possible, knowing Liam was right next door.

Thirty minutes later I was back in the relative peace and quiet of my suite, wearing lounge pants and sipping coffee. As much as I enjoyed clothing, I was tired of being trussed into a ball gown. I'd never make it as Cinderella. Even though it was just shy of eleven, it had been a very long and exhausting day.

As I was refilling my mug, I heard a couple of noises from Liam's room. I wanted to go to the adjoining door and knock, but I knew better. I was tired of pretending I wasn't attracted to him, and I knew if I made the first move, something that shouldn't happen would, three-wishes bullshit or not.

Summoning my courage, and switching from coffee to champagne, I changed into the silk nightie and matching robe I'd packed. I didn't want to think about why I'd packed the sexy getup. Wishful thinking?

I was tired of thinking and ready to act. I gulped the rest of my champagne and knocked on the adjoining door.

In a nanosecond it opened. Liam was gloriously bare-chested, wearing only a pair of jeans. The sight literally took my breath away.

"Need to borrow a cup of sugar?" he asked, with his head cocked and a sexy grin.

His eyes traversed the full length of my body, making me shiver. "I had something else in mind."

"So I see."

His arm snaked around me, and he pulled me close. The soft hair on his chest tickled my warmed skin. His mouth met mine, and then we were moving backward into my suite. I was lost in the pure sensuality of his tongue dancing with mine.

Gently, he lay on the sofa, bringing me tumbling down in his embrace. We were still lip-locked, but my brain was savoring the feel of his rock-solid body. My flimsy nightie was pretty much useless; I could feel every inch of him. He didn't need to tell me he wanted me, I could feel it and taste it as he drew my lower lip between his teeth and teased it with his tongue.

My hands went exploring. I touched every millimeter of his broad shoulders and torso, loving the way he moaned softly as I slipped my fingertips a hairsbreadth into the waistband of his jeans.

His hands were tangled in my hair, gently massaging my neck as he increased the pressure of his lips. My body responded with fiery waves coursing through my veins, sending heat to every nerve ending.

My heart skipped a beat when he looped his thumb and forefinger around my strap and slowly began to peel away the garment. All I could do was hold his head as he kissed his way down my shoulder and over my collarbone. Through the fabric, he teased my taut nipple with a combination of heat from his breath and gentle flicks of his tongue.

I wanted to be naked. I wanted him naked, too. I was filled with a sense of urgency and the promise of long-awaited fulfillment. I unfastened the top button of his jeans, as a small sound rumbled out of my throat when his fingers brushed my breast.

There was a ringing in my ears I originally chalked up to brain-addled passion. Eventually, I realized it was the phone in Liam's room.

"Let it ring," I whispered.

"I will," he said as he dragged me up his body and kissed me deeply.

The phone rang again and again until it couldn't be ignored.

"It's got to be important," he said. "Just give me a minute."

"Leaving me, eh?"

"How about you use the time to get into bed?" He kissed my forehead. "I'll meet you there."

Liam stood and went into his room while I went in the opposite direction. I closed the bedroom door, adjusted the lighting, then stripped and slipped beneath the sheets. My heart was pounding loudly. I was quivering as the first minute passed. Then another and another. Finally, Liam returned. This time he was wearing a shirt and shoes with his jeans. Had I really misread the signals that badly?

He took in a deep breath and let it out slowly. "I know I'll regret this, but I've got to go."

"Go where?"

"Back to West Palm."

"It's almost midnight."

"Can't be helped. If I stay, it will only make your life more difficult."

"Hooking up with you will not make my life difficult," I insisted as I bunched the covers up over my shoulders."

"You'll just have to trust me on this one." That said, he bent down and gave me one more mind-altering kiss, then left.

I scrambled out of bed and into some clothes, then raced into the living room. The door to his room was closed. I heard the muted sound of an exterior door closing, but by the time I reached the peephole, the hallway was clear.

I was confused and all worked up. The only cure?

Shop.

Powering up my laptop, I checked my eBay auctions and discovered that Tiara64 had bid all the items up over their appraised value. Combined, the three pins worth between twenty-four hundred and three thousand dollars were at nearly four grand. The bracelet was up from an appraised high of two hundred to two fifty, and the earrings were ten dollars over at two hundred ten. That was four thousand four hundred fifty. Even if the bids didn't go a penny higher, I was looking at making a cool five thousand with the selling bonus. Not too shabby for costume jewelry. The greedy part of me wished I'd listed the one good brooch as well. I could only imagine what Tiara64 would pay for a genuine Lucy Shaw piece.

With my almost-newfound wealth, I began searching for Rolex parts. I found the watch movement and placed a bid limit of twenty-five hundred on it. Then I grabbed up a couple of links on a "buy it now" for three hundred dollars. I could just hear Jane in my ear, reminding me that I needed to save the extra money and put it toward home expenses. At least then I wouldn't be drawing against the home equity line every month just to pay half of the monthly loan payment.

Satisfied that I'd done everything possible on the eBay front, I took my mug to the sink and rinsed it. Then, like some lovesick teenager, I tiptoed over to the adjoining door and placed my ear against it, listening intently.

All I heard was the sound of my own breathing. Dragging myself away from the door, I packed a lot of my things. I finally went to bed.

♦

In the morning, I took the SD card out of my camera and uploaded the photos I'd taken before the wedding and at the reception. Unconsciously, I had taken an awful lot of shots of Liam in his tux. I decided not to share all of them with Becky, Jane, and Liv, but I did want them to get the full flavor of the event. Both Liv and Jane called to comment on the photos and to see how my Liam time had gone. I filled them in, holding back the fact that I was over game playing and ready just to jump his bones to get it out of my system.

After showering, dressing, and finishing my packing, I went back to the computer to watch the auction clock click down to zero. As soon as it did, I totaled the amount and called Becky.

"Finley?"

"Yeah. Still willing to meet the tiara lady?"

"You're sure it's a lady and not some jewelry-collecting serial killer, right?" she joked.

Her mood seemed lighter. "Sounds like you got a good night's sleep."

"Don't know about good, but I managed five hours. That's more consecutive hours than I've had in almost a week."

"You're sure about meeting this woman?" I asked.

"Yeah. Just have her meet me at the corner of Chilean and

East Ocean. No sense in giving her your home address just in case she is a fruit loop."

I felt a pang of discomfort. "You know what, never mind. I can just e-mail her and tell her I'll ship her the stuff overnight tomorrow." *Good-bye, five-hundred-dollar bonus.*

"Don't be silly. I'm meeting her on a public street. She doesn't know me from Eve's housecat, so if I sense anything out of whack, I'll just drive away, and then you can make alternate arrangements."

"Are you sure?" *Welcome home, bonus bucks!*

"Positive. Besides, I'm meeting Jane and Liv for a late lunch afterward."

I felt a twinge of envy. While they were out lunching and chatting, I'd be battling my way through security at Hartsfield. I thanked Becky again, then sent the e-mail to Tiara64 with instructions.

I called for a bellman. I realized I had to pack the coffee gift basket, but it wouldn't fit in my luggage without some real creativity.

Thank heavens I'd brought a tote with me. I tried rolling up several items of clothing and tucking them into the tote, and then I shoved my laptop in my purse. It was too bulky. I gave up. I'd just have to go to the business center and have the items shipped home.

By the time the bellman arrived, I'd repacked, albeit in a disorganized fashion. As we walked out the door, I noticed a maid's cart blocking the door to Liam's room.

Following behind as the bellman pushed the luggage rack, I explained that I'd need to stop at the business center. While my basket was being wrapped and packed for shipment, I used the opportunity to print my boarding pass at one of the kiosks.

As soon as I was settled into a taxi, I called my mother's room. She still refused to get a cell phone. "Hi. I'm on my way to the airport."

"I'm staying an extra day. After this weekend, I need some time to relax from the stress."

"I thought the wedding was a huge success."

"Of course you would think that. You didn't have to be involved with the planning and logistics."

"That would have been a little difficult since I live six hundred miles away."

"I managed to make time for your sister. Yesterday was an important day for her, and you did nothing to help."

"What needed to be done that I missed?"

"How like you, Finley. Always thinking of yourself. You should have been thinking about how it felt for me to sit at a table with that private detective of yours. Really, you couldn't find anyone more appropriate?"

"What did Liam do that offended you?"

"Where do I begin?" she answered dramatically. "He's just not of our ilk."

"We have an ilk?"

"Don't take that tone with me," she warned. "You know exactly what and why I was mortified by his presence."

"I'm sorry you feel that way."

"Where is your pride? The man flirted with every girl there."

"He's a single man. Why shouldn't he flirt? And he wasn't the one flirting. Women like him. Seems to me you were a little flirty, too. Or did that single stockbroker end up at our table by accident?"

"The gentleman was coming unescorted. I arranged for him to sit near me to ensure he enjoyed the festivities."

"Whatever." I ended the hostile call and sent a text message to Becky. It was one forty-five, and I wanted to make sure she'd closed the costume jewelry deal. She didn't respond immediately. Either she was driving home, or to the office, or the battery in her phone had died. My money was on the battery drain. Becky was famous for neglecting to charge her phone. And now that she was overworked, she was probably even less attentive.

After I'd cleared security, I bought a half-dozen Moon Pies and found my gate. No way was I carrying on a six-pack of RC. Becky would just have to deal. I tried calling her. It went directly to voice mail, confirming my suspicions. I left a message, just in case she recharged. I remembered that she was meeting Jane and Liv for lunch and was about to call Liv when my flight was announced. Hoisting my tote up on my shoulder, I made my way down the gangway and into the belly of the aircraft. Like on the flight down, I was alone in business class, though I found myself wondering if Liam might magically appear. When he didn't, I wasn't sure if I was relieved or disappointed.

◆

Something was different when I got home. "What the hell?" I whispered as I deposited my second suitcase in the foyer. I hadn't noticed on the first trip in, but now that I was actually in, I saw little, disturbing details.

My sofa cushions were askew, as if someone had lifted them looking for spare change. The velvet jewelry bag was gone from the counter, but I didn't see any cash. I walked into the bedroom and found a few other things out of place. My comforter was bunched at the end of the bed. "Weird," I muttered as I deposited my purse and tote on the unmade bed. I couldn't imagine Becky going through my stuff, but I also couldn't imagine anyone breaking into my cottage. I checked the obvious stuff—jewelry and electronics—but everything was present and accounted for. As far as I could tell, nothing was missing.

"Maybe you're imagining things," I suggested as I slipped off my shoes. Maybe I'd been the one who'd left the cabinet doors in the kitchen ajar. And maybe I'd pulled back the comforter when I was packing.

"So where's the money?" I checked all the obvious places— kitchen drawers, dresser drawers, anyplace Becky could have hidden my windfall. She could still have it with her, I guess.

I made do with my coffeepot, missing the Cuisinart that would take three to five business days to arrive. I brewed a half pot and went to the refrigerator for cream. I smiled. There on the top shelf, right next to the French vanilla creamer was an envelope. "Clever," I said as I opened the envelope and began counting hundred-dollar bills. It also explained why my house looked disturbed. Becky must have been rooting around for a secure hiding place.

I was tempted to get naked and lie on the sofa covered in money, but that took way too much effort. Even though it was barely after six, I was exhausted and just wanted to call for Chinese and veg out in front of the TV for the night. After unpacking, I decided a nice soak in the tub would get rid of the travel cooties and help me relax. Okay, so it would probably work better if I hadn't taken a travel mug of coffee with me into the roman tub, but I needed the caffeine.

After a nice soak, I pulled on a pair of Gap Body shorts and matching cami top. My hair was twisted up in a ponytail, and I'd scrubbed my face clean of makeup. It was my relaxation ensemble, and it felt great. By rote, I dialed the Chinese restaurant and requested my usual—moo shu and an order of fried dumplings. I was almost salivating just ordering, so the twenty minutes they said I'd have to wait felt like an eternity.

When the bell rang, I practically raced to the door, opening it wide for the nice delivery guy who always slips me a few extra fortune cookies. Taking my two containers into the living room, I pointed the remote at the TV and started channel surfing.

I'd stop every now and then, just long enough to eat whatever happened to land on my chopsticks. My whole house smelled like sesame and hoisin. It was a beautiful thing.

I ate until I thought I'd explode. I was full, but it was a good full. That's one of the advantages to living alone—the ability to pig out without anyone seeing you.

With my belly full and my body exhausted, I made an early night of it.

The early night resulted in an early morning. I was up, showered, and on my second pot of coffee before *Today* came on. This meant I had to suffer through the local news sharing "pet pics," a parade of pampered animals, many posed in costume and driving golf carts.

While a photo of Godiva, the chocolate lab, filled the screen, I pulled my teal Ralph Lauren sleeveless matte jersey dress over my head. It had a slightly draped neckline and was pin-tucked on one side, making for a very flattering fit. I put large silver hoops in my ears and worked the matching bangles on my right arm. I chose a funky white-and-silver Swatch watch and a pair of Boutique 9 pumps to complete my ensemble. The shoes were discounted because there was a slight imperfection in the tonal straps over the beveled toe. You'd have to get down on your hands and knees to see the flaw, so I was pretty sure I could pull off the look without anyone noticing the difference. The dress was a worn-once find on eBay, and at eight dollars, I'd taken a chance, which had paid off nicely. It cost me more to have it cleaned and hemmed than it did to buy. But I was still under twenty bucks, total.

Even though it went against every instinct, I decided to go to work early. Well, that wasn't exactly true—I was going to my office, but I really had no intention of working until the stroke of nine. I just wanted to talk to Becky so I could thank her and get the scoop on Tiara64.

I had an image in my mind. A tall, bleached blonde with fake boobs and false eyelashes; toned, tanned, and a little trashy. Actually, I'd just described Liam's ex-wife. Now that I was thinking about it, Ashley, aka Beer Barbie, did look like a pageant person. She was always meticulously made-up and dressed in tight, revealing clothing. Grudgingly, I had to admit that she carried it off. What would have looked trashy on someone else looked sexy on her, in a Hooters kinda way.

"Great," I mumbled when I pulled into the parking lot, only to find that Becky's red BMW was nowhere to be found. The only other car was the big, banana-yellow Hummer H3 that belonged to Vain Dane.

Digging my phone out of my purse, I pressed the speed-dial

button for Becky's cell. It was still going directly to voice mail. Maybe Becky was just taking some personal time. If anything was wrong, I reasoned, Liv and Jane would have called me. It was already nearing eight, so I wasn't going to sit in my car for over an hour. I grabbed my tote and my purse, put my phone in my purse, unlocked and relocked the door, then took the elevator to the second floor.

Flipping light switches as I went along, I reached my office and dialed into the company mailbox system. "You've reached Finley Tanner. I'm unable to take your calls today, June seventh. Please leave your name and number, and I'll return your call as soon as possible." Then I dialed Margaret's extension and got her voice mail. I couldn't resist. "It's Finley, and it's eight thirty on Monday morning. When you get in, please check to see if a package was delivered for me last Friday. Thank you." I wasn't expecting a package; I just wanted to screw with Margaret. Lord knew she screwed with me often enough.

I turned on my computer and poured myself coffee while it booted up. When I clicked on my e-mail, I scrolled the list to find the most pressing. There was one from Becky time-stamped at 3:31 on Sunday. It read:

Left the money in the fridge. Working at home on Ellen's stuff from the drawer. I'll call you in a few days.

"In a few days?" I whispered. I couldn't think of a time when we'd gone days without communicating. Whether it be text, voice mail, or e-mail, we were always in touch. Something seemed hinky. Knowing Becky had had lunch with Liv and Jane yesterday, I picked up my phone and dialed Jane.

"Hello?"

"Hi, I—" My extension buzzed. "I'll call you right back." I switched over to the other line. "Finley Tanner."

"Please come to my office immediately," Vain Dane instructed.

"I'll be right up."

I'd have to wait to call Jane back. When Vain Dane said immediately, he meant like yesterday. Grabbing a pen and pad from my top drawer, I paused for a second. *Drawer.* Becky's message had mentioned Ellen's drawer. Could she have been referring to the Department of Corrections letter? That might explain why she was working from home. Maybe she'd come across something she didn't want anyone at the firm to know.

I couldn't stand there pondering, so I quickly made my way up to Vain Dane's office. The executive sentry wasn't at her desk, so I walked down the east hallway, stopping at Dane's door and knocking.

"Come."

Shake. Beg. Liver treat. "Good morning," I said.

"Morning. Sit."

Sit. Lie down. Heel. Liver treat. I sat in one of two leather chairs across from his glass-topped desk. As the seconds ticked away, a zillion possibilities went through my mind. Was he going to fire me for missing a half day even though I had given them notice? Was he going to praise me for showing up early?

"I spoke to Ms. Jameson yesterday. Have you completed everything in the Egghardt matter?"

How did he get in touch with Becky when I couldn't, and why on a Sunday? "All I have left to do is contact the people living on the property; if they haven't found the document guaranteeing their right to live on the property for life, the best solution would probably be to relocate them to the southwest edge of the land. Then they could have additional acreage for planting and their cattle can continue to graze. This option would prevent litigation and, if acceptable to Lenora Egghardt, settle everything."

"Contact the tenants and then set up a meeting with Lenora."

"Should I wait until Becky has free time in her schedule?"

"No. She'll be working at home, probably for a week or so, just to catch up on all the work left undone by Ellen."

"A week?"

"Possibly." He scrutinized me the same way he scrutinized his buffed, manicured fingernails. "Do you know something I don't?"

"No, sir. I'm just surprised. With Ellen gone, it seems like an odd time for Bec—Ms. Jameson to be taking time off."

"She isn't taking time off, she just didn't feel as if she could get up to speed and deal with the interruptions here at the office, all at the same time."

That didn't sound like Becky. She could multitask like a pro. Sure, she was probably overtaxed doing her job and Ellen's all at once, but Becky wasn't a time-out kind of person. "I see," I lied.

"Do a thirty-day notice to relocate to the tenants and send it up to me before you mail it. No, do it, and then petition to reopen the estate before you contact the tenants. Make the demand on behalf of the estate."

"Shouldn't I run this by Lenora first?"

"You can, with our recommendation that she take our advice to settle this as quickly and amiably as possible. Litigation could get expensive and won't get her equestrian center built."

"Yes, sir."

"Good, then we're done." He smoothed his hand over his gel-soaked hair.

"Okay." I stood. "I'm glad I came in early so I can get on this right away."

"Uh-huh," he mumbled as he picked up a letter and was already reading it.

Apparently, I was not going to get any props for coming in before nine. By the time I got back to my office, Margaret had left me a voice mail stating that no packages had been delivered, but she had held my mail downstairs and I was free to get it at any time. Margaret, one; Finley, zero.

I called Jane back. "Sorry. I was summoned to the inner sanctum. Listen, was Becky okay when you met her for lunch yesterday?"

"She didn't show up."

"What?"

"She was a no-show. But she did send a text."

"When?"

"Around three something. Said she was swamped with work from Ellen's drawer."

"She said Ellen's drawer?"

"Yes."

Shit.

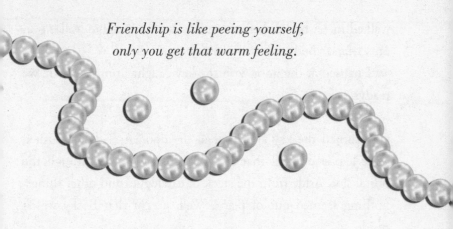

Friendship is like peeing yourself,
only you get that warm feeling.

fourteen

Becky hadn't answered a single text, e-mail, or call for more than three days, and I was starting to worry. Correction, I *was* worried. I was standing outside her condo in Juno Beach waiting on Liv and Jane. The sun was just beginning to set, but it was still warm, low to mid eighties.

Liv's champagne-colored Mercedes pulled into one of the visitor's parking spots. Jane was right behind her, and she pulled into the space next to my bright, shiny pink convertible. Liv and Jane both wore their concern on their faces.

"Okay. Have you knocked?" Liv asked.

"For about ten minutes," I said.

"Then let's go in," Jane said.

Taking the elevator up to the fifth floor, I kept fidgeting with the spare key I had in my hand. I didn't want to go in alone because, quite frankly, I was afraid of what I might find. I've walked in on bodies before, and I couldn't imagine walking in on a friend's body.

I paused at the door with the key caught in midair. "Are we ready?"

"Yes."

I turned the key and opened the door. As I did, I pushed aside a pile of mail that had collected as it fell through the postal slot. Aside from the stack of catalogues and other things, nothing seemed out of place. Well, except that Becky wasn't inside.

"Now what do we do?" Jane asked.

"Look around. See if anything is weird."

"All this mail is weird," Jane said as she gathered it up and placed it on the kitchen counter.

While Jane went through the mail, Liv did the guest room and I took the master. The bed was made. The little dish that Becky kept her keys in was empty. I didn't see her purse, nor did anything look disturbed. I went into the master bath, and it too was neat, but what I saw gave me a chill. There on the vanity I saw Becky's toothbrush and all her makeup. There was no way she'd go anywhere without those.

"Nothing here!" Liv yelled.

I caught up with her in the hallway and told her what I'd discovered. "Becky would never leave her MAC behind," Liv said.

"I know. So where is she?"

"Her purse and her car are gone. If anything happened to her, I doubt the suspect would allow her to grab her purse before being kidnapped," Liv said.

"Her car may not be missing," Jane called from the kitchen.

When we went in to see what was up, we found her waving an official-looking envelope. "This is from the Palm Beach Police. Traffic Division."

"Becky got a ticket?" I asked.

Jane shrugged and held the envelope up to the light. "It looks like one. Why would she get a ticket in Palm Beach?"

"She met someone for me on Sunday," I said. God, what if Tiara64 really was a serial killer? I shivered. "Now I'm sure we should call the police."

Liv had her phone out. "Palm Beach or Palm Beach County?"

"Palm Beach County." I watched as Jane's expression dimmed. I couldn't blame her. Not when she had such bad memories from her last encounter with law enforcement.

"Let's open the ticket first," I suggested.

Jane ripped along the perforated lines and unfolded the form. "Illegal parking. And her car was towed by Lawson's Towing."

"When?"

"Sunday at three-oh-five p.m."

"Now we have to call the police," I insisted. "What have I done?" I felt tears well in my eyes. "She was supposed to meet the tiara woman at one."

"But she sent us a text after three," Jane reminded me. "After the car had been towed."

"And I got an e-mail," I added. "And she talked to Vain Dane. All that happened after three as well."

"Maybe her car wouldn't start," Liv suggested.

"Then she would have called one of you for a ride. She wouldn't just leave it on East Ocean. She knows the trash trucks come once a day and the streets are narrow." I sniffed as I tried to keep my composure. "I definitely think we should call the sheriff's office."

Liv dialed and then said, "Yes, I'd like to report a missing woman." Then a pause, and then, "Rebecca Jameson. She's twenty-nine, five-six, red hair, green eyes. No one has seen her since Sunday afternoon." Then Liv's brows pulled together. "No, it is not voluntary. She left her makeup and toothbrush and allowed her car to be towed." Then, "Fine, we'll come down and fill out a report."

"Why?" I asked when Liv snapped her blinged-out clamshell phone closed.

"They won't send a detective because they don't consider a missing adult a big deal."

"Then let's go to them."

Liv rubbed her forehead. "I have a meeting at nine with a client."

"Nine p.m.?" Jane asked.

"The groom works long hours. He's a yacht broker, and his business is open until eight."

"Then Finley and I will handle it," Jane said. "C'mon, Finley. I'll drive."

After locking up, we went down in the elevator. I got into the passenger side of Jane's Escalade. Not an easy task in high heels. I had to hike up my skirt to grab the leather strap above the window so I could reach the seat.

"It's weird that both Ellen and Becky would go missing less than two weeks apart."

"Anything happening at work?" Jane asked.

"They do contracts. Real estate mostly. Hardly a hotbed for nut jobs."

"She took her purse, Finley."

"Unless her purse is in her car at Lawson's tow yard."

"We can have the detectives look there."

We went to the Pine Trail satellite office of the Palm Beach County Sheriff's Office and parked, then went inside. The place smelled of stale coffee and cherry deodorizer. I'd take some stale coffee. My caffeine level was plunging. I went to the glass window, and a uniformed man slid it open.

"May I help you?"

"We'd like to file a missing person's report."

"Is the missing person a minor?"

"No, she's twenty-nine."

"Take a seat. Someone will be with you shortly."

Jane leaned close to me and whispered, "They don't seem to be overly worried. Maybe we're overreacting."

"I'd rather overreact than not react at all."

Nearly thirty minutes later a middle-aged man in a white short-sleeved oxford shirt, striped tie, and khaki pants opened the veneered doorway. "Ladies? This way." As we stood, he raked his fingers through is salt-and-pepper hair.

We entered the office, where phones were ringing and there was a din of conversations sometimes punctuated with laughter. It was a small office with maybe a half-dozen employees, including the guy at the front. Most of the space was divided with temporary walls creating three-sided cubicles. There was an office at the far end of the rectangular room and another room next to the office that had a plaque that read INTERROGATION.

"I'm Detective-Sergeant Michael Wilkes."

Jane and I attracted some attention from the male officers. It was probably Jane, since she had on a black leather miniskirt and a red corset top. You could see the black lace of her bra and a whole lot of cleavage. Add that to four-inch stilettos, and that was Jane in a nutshell. She was the Erin Brockovich of accounting.

"I'm Finley Tanner, and this is Jane Spencer."

"Right here," the detective said when we reached his cubicle.

Jane and I each took a seat opposite the detective. "May I get you anything?"

"Coffee for me," I said.

"Water would be nice," Jane answered.

The detective left for a minute and came back with two Styrofoam cups. He'd also brought powdered cream, sugar, and an artificial sweetener. I was good with straight black. Well, I was until I tasted it. It was strong enough to melt the fender off a midsize Toyota. "I'll take that cream after all." I sprinkled the creamer into the cup, then picked up the swizzle stick and tried to stir it into the tarlike coffee.

Detective Wilkes reached into a drawer and pulled out a pad with forms on it. "Name of the person you suspect is missing?"

"Rebecca Jameson."

"Date of birth?"

Jane answered. It took almost twenty minutes for him to take down the most rudimentary information. He seemed almost bored as he asked each question.

"So, Ms. Jameson was overwhelmed at work?"

I shook my head. "More like super busy. Becky doesn't get overwhelmed."

"Is there any other reason you can think of that would cause Ms. Jameson to want to disappear?"

"I don't think she'd want to disappear. I think she met the person from eBay for me, and something went terribly wrong."

"But the cash from the transaction was placed safely at your residence?"

"Yes."

"And you did receive a text from Ms. Jameson?" he asked Jane.

She nodded. "Late Sunday afternoon. Here, I saved it." Jane dug her phone out of her purse and scrolled through her text messages, then handed him the phone.

"Is this Ms. Jameson's phone number?" he asked, pointing to the identifier at the top of the message where the date, time, and source of the text were listed.

"Yes."

"And you received an e-mail?" he asked me.

"Uh-huh. And before you ask, yes, it was sent via Becky's private e-mail account."

"Ms. Jameson called her superior and informed him that she would be out for a week or more?"

I nodded. "You're making it sound as if Becky chose to go missing."

"It does seem that way. A lot of adults opt to disappear."

"Wouldn't she take clothes and toiletries?" I argued.

"Maybe she planned on buying new when she arrived at her destination."

"What about the fact that one of the partners at my firm went missing nearly two weeks ago?"

"Again, that woman communicated her intention to quit her job, correct?"

"Correct. But that doesn't mean the two things aren't related," I said.

"Do you have any reason to think the two women are together?"

"Becky isn't a lesbian, if that's what you're trying to get at," I said.

"Sometimes people aren't always open about their sexuality."

"She was my college roommate. Trust me, she's not gay."

The detective rose. "Thank you for coming in."

"That's it?"

"We'll see what we can find out, and we'll keep you abreast of any developments." He had moved close to the entrance of his cubby.

"You can check out the car. And maybe dump the local-usage details from Becky's phone for the last three days," I practically pleaded.

"We will do what we can," Detective Wilkes insisted without a discernible trace of sincerity. "But without sufficient probable cause that something has happened to Ms. Jameson, we do have an obligation to respect her wishes to check out from her own life. Somewhere around two hundred thousand adults go missing every year. Any adult has an absolute right to disappear. But as I said, we'll check out these leads."

"What about . . ." Jane hesitated. "What about dental records?"

"That would be premature," the detective said. "We have absolutely no indicators that Ms. Jameson is in any danger."

"Well, that was a waste of time," Jane muttered as we walked through the lighted parking lot to her car. "He didn't seem to give a single shit."

"He was rather blasé about the whole thing."

"I think we should call Liam," Jane suggested rather adamantly.

"You call him," I said. "I'm sure he'll help, but I'd rather not be the one to ask. I'm already into him for three wishes, remember? You're the one he got naked."

I watched as Jane's shoulders slumped. I immediately felt bad for my caustic remark. "Sorry. I'm just tired. I know Liam was just getting you out of that bar before some weasel could take advantage of your intoxicated self."

"Thank you. He really was just looking out for my welfare."

"I know." A long silence followed. My mind was racing along with my heart. I had an idea, but I didn't dare tell Jane because I knew she'd tell Liam and then I'd probably get some long lecture from them both. Better to have Jane distracting Liam while I made a slight detour for the cause. "I'd still like it better if you called him."

"I will. As soon as I drop you off at your car."

♦

The gravel road leading up to Lawson's tow yard was pitch-black. The only light shone like a beacon up ahead. Floodlights bathed the area immediately around the fenced and razor-wired lot. As soon as I drove within a hundred yards of the place, I heard the chilling sound of two dogs barking.

"I hate guard dogs."

I kept reminding myself that this was all for Becky, hoping to bolster my courage. Leaving my high beams on, I exited the car and went directly to the padlocked gates. A slightly rusted sign explained that the yard was open from seven a.m. through seven p.m., and that cash was the only acceptable form of payment to release cars from impound.

"Jesus!" I screamed when a fierce-looking black dog threw himself at the chained gate. Reflexively, I took a step backward. "Bad dog."

It continued to snarl and growl. "Bad, bad, scary dog!"

The growling stopped. The fear coursing through my veins did not. The dog shadowed me as I walked along the fence line. It took only a matter of seconds for me to spot Becky's BMW. It was in the front row. However, I had to find a way past the dogs and into the car, since I didn't have any hope that Detective-Sergeant Wilkes was going to get his happy ass in gear any time soon.

I got back in my car, turned around, and headed back out east on Okeechobee Boulevard. I went into an all-night Walgreens and purchased one of those things that puncture glass—whatever it's called. My next stop was the McDonald's drive-through, where I purchased sandwiches and a large frappe to go.

I drove home, took off my dress and heels, and slipped on yoga pants, a top, and some barely used tennis shoes. There was no way I could accomplish my goal in four-inch wedges. Jane had gotten me the yoga outfit as a present and an incentive to join her sweaty yoga class. I'd passed on the class, but kept the outfit because it was comfy. And black, an added bonus because it was good camouflage. I went to my computer and did a Google search. I smiled when I found the answer I was looking for on Ask.com. I went to my medicine chest and grabbed my secret weapon: Xanax.

I thought about calling Tony, but decided it would be better if I put that off. As an officer of the court, he couldn't sanction what I was about to do, so keeping him out of the loop was crucial. I'd tell him when and if I found a significant clue.

Armed with my implements, I drove the twenty minutes back out to Lawson's. I'd already had one very unpleasant experience with a dog, and I didn't intend to repeat it. This time I came prepared.

Taking a long sip of my coffee for fortification, I tried to ignore my shaking hands. Hell, my whole body was shaking. Breaking and entering wasn't exactly one of my strengths.

Dressed for the part, I parked my car with the lights shining on my target and grabbed up the McDonald's bag. This time both dogs showed up at the gate, trying—and succeeding—to intimidate me. I was intimidated, but I was more worried about Becky.

Opening the bag, I unwrapped the first of a dozen cheeseburgers, added a Xanax, and then placed it on the gravel. I did the same for a second one. "Good doggies," I cooed as I let them get the scent through the chain link. They stopped snarling, so I figured my plan might just work. And since I'd checked, the Xanax wouldn't harm them in any way, so if I got caught, no one could tack on a cruelty-to-animals charge.

Like a minor-league pitcher, I threw those sandwiches as far away from Becky's car as possible. The dogs raced after them, fighting between themselves before each got his own sandwich. While they ate, I climbed up about three feet, the McDonald's bag clenched in my teeth. The dogs had finished their sandwiches and started running toward me, barking wildly.

I was ready. I tossed two more Xanax-laced burgers in the distance and bought myself enough time to reach the top of the fence and carefully negotiate the razor wire.

"Geez, don't you guys chew? Aren't you getting sleepy yet?" I asked when they came racing back for more. I unwrapped two more of the prespiked sandwiches, threw them, and off they went. I jumped the five feet to the ground and made a dash for Becky's car.

My heart was pounding in my chest and ears. I'd seen how the dogs had ripped into the burgers, and I sure as hell didn't want to be dessert. When I reached the car, I went around to the passenger's side so I could keep one eye out for the Hounds of the Baskervilles. Using the center punch, I shattered the window. Immediately, the car alarm started blaring. I was depending on the fact that these days, most people ignored the sound of an alarm.

People did. Dogs did not.

They came back toward me, though neither one seemed to have the energy to run. "Thank you, Xanax." I quickly unwrapped two more burgers, and then tossed them to the dogs. They began to eat, just not with the same enthusiasm as before. I only had two burgers left, so I had to make my search of Becky's car fast.

My heart sank into my toes when I spotted her Prada bag on the console. Reaching in, and being careful not to cut myself, I pulled the purse out, carefully shaking off shards of glass.

The blaring horn was giving me a headache. I debated whether to leave the purse for the police to find or just to take it with me. I decided to go through it and then put it back where I'd found it. Maybe when he saw her purse, Detective-Sergeant Wilkes would work a little harder on finding Becky.

The dogs were still chomping on their burgers as I tilted the purse toward the light and began surveying the contents. All the usual stuff was there. Makeup, compact, datebook. Then a chill ran along my spine. Her wallet was still inside. It would have been impossible for Becky to go missing voluntarily without taking along her debit card, checks, and credit cards. I slipped the debit card out and stuck it inside the strap of my sports bra.

I also noticed something else missing. Becky's cell phone. That was a positive sign. If she'd been snatched by the tiara lady, I doubted she would have asked permission to take her phone along. Her phone had a GPS chip, so maybe someone could triangulate the cell towers and get her location. I didn't know if that was possible or just something they did on CSI. Still, it was worth further investigation.

The two lethargic dogs staggered toward me as I went back to my point of entry. They were definitely buzzed, but the information from the Internet clearly stated that Xanax, in small doses, would not hurt them at all. Make them tired, yes. Cause them any long-lasting residual effects, no. I couldn't be miffed at the dogs; they were there for protection. But I didn't want protection. I just wanted to get out of there in one piece. Before I placed my foot in the fencing, I tossed the last set of burgers to the dogs. They sniffed them, but didn't seem very interested. Time to climb before they remembered they were actually supposed to keep people like me out of there.

I had just cleared the razor wire when I spotted a car coming up the gravel road.

Damn!

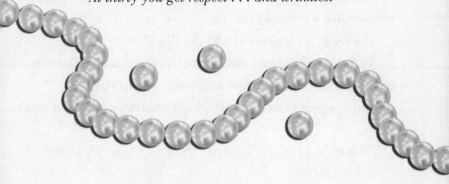

At thirty you get respect . . . and wrinkles.

fifteen

I jumped down and raced toward my car, adrenaline pumping through my whole body. I guess some people do still pay attention to alarms.

Too late. The car had me blocked in. Damn. I was probably going to jail for trespassing.

The bright headlights from the car made me shield my eyes as I watched the black silhouette in my rearview step out of the car and begin to walk toward me. I'd know that silhouette anywhere.

I stepped out of my car. "What are you doing here?"

"Saving your ass," Liam yelled over the car alarm, his tone laced with amusement.

I placed one hand on my hip and said, "Too late. I already got what I came for."

"And it's all memorialized on candid camera," he said, pointing to a place just below the roofline of the building. There, big as life was a security camera with its red blinking light laughing at me.

"Now what do I do?" I asked, my sense of accomplishment deflated like a week-old balloon.

"I have to get inside and take the tapes."

"Why you?" I asked defensively. "Just tell me what to do, and I'll do it. I've already got a rapport with the guard dogs."

Liam looked over at the sleeping Dobermans. "What'd you use?"

"Xanax," I admitted, because I thought it was very clever.

"How much?"

"One and a half milligrams. Why?"

"Well, that doesn't give me a lot of time."

I followed him over to the fence. I was treated to a nice, unobstructed view of his butt as he made quick work of scaling the fence. "What do you think you're doing?" he asked.

"Coming with you. Becky is my closest friend, and I'm going nuts trying to find her."

"You'll only slow me down," Liam said as he jogged over to Becky's car, reached across to open the driver's-side door, and then, in a matter of seconds, silenced the irritating car alarm. The dogs were snoring, so I felt a little more comfortable going past them as I followed Liam to the small shack that served as an office.

Using a credit card, he managed to make quick work of the lock. The minute the door was opened, a beeping sound alerted. "What's that?" I asked as Liam dashed around the room opening cabinets.

"Alarm system. We have less than ninety seconds to find the recorder, grab the tape, and get out of here. Start looking."

In under ten seconds I located the machine mounted in a

cabinet behind the desk. "Here it is." I pressed Stop and then Eject. The machine slowly coughed up the tape. "Got it!"

"Let's go," Liam said as he used the hem of his shirt to wipe away any fingerprints.

I could still taste my own fear, terrified that the dogs had awakened from their catnap—if dogs can actually catnap—and were waiting just outside to maul me to death. However, mostly I was terrified for Becky. I kept reminding myself that in her call to Vain Dane she had said she'd be gone a week or so. Her purse was in the car, which didn't bode well, but her phone and keys were missing. Maybe she did just need time away.

Luckily, the dogs were still asleep as Liam and I moved quickly back to the fence. I climbed up again, aided by Liam's hand on my butt. Well, it wasn't so much aiding me as it was making me hot from the inside out.

Jumping down, I went directly to my car and started the engine. Liam did the same, and then we both did a series of Y turns until we were ready to traverse the gravel road.

Adrenaline didn't stop pumping in my body until we were safely out on Okeechobee Road, headed east. I was following Liam, fully expecting him to take the I-95 exit back to his place in Lake Worth. Instead, he went over the bridge, and I knew he was on his way to my house.

Just once I'd like it if he asked first. But I didn't think that would happen anytime soon. He pulled his ratty Mustang into the horseshoe-shaped drive and opened the driver's-side door. The door, like the rear right quarter panel, was primer gray. I couldn't imagine restoring a car when there were so many good ones out there to buy. New car smell is intoxicating.

"Why did you come here?" I asked without preamble.

"To stare at you in exercise clothes. That Lycra really hugs your body, doesn't it?"

"Try to act like a grown-up."

"I just wanted to hear how things went at the tow yard so I can get a better handle on Becky's disappearance."

"So you believe me? Us? Jane and Liv, too?"

"I don't buy Becky just picking up and taking off. But it's not out of the realm of possibility."

Buzzkill. I walked him to the front door. "It's late."

"It's eleven," he corrected. "I want you to tell me everything you found in the car."

"C'mon in."

While I brewed a pot of coffee, I asked, "Want something?"

He grinned slowly.

I rolled my eyes. "Now you get nothing. By the way, nice disappearing act after the wedding."

"What?"

"You snuck away in the middle of the night."

"I was asked to leave."

"What?"

"Your mother asked me to leave, so I did. I figured if I didn't, she'd take it out on you."

"Thank you, but my mother can *always* find something to take out on me. I'm sorry she was rude to you."

"Not a problem."

The coffeepot was taking its sweet time. I was leaning against the counter, mug readied in my right hand. I couldn't help but notice that Liam's perpetual five o'clock shadow was back and, as yummy as he might have looked in a tux, the casual shirt and jeans just seemed to suit him better. To the untrained eye, it might appear as if he'd subjected his pale blue and pale yellow shirt to multiple washings over the years. But I recognized Tommy Bahama, and I knew the shirts weren't cheap. PI work obviously paid better than being a paralegal.

"What did you think of the wedding?" I asked, since the bouquet was lying atop my counter.

"Nice, but excessive."

"It was that," I recalled with a grin. "The Huntington-St. Johns didn't spare a single expense. Lisa hated it."

One dark brow arched toward that always-mussed lock of hair that practically called my name. "Then why'd she do something so over-the-top?"

"She didn't. That was all Cassidy Presley Tanner Rossi Browning and Tenley and Tripp Huntington-St. John. The only thing Lisa selected was her shoes, and I doubt she'll ever wear them again."

"Not a shoe junkie?"

"She's a clogs kinda girl." *I can't imagine having a wardrobe of rubber shoes.*

"The two of you are very different."

"I know." The coffee was finally finished. "Want some?" I asked, rescinding my earlier edict.

"Sure. Can we move over to the sofa and watch the tape?"

"Fine by me." I handed him a mug of coffee with just a splash of cream without asking. That felt a little familiar, and I wasn't sure if that was good or bad.

Liam's broad shoulders made my great room seem slightly

less great in size. He had the tape in one hand and a mug in the other. He placed both on the table. "So what was in the car?"

"I'm so worried. I feel totally responsible. Becky's purse," I said, then listed all the other items. "I can check her account balance in the morning. I took her debit card."

"You had no way of knowing she was going to disappear; stop beating yourself up over it. For the bank card, don't you need to know the PIN?"

"I know her PIN."

"She's a trusting soul."

"She's my best friend," I snapped, irritated by the implication. "She has mine, too. That way we can run banking errands for each other if necessary. In fact, I'll bet I can access her account online." I powered up my computer and went to the Bank of America site. As I guessed, Becky's account password was her Social Security number backward.

"Look at this. Becky took one hundred dollars out on Sunday afternoon at twelve twenty."

"Is that unusual?"

"No, that's about what she carries around."

"Crap," Liam groaned.

"What?"

"She made the withdrawal from an ATM in Publix on the Island."

"So?"

"No cameras on those machines. No way to see if Becky had anyone watching her. If you're right and the eBay woman took her, maybe she was stalking Becky."

God, I was feeling worse by the minute. "What about store cameras?"

Liam shrugged. "I can check into it." He took a small notebook out of his breast pocket and made some notes. "You shouldn't have taken the bank card."

"Why?"

"You should have taken the purse and not just one card. The detectives will wonder why Becky's car was the only one disturbed and probably chalk it up to Becky sneaking in to retrieve an item."

Okay, now I felt like a breaking-and-entering fool. "What if she doesn't take any more of her money out? Wouldn't that prove she didn't just waltz away from her life?"

"Maybe, but the sheriff's office would need a few months of inactivity to raise a red flag."

I felt defeated. "I didn't think about that. What about Becky's phone?"

Liam took a sip of coffee. "What about it?"

"It wasn't in the car, but isn't there some way to triangulate the signals off the towers and get a location?"

He nodded. "I've got a friend at the phone company. She owes me a favor because I did a thing for her."

The famous *thing*. "Of course she does."

"Jealous?"

"Delusional?"

He laughed. "Let's watch the tape."

After viewing the video, I was hugely thankful that Liam had come along. My face was splashed all over the place, as was my car. Luckily, Florida doesn't have front license plates, but it would have been easy for the police to link my face with my car. "I would have been toast."

"Explain this whole eBay thing to me."

I reopened my laptop and ran my finger across the touchpad to wake it up. "You select an item, then place a bid. You can either watch the listing or enter a maximum bid and let the computer do it for you."

"How do you know who you're dealing with?"

"It isn't until payment is made that you get the physical address of the buyer."

"So you have that on the eBay woman Becky met, right?"

I shook my head. "Since she brought cash, there was no reason for her to go through the PayPal process. All I know is what's on her profile."

"Profile?"

"Here," I said, pulling up the page for Tiara64. "Lives in Palm Beach County. Damn," I muttered as I looked at the other important detail.

"What?"

"She has no feedback."

"Is that bad?"

"Yeah. It means the only thing she bought on eBay was the stuff she bought from me. See here where it says "Member since 2012?"

"Yes."

"That means that until a few days ago, she didn't exist on eBay."

"Can someone find out who you are?"

I nodded. "If someone knew my area and did a little digging, it would be pretty simple to back trace me through either my ISP or my screen name. If you know what you're doing, the IP thing is more efficient. If you're using my screen name, then you have to go through all the telephone directories for someone matching 'F. A. Tanner.'"

"Can you do the back trace?"

"No. My skills don't extend that far."

"But an IT guy could do it, right?"

"Sure. But the only IT guys I know are the ones who work on the Dane-Lieberman computers. I'm not sure the firm would like me confiscating a computer expert for my own purposes."

"I know a guy who could do it. He owes me because I did—"

"A *thing*. Got it. Is there anyone in Palm Beach County who doesn't owe you a favor?"

"Possibly." His expression grew more serious. "I think you should bring Tony in on this."

"Why?"

"He's got some pull at the sheriff's office. He might be able to move the cops off their asses, and find out if they have any holdbacks."

"What's a holdback?"

"Something only the police know that they don't release to the general public so that when they catch the person, they know it's the right guy."

"Do you think she's in danger?" I asked.

"No, not until I have proof to the contrary. If this was just a thrill kill, we'd already have found Becky's remains."

I shivered. "Not if they threw them into the everglades."

Liam wrapped me in the comfort of an embrace. "Think positive thoughts. We haven't even reached the date when Becky told Victor she'd be back."

"But that doesn't explain her car or her purse."

"Taking her phone and her keys is a good sign."

Moving away, I stifled a yawn. "I've got a meeting first thing in the morning."

"Kicking me out?"

"You bet."

He moved closer to me on the sofa. He picked up several strands of my hair and tucked them behind my ear. "Sure you want me to leave?"

His breath was warm against my exposed neck. I could feel the heat pooling in my stomach, and it took all my efforts to move away from him and stand up. "I'm completely sure. What should I do with the tape?"

"Burn it."

"Seriously?"

"Yep. They might have had more than one video setup, so you don't want that thing lying around just in case the police come sniffing around."

"Why would they sniff?"

"Because I'm assuming you didn't wipe your prints off Becky's purse or wallet. They may want to talk to you. We did break and enter, and you defaced private property when you shattered Becky's window. Lemme take your computer with me."

"Great. No computer and the possibility of being arrested. *Again.*" I grumbled.

Liam stood, drained the rest of his coffee, and headed for the door. "Good night, Finley. Remember to lock up."

I did, but I realized that my motion-sensor lights hadn't fired up when Liam left. Obviously, I had a blind spot. I really did need to call Harold.

I was tired, but too worried about Becky to go to sleep. I busied myself making notes regarding the letter to Wanda Jean and Sleepy. I shook my hand, trying to relieve the cramp caused by writing longhand. Life without a computer was almost as bad as life without Spanx. I could input the finishing touches on the letter first thing and e-mail it to Vain Dane. I only hoped he'd read it before Lenora arrived tomorrow at nine.

◆

I was up early. Again. Becky's absence weighed heavily on my mind. If she used the ATM on the island, then she must have needed cash. Like for lunch with Jane and Liv. So why didn't she show? Other than a voluntary walkaway, there was no answer except that the person known only as Tiara64 had done something to her. Only if that were true, then why would a kidnapper pay for the eBay items before abducting Becky? Nothing seemed to be gelling. Maybe Liam was right. Maybe she had just taken a break and was lying low in some hotel room living off room service. I had no way of knowing if all her credit cards were present and accounted for. Maybe having her car towed was the proverbial straw that broke her back. As much as I adore my friends, there have been times when I've wanted to just get away.

I promised myself that I wouldn't fall apart. At least not until there was any reason to think Becky was *someplace*. Preferably safe.

I dressed in one of my favorite Lilly Pulitzer skirts and tops, then accessorized with the pearls my sister had given me as my maid-of-honor gift. The look was very Jackie O, especially when I paired it with my knockoff Chanel sunglasses I'd picked up on my last visit to New York.

I was so worried about Becky, and a tad worried about Ellen, that I actually missed the turn to my office and had to drive around the block just to get back to Clematis. As I was backtracking, I noticed the baseball-capped traffic enforcement chick I'd seen a couple of weeks ago. I only noticed her because I made a left turn on red and was afraid I'd get a ticket on the spot. I saw the blonde watching me. I was in my office by eight thirty, resenting the extra thirty minutes of course. I quickly typed and proofed the letter, then sent it to Vain Dane via e-mail attachment. I knew he was in the office because his Hummer H3 was in the parking lot. I also reminded him that Lenora Egghardt was due in at nine.

I didn't want to be wasting time on the Egghardt thing. I wanted to be out there looking for Becky. Except I had no idea where to start. On a whim, I sent an e-mail to eBay asking for any information they may have on Tiara64. I erroneously claimed that she was the high bidder and had yet to pay me, so I wanted the home or business address listed on her profile. I knew it was a long shot, but hell—you don't ask, you don't get.

At ten before the hour, Vain Dane sent the letter back to me without a single correction. Of course, it didn't mention any praise or recognition, either. Just once I'd love to hear him say, "Good job, Finley." But that was about as far-fetched as Lindsey Lohan getting off probation.

Lenora arrived right on time. I met her at the elevators and took her into Ellen's conference room, except that I didn't know if I should still call it that now that Ellen was gone. Just thinking about that caused a chill to creep up my spine. What if my suspicions were right and Becky's disappearance was somehow linked to Ellen's absence?

"Where's the red-headed woman?" Lenora asked.

"I'm afraid Ms. Lieberman is no longer with the firm."

"Did she go back to TV?"

I looked quizzically at Lenora. "Ellen was on TV?"

She nodded. "Long time ago. That's where I recognized her from. Only I can't place the show. Something to do with her looks maybe."

Jeopardy, probably. I didn't really care about Ellen's intellectual prowess, but I did want to get this over so I could talk to Tony. "Here's the plan we've come up with. . . ." I spent the better part of three hours explaining all the pluses and minuses for allowing the Bollans to stay on the land subject to a new location as described in the rental agreement.

"Do you think it's a good idea?"

"Mr. Dane does, and he's the senior partner here."

Lenora was holding a locket and sliding it back and forth on its chain. "I want to know what you think, Ms. Tanner."

"I'm not in a position to give you legal advice. But I'd be happy to get Mr. Dane down here to answer any questions or address any concerns you may have."

She frowned. "Almost all of my dealings have been with you. I want to know what *you* think."

God, I hoped this didn't come back and bite me in the fanny. "I think it's fair and equitable and that you should make the offer."

"And if they say no?"

"It wouldn't be in their best interests. The alternative is eviction from the property."

Lenora dropped the locket. "Okay then, let's do it this way."

I went back to my office long enough to pick up the Egghardt estate file, and then headed over to the courthouse to get new Letters of Administration. With a half-dozen in hand, I walked back to the office, trying to hold my fears in check. What would I do if Becky had met with foul play because she was doing me a favor? I shivered even though I could see the heat wafting off the concrete.

As soon as I made the turn toward the Dane-Lieberman office, I noticed three sheriff's cars parked in the lot.

My first thought was that they'd found Becky. I picked up my pace. I refused to think of the alternative. No, all I wanted was to hear that she was just fine and had some plausible reason for dropping off the radar for nearly a week.

A man and a woman, each dressed in a khaki uniform, were seated in the lobby. Margaret was behind her half-moon-shaped desk, a smug smile in her eyes. That was a good sign. Margaret wouldn't be going all snark on me if she knew something horrible had happened to Becky.

"This is Ms. Tanner," Margaret announced.

The male rose and swiftly took the file out of my hands and

my purse off my shoulders. As he was doing that, his female partner twisted my free arm up behind my back, nearly causing me to lose my balance.

"What the hell are you doing?" I half yelled, half winced.

"Finley Tanner, you are under arrest for breaking and entering. You have the right to remain silent."

Handcuffs snapped tightly around my wrists.

"Anything you say can and will be used against you in a court of law."

"Call Tony," I said to Margaret. She looked so pleased I half expected her to whip out her cell phone to take pictures of me being handcuffed and led away.

"You are entitled to a lawyer. If you cannot afford a lawyer, one will be appointed to you. Do you understand these rights?"

"Margaret, please!"

"He's at lunch, then meeting with a client. But I will tell him you've been taken into custody when he gets back into the office."

Bitch.

Friends don't Google other friends.
Enemies are fair game.

sixteen

Sadly, the holding area of the Palm Beach County jail was not a new experience to me. It was, however, the first time I'd been there fully clothed. The last time I'd been taken in by the police, I'd been wearing my spending-the-night-alone jammies. Those consisted of a pair of boxers and a cami. They hadn't even allowed me to find my shoes first. That had been one huge misunderstanding, but I learned a lot about the police mind-set.

Now I sat in the center of a long wooden bench with my wrists shackled to large iron circles and chains suspended from high up on the wall. I could smell tobacco, alcohol, and sweat, and the combo wasn't pretty.

I'd already been photographed, fingerprinted, and interrogated. The interrogation had lasted only a few seconds since I invoked my right to counsel immediately. I'd learned that the hard way last time, when I willingly allowed myself to be interrogated and it blew up in my face. Now I was just waiting for an arraignment in front of the judge. A large round clock guarded by a cage of metal clicked loudly. It was already four thirty; I was supposed to help Izzy with her hair and makeup, *and* I desperately wanted to know what had happened to my best friend.

"Tanning?" a large officer with a thick neck called.

"I'm Tann-*er*," I said as I attempted to raise a hand, but instead just jerked painfully on my wrists.

The officer came over and freed me from the wall. Several of my bench mates took issue with what they called special treatment for me. I was escorted through two sets of locked doors, then brought to caged areas marked PROPERTY CLERK. That officer slid a large brown bag under the concave spot on the counter.

"Check to make sure all your valuables are there, then sign at the X on the bottom of the page."

My purse, watch, necklace, and bracelets were all accounted for, so I signed the paper. The guard then led me through the last door, where I saw Tony waiting.

I wanted to rush up and put my arms around him, but I settled for "Thank you." I rubbed my wrists, trying to soothe the red welts left by the handcuffs.

"No problem."

"How did you get me out without me having to go before a judge?"

"Liam convinced the owner to drop the charges."

"Do I want to know how?"

"*Why* is the better question? Seems someone reported you to Crime Stoppers before the tow yard opened this morning. Anyone mad at you besides Victor?"

"My mother isn't very fond of me, but I doubt she even knows what Crime Stoppers is, and she had no way of knowing what I was going to do. No one knew."

"Liam did."

"Lucky guess."

Tony took off his suit jacket as soon as we got outside. When we reached his car, he held the door for me, went around and tossed his jacket in the back, and then got behind the wheel.

"Do you want to swing by and pick up your car or go straight to my place?"

I gaped at his profile. "That's pretty direct for a guy who doesn't want to date me."

"I wasn't inviting you as a date. You promised Izzy you'd do her hair and makeup tonight."

I was glad he was driving because then he couldn't see my cheeks burn from embarrassment. I checked my watch. "I need some stuff from my house, so just drop me at the office." Not to mention the fact that I was still in the same clothes I'd had on yesterday, and I needed to wash all the jail cooties off.

"Victor was still there when I left, and he's not very happy with you."

I shrugged. "He's never very happy with me."

"No, this is serious. He wants you suspended without pay."

"You have got to be kidding me. After the efficient and creative way I dealt with the Egghardt case? I spent time in a greasy trailer"—I paused to tick each item off as I spoke—"I found a way to make the whole thing work and dumped the solution in his lap. Gift-wrapped. It wasn't my fault that the police came looking for me at the office."

Tony smiled. "I think the fact that the police were looking for you in general is the part that pissed him off. Just be grateful that there weren't any clients in the waiting area. If anyone had witnessed your being carted off to jail, being read your rights, Victor would fire you right now."

"He can't fire me without a consensus of the partners, so with Ellen gone, he can't touch me."

"Why are you assuming I wouldn't vote with Victor? What you did was illegal and impulsive. You could have easily waited until this morning and asked the tow guy to look in the car." Tony paused as he turned on Australian. "Then you wouldn't have spent the night in jail."

"Then side with Victor if you feel that strongly."

"You're about to help my daughter," Tony said. "Tough for me to suspend you when you're doing me a favor."

"I'm doing the favor for Izzy."

"Do you want to be suspended?"

"I want the freedom to find Becky."

"The police are on it," Tony assured me.

"They didn't seem very interested last night."

"Finding her purse in the car sent up a real red flag."

Relief washed over me. "See, I knew she didn't just walk away."

"Do you know if she had any enemies?"

"Enemies? She hardly had time for friends."

◆

I grabbed a quick shower and changed into a simple shift dress and some cute ballerina flats; I twisted my towel-dried hair up and secured it with lacquered chopsticks that matched my shoes. Next I packed a small tote with whatever I could think of—curling irons, flat iron, wave iron, and makeup.

I'd gotten Izzy a few gifts at Walgreens that I thought would be a perfect complement to her pink bunny Betsey Johnson dress and her olive complexion. I was tired from lack of sleep. Jail wasn't conducive to rest, so I downed most of a pot of coffee before filling my travel mug and hitting the road.

Someone buzzed me in at the gate, and I drove through the manicured community until I reached Tony's house. Looking in the rearview mirror, I was pleased that my hair had dried during the drive. Still, I twisted it back up in the chopsticks and went to the front door.

"Hi," Izzy said, excitement oozing from every pore.

"Ready for your transformation?"

"You have, like, no idea."

I followed her upstairs. I still hadn't seen so much as a glimpse of Tony. Too bad, he was pretty easy on the eyes.

"Hello?" Izzy called.

"Sorry. Guess I zoned out there for a minute," I admitted.

"I said Lindsey Hetzler got braces yesterday. I'm talking total full metal jacket."

I smiled. "Can't cover that with concealer, can you?"

"But she still has a boyfriend," Izzy whined.

"Believe me, boyfriends are way overrated."

"Do you have one?"

"Put on all your undergarments and a robe. We'll do makeup first."

"You're so ignoring the question." Izzy pulled a robe off

a hook next to the door leading to her bathroom. Then she reached in her drawer and took out the bra and panties we'd bought at Victoria's Secret. "Well, do you?"

"No. I'm happily single."

"Aren't most women your age married?"

"That was snarky. I'm only twenty-nine, hardly an old maid."

"Well, I want to get married and have kids when I'm young." She slipped into the bathroom.

"Define young!"

"Early twenties. Why? Did you think I meant teen mother or something? I'm not that dumb. I need to finish college first. But right after that . . . ."

I shook my head. "Sometimes things don't turn out the way we envision."

"Did you think you'd still be single at your age?"

No. Maybe. Engaged at least. "I didn't give it much thought."

"You're totally lying." Izzy emerged from the bathroom.

"You're being a pain. Now, let's take your desk chair into the bathroom. Makeup first, hair second. Have you thought of what you'd like to do with your hair? Up, down, curly, straight, waves?"

"Wait! I cut a picture out of a magazine." Izzy bolted into her room and came back with a folded picture of Scarlett Johansson. "Like this. Soft waves. Can you do that?"

"Sure, but we'll have to use hairspray. You've got a lot of hair."

Setting my tote on the floor, I pulled out a wide cloth headband and used it to keep all the hair off Izzy's face. Then item by item, I took out the makeup I'd bought for her. It wasn't MAC or Chanel, but she was only thirteen.

"Why all the new stuff?"

"You need makeup that works with your skin tone. All my stuff is for blondes."

"This is for me?"

"Yep. All yours. Now, be still so I can do this. You can watch in this mirror." I pulled a small handheld from the bag. "With some practice, you can do this all by yourself."

I spent about twenty minutes applying, painting, swiping, and smudging until she looked dewy and not slutty. I spent extra time on her mouth, since that was going to be the focal point of the makeup. Bright pink lips toned down with a pale bronze gloss.

"You like?"

"I love!"

"Time for hair." I pulled large clips out of my bag and segmented her hair while the wave iron heated up. I was really glad I'd tossed hairspray in the bag since Izzy didn't have any. I held each section out and worked the iron down to the ends of her hair. The end result was stunning. Her dark brown hair was shiny and didn't look at all like it had been styled. The waves looked completely natural. "Close your eyes."

She complied and I doused her hair in spray. It wasn't going to lose its curl anytime soon. Next I had her put on her dress, and then we tended to her necklace and earrings. The last thing she did was slip on her shoes.

"You look perfect."

She went into the bathroom and checked herself in the mirror. "I can't believe this is really me."

"It's really you," I insisted. "Now, put the gloss, blush and the blush brush in your purse for touch-ups. Remember, no re-applying in public. You only do that in the bathroom. Oh, and fluorescent lighting changes the way makeup looks, so don't go nuts or you'll look like a clown."

"How did you learn all this stuff?" she asked as she filled her purse, and then got the sweater out of her walk-in closet.

"My mother puts on a full complement of makeup just to take a shower. I learned from a master."

"I wonder if my mother was good at makeup."

"Sorry," I said. "I didn't mean to bring up—"

"Don't be sorry. Not having a mom around is like part of who I am."

"I can see where it could be. I don't know who my biological father is, but it does become part of the definition." After a brief pause, I stood and asked, "Ready to go downstairs for the big reveal?" Now I was the one full of excitement.

"What if Dad hates it?"

"He won't. You look very nice, and I'm sure he'll be happy for you."

"Let's hope."

Using the intercom, Izzy announced her intention to come down the stairs. It was very theatrical and kinda cute.

I went first, finding Tony at the base of the stairs with one hand behind his back and the other armed with a digital camera.

"Okay!" I called.

As if she was working a catwalk, Izzy descended regally. I turned to see Tony's eyes grow wide and he wore a dimple-showing smile, all the while snapping shot after shot of Izzy. Izzy was only halfway down when Tony dropped the camera to the side and said, "You look beautiful, baby."

"Thank you. And thank Finley."

Tony turned to me. "Thanks, she looks very nice." He leaned close to me and whispered, "And she looks her age, so thanks for that, too."

As soon as Izzy reached the bottom step, Tony took his hand from behind his back. In it, he held a small jewelry box.

"This is for you. In honor of your first school dance."

Izzy opened it quickly and inside was a very pretty rose quartz ring in a simple cabochon setting.

Izzy threw her arms around Tony. "Thank you! But how did you know it would match my dress?"

"I didn't. I just had a feeling that with Finley in the picture, pink was a safe bet."

Izzy took it out and slipped it on her finger. "I totally love it!"

"Does this mean you've forgiven me for not going to Atlanta last week?"

"Of course," Izzy said as she placed a feathery kiss on his cheek, and then wiped the pale pink lip imprint off his face.

"Ready to go?" he asked.

Izzy seemed to shrink back a bit. "Would you mind if Finley took me?" Then she turned to me. "Would you mind driving me? St. Joe's is only five minutes away."

"If it's okay with your father."

"Fine with me," Tony said, though I sensed his disappointment.

"Let me just run upstairs and get my stuff."

With my tote packed, Izzy and I headed out to my car. Once we were nearing the gate, I asked, "Why did you want me to drop you off?"

"I need to know what to do if a boy wants to kiss me."

I was glad it was dark so she couldn't see my face flame. "Depends on the guy."

"What if it's, y'know, a guy I kinda like."

"Then you can kiss him, but no tongue."

"Ewww, that is so gross."

That was my point. "Just remember this simple rule. No touching between the knees and the neck."

"That'll be easy. Our chaperones are parents, nuns, and priests. The only safe zone is the space between the lockers and the girls' room. It's like totally secret, and no one can see you there."

"Oh, and the other rule is never kiss more than one boy a month."

"Why?"

"Because at your age, that's considered slutty behavior and you don't want that reputation, do you?"

"No. What if a boy you like won't talk to you because you won't have sex with them?"

This was turning into the longest freaking five minutes of my life. All I wanted to do was turn up Wild 95.5 and listen for the next Lady Gaga song.

"Any boy who insists you have to have sex with him to be his girlfriend is an ass. Someone who cares about you will never ask you to do something you don't want to do."

"What if I want to have sex?"

I damn near drove into a canal. "If that's your plan, I'm turning this car around right now."

"I didn't mean like tonight, I just meant, how do you know when you want to have sex with a guy?"

"The stars align."

"Huh?"

"First, you have to be old enough to understand what you're doing. Second, you should have feelings for the guy. Third, you should think about it for months before you actually do it. Fourth, you'll know when the right guy comes along. No one ever died from lusting after someone else."

"Months? But I know people my age who've already had sex."

"And do you respect them for it?"

"I guess not."

"Then that's your answer. Don't be like the crowd. Be you."

"Turn in here."

I did and found a few dozen kids standing outside. Izzy thanked me again for the makeover, and then got out of the car. Two girls squealed her name, so I figured she was all set.

◆

I saw Liam before I saw his excuse of a car. He was seated on my front step with my laptop next to him. He looked fabulous in his casual shirt and thigh-hugging jeans, but I immediately reminded myself that he had to be off-limits. As much as it pained me to say, there was a possibility my mother was right, and I should keep my distance from him.

Liam was nothing like any of the other men I've dated. Not that we've had a date. What did we have in common? Probably nothing more than a strong physical attraction. And here I'd just spent time telling a thirteen-year-old when to kiss and when not to have sex. Maybe I needed to take my own advice.

"Have fun playing dress-up with Izzy?" he asked as soon as I was out of my car.

"It went well, thank you. Why are you here?" That question was getting redundant.

"Returning your laptop—and I thought you might want to know what the IT guy had to say. Oh, and I got to listen to the recording of the Crime Stoppers call." He held up a micro-recorder. "Wanna know what I found out?"

"You know I do. Come on in."

Liam carried my laptop inside the house while I took the tote bag in and put it in my bedroom. When I came back, he had his head in my fridge.

"Try the veggie drawer."

"You keep beer in the veggie drawer?"

"Want one or not?"

"Don't get snippy."

As soon as he finished rummaging through my refrigerator, I went over and uncorked a bottle of red from Australia. After pouring myself a large glass, I stood in the kitchen while Liam took one of the bar stools. "So what did you find out?"

"Tiara64 is no slouch. She routed her IP through about seven countries. But it looks like the site of origin moves in and around West Palm."

"In and around?"

He nodded and then took a drink. "She's using Internet cafés all over the county."

"Tiara is a total stranger. How would she know to find me on eBay?"

"Don't know yet."

"Do you think she mistook Becky for me?"

"Possibly. But I think all this tracks back to Ellen's sudden departure."

"What about breaking into Ellen's apartment?" I asked.

"Speaking of break-ins, you owe me five hundred dollars."

"For what?"

"That's what it cost me to get the tow yard to drop the charges."

I went into my bathroom, took the envelope out of the tampon box, and counted out five hundred in twenties. "Here," I said when I returned with the cash. "Are you going to play the Crime Stoppers tape for me?"

"I was saving that for last."

"So now we go to Ellen's place?"

"Not tonight. I have a thing. You really need to learn patience."

That blasted *thing*. "And you need to learn when you've overstayed your welcome."

"Okay, don't get your thong in a twist." He pulled the recorder out of his pocket, laid it on the table, then pressed the Play button.

A female voice asked. "Palm Beach Crime Stoppers, may I help you?"

"I'd like to report a crime that I just witnessed," a second female voice stated. Only the second voice wasn't as strong or as commanding as the first.

"For that you'd need to contact the police directly."

During the brief silence, I heard some muffled sound I couldn't place.

"No police," the scared woman said with urgency. "Finley Anderson Tanner just broke into Lawson's tow yard and broke the window on at least one car."

"Oh my God," I said as I brought my hands up to my face. "That's Becky's voice."

"I thought so, but I wanted to confirm it with you."

"So now what?"

"So we keep it to ourselves. If the police find out she's made contact, they'll call off any kind of search."

"How would Becky know I went to the tow yard?"

"I was going to ask you that."

I shrugged as my brain swirled, trying to get a grip on this latest piece of the puzzle. "No one knew. It was a spur-of-the-moment thing."

"Tell me how you came up with the idea to break in. Did Jane and Liv suspect?"

I shook my head. "I didn't tell anyone."

"Well, at least this is good news."

"How? My best friend ratted me out to the authorities."

"Yes, but your best friend is alive." He tipped his drink to me. "Try to have a good night."

"You too."

As soon as he left, I curled up on the sofa with my computer in my lap and a box of Lucky Charms to my left. I went to Google and typed in my own name. About seven entries later, I found that my Facebook profile listed my eBay addiction but didn't have a photograph of me. I thought that was secure enough to keep the loons at bay. I did a quick scan of my posts, and sure enough, I'd posted my eBay screen name in one of my entries.

"Stupid, stupid, incredibly stupid."

No wonder Tiara found me. "Well, that solves one element of the mystery." I was so anxious about Becky. Even though Tony had faith in the police, I wasn't so sure. Something was wrong, and Liam might be right. It all started with Ellen. The problem was, I had no idea what *it* was.

On a lark, I Googled Ellen Lieberman. The first fifty entries had to do with various newspaper articles, all relating to her work with the bar association and/or cases for particularly high-profile clients. Then I came across something very strange. It referenced an Ellen Becker, but the link to that page was broken. I'd gotten to that Google place where it just started listing every instance of "Ellen." Then it gave me all the possibilities for "Lieberman."

Not really helpful. Then I thought about the Department of Corrections, so I typed in Ellen Lieberman and Department of Corrections. Nothing. Next I tried Tiara64. That gave me nothing but pageant results. Another useless path. In a last-ditch effort, and using my Dane-Lieberman password, I went to one of the credit-reporting places and typed in Ellen's name. Her report was spotless. Only problem? It went back only as far as 1988. No loans or debts of any kind until she was twenty-seven. Not even a store credit card. Nothing. It was as if she was born in 1988. Only I knew she was forty-seven, so where did the other twenty years go?

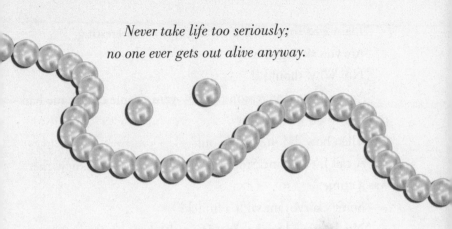

Never take life too seriously;
no one ever gets out alive anyway.

seventeen

"She didn't exist," I told Jane over the phone. "I'm going into the office so I can access the census and Social Security databases."

"What can I do to help?" she asked.

"Know anyone at the IRS who will tell you if Ellen filed taxes before 1988?"

"Maybe. But it's Saturday. I might have to wait until Monday. Are you okay from your night in jail?

"As good as I'm going to get. At least Steadman and Grimes weren't on duty." I'd had a brief but memorable encounter with those detectives, and even though it all ended well, they still held a grudge.

"How'd you get out? Liv and I were already pooling our resources to cover your bail."

"Thanks, but Tony and Liam got the charges dismissed. The guy from Lawson's declined to prosecute if I paid him five hundred dollars."

"Liam *and* Tony. This is getting *way too* interesting."

"Are you sitting down?"

"No. Why, should I?"

"Yes and yes. The reason the tow-yard people caught me had nothing to do with security."

"Then how did they find you?"

"A call into Crime Stoppers even before anyone knew there was a crime."

"Some clairvoyant with a hunch?"

"No. I listened to the tape. It was Becky."

"That's great, right?" Jane said on a single breath.

"Yes. Proof of life is good. Or so Liam tells me. But the call to Crime Stoppers can mean only one thing."

"Which is?"

"Someone is following me. I didn't tell anyone I was going to the tow yard. Hell, *I* didn't even know I was going until I was halfway home."

Jane made a *tsk*ing sound. "You really need to stop this. You could have been hurt. I'd bet Lawson or whoever had a nice collection of guns."

I told her all about Becky's purse still being in the car. "It looked as if nothing was disturbed."

"Were her keys inside?"

"No."

"Phone?"

"No."

"Then it does seem more plausible that she just took some time away. Remember last year when she went to the Bahamas with nothing but her ID and passport?"

"But things were slow at the office, and she knew no one would care if she took three days off. And she did tell the three of us. This feels different. Besides, why would she turn me into the police when she has to know I'm worried sick?"

"I'll call Liv and cancel lunch."

"Oh, that's right!" I slapped my forehead. "No, no, don't cancel. I'll be at Thai Jo at one."

"Want me to come by and pick you up?"

It did feel a little creepy knowing someone had probably been following me. "No, thanks. I'll spend some time at the office and then meet you at the Thai place. But Jane?"

"Yes."

"Call me on my cell every fifteen minutes. I don't want to end up like Ellen and Becky."

◆

The place was dead. It didn't used to be this way. Ellen and Becky usually worked on Saturdays, and often Vain Dane would come by to get some things done. But this Saturday morning, I was the only one in the building. Which is why I was super careful to lock the door and reset the alarm code the minute I'd stepped inside. Even after taking all those precautions, I still felt like Janet Leigh walking into the Bates Motel.

Following my standard procedure, I made myself some coffee and then hunkered down to business. Checking the census records was tedious, but in the end, I was satisfied with my results. Ellen Lieberman was not counted until after the 1990 census. The woman was a ghost, but why?

My mind immediately went to something sexy like a spy, or a material witness in some big trial. But then I remembered Ellen—nothing sexy about her. "So what are you hiding?" I thought aloud.

In order to continue my search, I'd have to go to the Human Resources office. One of the perks of being a paralegal was that I'd been entrusted with a master key. The key was supposed to be used in emergencies—like if one of the partners forgot to sign something or I needed to retrieve a file from one of their offices. I considered finding Becky an emergency.

HR was on the first floor, an area I try to steer clear of. It's usually occupied by Maudlin Margaret's minions, who share her resentment over my salary. Most of the ladies had worked for Dane-Lieberman a decade longer than I had, but they were administrative assistants, so of course we had a pay inequity. This made Margaret nuts. She'd been seated at her post for nine and one half hours with an hour for lunch for more than twenty-five years.

I slipped my key into the lock of the HR office. There was a small waiting area with a desk and a few chairs. The second door led to the actual office, where all employee information was safeguarded.

I yanked on the cabinet marked with the letters "L" through "P," but it was locked. I tried all the other drawers with the same result. Time to go hunting. I checked the obvious places first—the desk, the credenza behind the desk, then even ran my hands under the three chairs, all in the name of thoroughness.

I was about to give up when I noticed a plant atop the file cabinets. The room had several potted plants in it, but this one was fake. A really bad plastic fake of an African violet. I went over, felt the bottom, and realized I'd found the prize. I removed the small silver key from the bottom of the flowerpot.

I had only to unlock the top vertical file for the others to open. I pulled out the drawer and easily found Ellen's file. I took it over to the desk and sat down. Flipping through the pages, I learned that she was a graduate of Yale Law, after having completed her undergrad work at Harvard. I scrutinized the college transcripts. Something didn't seem right.

Then it hit me. Either I couldn't count or Ellen had gotten her bachelor's and her JD all at the same time from two different universities. Everything was dated May or June, 1988. And Ellen's Social Security number didn't match up with her credentials. Doing trusts and estates for eight years had made me somewhat familiar with the portion of a Social Security number that identifies state of issue. Based on the first three digits of Ellen's number, hers had been issued in Massachusetts on her transcripts, but she had one assigned in South Carolina as well. The numbers didn't match. There was no way she could live for twenty-plus years without a Social Security number, and the Social Security Administration didn't just hand out numbers on a whim. The only thing that made any sense was that Ellen had, for whatever reason, had her Social Security number changed. Legally, by the looks of her transcripts.

"What else are you hiding?" I thumbed through her file, stopping on the page listing former employers. None. Nada. According to this, Ellen hadn't worked a day in her life until joining Dane-Lieberman. And that didn't make sense, either. Lawyers always had summer internships or they clerked for judges, something to garner experience before they went out into the real world. But not Ellen.

Reading through her personal information, I found what might be a clue. She'd grown up in South Carolina. I instantly remembered the Department of Corrections letter that had the letters N-A. "Were you a bad girl in South Carolina?" I asked.

That would explain a lot. So long as there was no fraud involved, anyone could change her name and Social Security number with a simple request to the court. Maybe she was some sort of witness in some big case. Or a parolee—naw, too much time had passed. The possibilities were endless, and they also lifted my spirits.

It would be just like Becky to help Ellen out of a jam. Now I felt a glimmer of hope that my trusted friend was off doing whatever it took to save Ellen's muumuu-covered ass. And it would make sense that Ellen went for a new Social Security number, harder for anyone to trace her that way. Although there were a zillion sites on the Internet that could find a person in no time. But for me, she would now be known as Secret Ellen.

I was careful to place the file back in the drawer just as I had found it after I'd copied down some important dates and places she'd lived, her college information, and the conflicting Social Security numbers. No sense in working the HR director into a frenzy. She'd have a fit if she knew someone had rifled through her things.

I needed to make an Ellen flowchart. After carefully taping the key back under the flowerpot and locking the doors so that nothing looked disturbed, I went back to my office. I got out a large file folder and proceeded to create smaller files for the different aspects of Ellen's life. I was intrigued by her lack of identity, so I put that one in one folder. The conflicting Social Security numbers went into another. I stopped long enough to send Jane a text with the two numbers to see what, if anything, her Social Security buddy could find.

She texted back:

Cooprting w me. Callng him @ home now.
Will give updt soon.

The text reminded me of something weird in Becky's e-mail. She'd specifically said she was working on things from Ellen's drawers. When we'd jimmied them open, all we found was personal files and the torn letter from the Department of Corrections. It was worth checking out.

I logged into LexisNexis and did a search for Ellen Lieberman. I couldn't find any record of her in the South Carolina database. I tried checking Florida. Same result. I tried Massachusetts. Same result. I was frustrated. I was missing something, but what?

Lacing my fingers behind my head, I leaned back and looked at the screen. I guess I wanted it to magically spew out answers. I wanted something to make sense.

"What else was in those drawers?" I thought back and recalled labels like STORAGE, BANKING, HEALTH INSURANCE, VEHICLE INSURANCE, and a few other completely normal folders. Since I wasn't getting anywhere on the computer, I went up to the fourth floor and walked directly to Ellen's office. If Vain Dane showed up, I was totally screwed.

I opened the top drawer and found pens, pencils, small legal pads, and the torn envelope from the Department of Corrections. I held it up to the light but there was no ink transfer. I reasoned it had to be important or Ellen wouldn't have kept it.

Switching to the larger file drawer, I ran one finger over the neatly typed labels. BANKING held banking information. CAR INSURANCE held car insurance information. And on and on. The only thing that seemed to be the least bit unusual was the file labeled STORAGE. Inside I found a contract for a storage unit in Hobe Sound. The reason it attracted my attention was that Ellen had saved every annual lease agreement. She had first rented the space in 1988, the year Ellen Leiberman had first appeared. It was a five-by-ten-foot unit, roughly the size of a walk-in closet. What? Did she have an excess of muumuus she saved for special occasions? More likely she'd moved from a larger place and, like a lot of people, rented storage instead of just getting rid of things.

Not me. I'd much rather have new. I thought of my stunning cottage on the beach and couldn't imagine dragging any of the furniture from my condo into the gorgeous new house. I'd donated everything to Faith Farms at Sam's strong urging. He was right; my condo did look more like a dorm room than a home.

At the bottom of the STORAGE file I found a key. It wasn't exactly a Mensa moment to deduce it was a spare key to the storage unit. I slipped it into my pocket, not sure if it was relevant, but I copied down the address and unit number from the rental agreement.

I sat in Ellen's chair and looked at every item in her office. The walls were painted dull celery green. The furniture was teak, very IKEA looking. Everything on the walls was generic. Several paintings of the beach. Even though I'd been in Ellen's office, I never paid much attention to the details. Now I was, and I realized that one of the paintings was not like the others. One was a lone beach chair and umbrella looking out on a brownish ocean. Unlike the others, which clearly portrayed the clear, turquoise Florida oceans, this one was different.

I went over to the painting and took it off the wall. Penciled on the backing were four words: Folly Beach, South Carolina.

"A tie to South Carolina? Definitely." *But why?*

I rehung the painting and left Ellen's office. I went to my office and did a quick computer search for Ellen Lieberman, Folly Beach, and South Carolina. Nothing popped. I got results for every mention of the name Ellen, but I wasn't going through a thousand useless entries. Besides, I didn't have time. I needed to get to the Thai place to meet Jane and Liv. Jane would be relieved since she was probably tired of dialing my number just to hear me say "I'm good" every fifteen minutes.

As I left the office, I noticed the traffic enforcement blonde lurking around the corner of Australian and Clematis. Maybe that's how Becky's car got towed, I reasoned. While she was at my place dealing with Tiara64, the tow company grabbed her car. Maybe she took Tiara64 to my place, and her unattended vehicle was spotted by the Palm Beach Police. It would explain why she had her keys and her phone.

◆

I was the last one to reach the restaurant. Liv and Jane were sipping pomegranate mojitos and had one waiting for me. "Sorry, I got hung up by a train," I explained as I took my seat. In Florida it wasn't uncommon to get stuck for several minutes at a railroad crossing. Nor was it unusual to start counting cars as they chugged by. My train had 107 cars and took nearly seven minutes to clear the crossing.

Jane had on a cute sundress, a pretty salmon color that highlighted her dark complexion. Perfectly coiffed Liv was wearing a Lilly Pulitzer sheath dress from the new summer collection. I had dress envy. I couldn't wait until that one popped up on eBay.

"So what's the deal?" Liv asked.

I took a sip of my refreshing, red mojito. "There's something freaky about Ellen." I went on to explain the dual Social Security numbers; the lack of a work history; the painting of Folly Beach in Ellen's office; the degrees bestowed in the same year; and the storage unit she'd been renting since Tracy Chapman topped the charts with "Fast Car."

"So should we check out the storage unit?" Jane asked.

"I think we should check her condo first, and then go down to Jupiter Island Marina and Storage. I'm not looking forward to checking out a place that will reek of boat diesel," I answered.

Liv said, "Here," as she reached into her purse and pulled out a CD. "Liam got this copy from someone he knows at Crime Stoppers. I guess he just wanted us all to be comforted hearing Becky's voice."

"Did you two listen to it?" I asked.

They both nodded, then Jane said, "It's definitely Becky.

There's not much in the way of background noise, so I don't think it has any clues as to where she is."

We all ordered pad Thai and a second drink. "I've crawled all over the life and times of Ellen Lieberman, and I can't find anything," I lamented. "What about your IRS guy?" I asked.

"Waiting for him to text me," she said, patting her phone as it rested next to her utensils.

"How does a person get two Social Security numbers?" Liv asked.

"You can't," Jane suggested. "Unless you do something ghoulish like search a cemetery to find a child who died around the time you were born."

"Why go to all that trouble?" Liv asked.

"To change your identity."

I tapped my fingernail on the table. "Technically, that's not true," I explained. "You can do it all nice and legal for cause. What if Ellen is in the witness protection program or something?" I suggested. "Or maybe she's been living one big sham since 1988. But she really doesn't strike me as the type."

"But why would she go to all that trouble?" Liv asked again.

"If we figure that out, then I think we'll find Ellen, and if we find Ellen, we'll find Becky." I hoped.

"Shouldn't we call the police?" Jane asked.

"And tell them what?" I asked. "That Ellen has a storage unit? That she has two Social Security numbers? Remember, they're only investigating—and I use that term loosely—Becky's disappearance. And after the Crime Stoppers tape, they are more convinced than ever that Becky disappeared intentionally."

"I still think I'll stop in," Liv said. "Maybe I can light a fire under them."

"Speaking of fire," I said, as three bowls of pad Thai were placed on the table. We all switched to water, then dug into the stir-fried rice noodles with eggs, fish sauce, tamarind juice, red chili pepper, and, in my case, bean sprouts and shrimp. The garnish was crushed peanuts, lime juice, and coriander.

Jane had just captured some noodles on her chopsticks when her phone vibrated toward her bowl. "It's Justin," she said. "According to him, the Massachusetts Social Security number definitely belongs to Ellen Lieberman and was issued in 1988. The one from South Carolina was issued in 1977 to thirteen-year-old Ellen Marie Becker."

"I recognize that name!" I said enthusiastically. "It came up when I Googled Ellen."

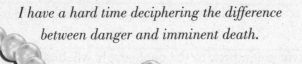

*I have a hard time deciphering the difference
between danger and imminent death.*

eighteen

Once I was back at my place, I powered up my laptop and began to search for any and all information on Ellen Becker. There were a few mentions about an Ellen Becker being a homecoming queen and a prom queen and Miss Low Country, but I skipped all that. No way was Ellen a beauty queen.

I finally found a reference to an Ellen Becker who was involved in a car accident. Unfortunately, the driver was killed after lingering in a coma for three weeks. I kept digging and it paid off.

"Holy shit!" I exclaimed. It was grainy and twenty-two years old, but it sure looked like Ellen. And she was wearing the Miss North America crown. How did someone go from beauty queen to frump?

According to the article, on the night Ellen Becker crowned her successor in Massachusetts, she had been in a car accident. Her fiancé was killed in the crash, but Ellen walked away without a scratch. She'd been wearing a seat belt; the boyfriend had not.

I kept going back to the photograph. My brain was having trouble grasping the idea of her as a beauty. It looked like Ellen, but I couldn't be sure. Same red hair, same pale skin, same height, but the picture was just too blurry.

I went back to the Google hits I'd ignored and saw more photos of Ellen Becker being crowned everything from Shrimp Princess to Miss South Carolina. Sadly, all the photos were grainy and hard to see. I wanted to check for myself.

Even though it was after one in the morning, I decided it was important for me to get inside Ellen's house. If she was Ellen Becker, then why hide it? Why become Ellen Lieberman? Why go out of your way to be as homely as possible?

I drove to the condo and went up to the third floor. Thanks to Becky, I knew Ellen kept a spare key beneath the hallway table by the elevators. I felt around, then found it and pulled it off, tape and all.

Ellen's condo was in shambles. Every cushion was cut and the stuffing had been pulled out. Every drawer had been dumped on the floor. I got scared, wondering why I hadn't told anyone that I was going to Ellen's. Just to be on the safe side, I called Jane.

"Sorry if I woke you."

"That's okay. What's wrong?"

"I'm at Ellen's, and the place has been torn apart. I just want someone to be with me while I check the bedrooms."

"Want me to come over?"

"No, just stay on the phone. I'm going to put you on speaker."

I clipped my iPhone to the pocket of my black Lycra yoga outfit. "Can you hear me?" I asked.

"Loud and clear."

Careful to step over the mess, I made my way through the maze of broken china and went into the back hallway. I reached the first bedroom, and it too had been tossed. Since I'd never been there before, I had no idea just how extensive the damage was. It just looked like a hurricane had ripped through the condo.

"First bedroom a mess, but it's all clear."

"Okay."

"I'm going into the next one."

I poked my head in and found the same thing. "Someone totally trashed this place."

"Maybe you should get out of there. What's the address? I'm calling the police on my landline."

"Hang on, let me check the master before you call the sheriff's office."

"Why?"

"I want to see if there's anything here that will tell us what happened. Oh God!"

"What?" Jane cried.

"There's blood."

"That's it. I'm calling the cops."

♦

Detective Wilkes arrived about twenty minutes after Jane's call. If his expression was any indication, he wasn't too thrilled with me.

"Why did you enter when you saw the condition of the apartment?" he asked.

"Because I was looking for something that might tell me where my friend is."

"I told you we'd investigate the matter."

"And so far, you haven't done a thing."

At that moment, Liam came into the room. "Mikey," he greeted, shaking the detective's hand.

I swear, he *did* know everyone in Palm Beach County.

Liam shot me a glance, then asked the detective, "Got any theories?"

"Someone figured out the apartment was empty. Must have gotten frustrated when there weren't a lot of high-value items." He pointed to wires hanging out of the wall. "Took the TV and the stereo. Easy pawns." He turned to me. "Did Ms. Lieberman have a laptop?"

I nodded. "Two. One was for work and the other was for her personal use."

"Neither of those are here, either. Jewelry?"

I shook my head. "I've never seen her wear anything but a watch." I wondered if now was an appropriate time to mention that I had Ellen's pricey brooch. Nope. "Ellen gave me some jewelry a few weeks ago."

"Can we see it?"

"I auctioned it off on eBay. Well, all but one piece."

"We'll need that."

"Okay. I'll go home and bring it to the sheriff's in the morning." It was already nearing three a.m., and I was tired.

"That'll work."

Liam followed me out of the condo. His expression conveyed his disapproval. "Did you even consider calling me before you went into Ellen's place?"

"How was I supposed to know it would be trashed?"

"You knew when you opened the door."

I stepped into the elevator. "I don't need an escort, Liam."

"No, you need a keeper."

◆

"You need a keeper," I mocked to myself. "God, that man makes me nuts."

There had to be a reason why a person or persons tore through Ellen's place. And a reason why they hadn't touched Becky's home.

Unfortunately, I was far too brain dead to come up with a cohesive answer when my bedside clock read three thirty-five. As soon as I got some sleep, I would keep digging into Ellen's dual life.

In what felt like ten minutes since I'd fallen asleep, my cell phone rang. I picked it up, but didn't recognize the number. I slid the bar to unlock the phone, then I accepted the call. "Do you know it's eight ten in the flipping morning?"

"Do you know that I'll kill them both if you don't bring me the brooch?" a woman said.

I sat up. "Who is this?"

"Doesn't matter. No cops, no boyfriend, just you."

"I don't have it, I gave it to the sheriff."

I heard a bloodcurdling scream. I couldn't tell if it was Becky or Ellen, but it made my stomach churn. "Okay, okay! Tell me where to drop it off."

"Go to the Carlin Park. I'll call you with additional instructions."

"Okay."

"And Finley? Remember my instructions. I'd hate to have to kill the boyfriend who thinks you need a keeper and makes you nuts."

"How did you—"

"It doesn't matter. But if you must know, I bugged your house when you were out of town. I bugged your car, too. Be at the park in twenty minutes."

I leapt out of bed, desperate to find whatever listening device was in my house. That was the only explanation for her repeating what I'd said a scant few hours earlier. But twenty minutes was a tight deadline, and I didn't dare miss it.

I didn't dare call the cops, either. I didn't want to be responsible for getting anyone killed, myself included. I thought about calling someone but I wasn't sure who. Liv and Jane couldn't help, and Tony and Liam would just call the police. Unfortunately, I was on my own.

Pulling on a pair of shorts, T-shirt, and flip-flops, I stuck my cell in my purse and started for the door. I retrieved the brooch. For some reason I grabbed the key to Ellen's storage unit and stuffed it in my front pocket. I was out the door in five minutes. Making it to Jupiter was going to be a challenge.

I managed to pull into the parking lot with two minutes to spare. I looked around. Nothing but surfers in board shorts carrying surfboards toward the wooden walkway that led to the beach. Mine was only one of a half dozen cars in the lot. The others were unoccupied. Did that mean the woman was running late or— My cell rang, and I noticed my hands shaking as I answered the call.

"Very good, Finley. Now, come to the Jupiter Marina and park by the manager's office."

Now I was really scared and decided I didn't want to fly solo. I did as instructed by the tormentor, trying to text and drive at the same time. I was so afraid that the crazy woman was watching me that I texted without looking down. When I sent the message to Jane, I wasn't sure it made any sense.

I found a visitor's parking spot and pulled in. As I cut the engine, I heard three dings from a brass bell. Immediately, I thought of Becky's call to Crime Stoppers. You could hear the bells in the background.

There was a tap on the window, and a woman was bent over, flashing a really big knife from inside her overblouse. She was a hard-looking woman. Maybe five-five, a hundred and ten pounds, with dyed blond hair. Her eyes were blue and threatening. I knew her; I just couldn't place her. I could only think about fear.

"Unlock the door and get out of the car," she instructed.

I grabbed my purse and was about to get out when she said, "Leave everything but the brooch, your keys, and your cell phone."

As I put my keys in my back pocket, I took out the storage key and left it on the front seat. Maybe she wouldn't notice.

Luckily, she didn't. Hopefully, someone else would.

She walked next to me, allowing the point of the knife to

scratch my skin with every step. By the time we reached the storage units, blood stained the right side of my T-shirt.

She unlocked the corrugated aluminum door, sliding it partly open, then shoved me through the opening. The tight space smelled of bodily fluids and fear.

It was surreal. Along the sides were gowns, trophies, and crowns. In the center, Becky and Ellen were duct-taped at the arms and the ankles. They were in plastic Adirondack chairs with their mouths covered with more duct tape. Fast-food wrappers and a Porta Potty filled the small space. Evidence that Ellen had spent every second of her two weeks held captive in the unit. Smart move since the marina was a favorite for storage and few, if any, locals stored their boats there.

Another chair stood empty, and I had a sinking feeling that it was for me.

She shoved me toward the chair, and I stumbled in the direction. "I brought you what you wanted. I don't know your name or anything about you, so why tie me up? Why not let me go?"

"Because I need Ellen to watch."

"Watch what?" I asked.

"First you text the boyfriend."

I read the panic in Becky and Ellen's eyes, so I complied. "Wait! You're the traffic chick that's been hanging around the office."

"Smart girl. Now text."

"What do you want me to say?"

"Let him know you're okay and that you are working too hard to see him for a few days. Don't send it without letting me see it first."

I carefully typed:

Sweetheart, sorry but I'm swamped with work from Ellen's desk drawer. The spare key is in the driveway. I left your CD on the dining room table.
XOXO Fin.

"Here," I said handing it to the woman. Silently, I prayed she wouldn't get it.

"Good job. Now tell your boss something similar."

Again I typed:

Out of the office Monday working on the Bollan case. Transferring all the land in Jupiter to Sleepy and Wanda Jean. Finley

"Here." I handed her the phone again. God, was it enough? Would Vain Dane and/or Liam pick up on the lame clues I was trying to give?

"Send it."

I did as instructed. Then she took my phone, tossed it on the ground, and stomped it until the face shattered.

"What is it Ellen is supposed to watch?" I asked, hoping to buy time.

"I had to watch when she killed my brother. Course back then she was Ellen Becker, the beauty queen. My brother loved her, and she didn't give a passing thought when she had his life support terminated."

Ellen strained against her restraints. "Shut up! See, my brother was so besotted with her that he gave her power of attorney. It should have been a family decision, but no. She went against my wishes and killed him. Now that I'm out of jail, I thought I'd return the favor." She poked the knife in my direction. "I would have preferred a husband and some kids, but after watching Ellen for a while, I realize you two are the only ones she seems to care about."

"She has a lot of friends. We all do."

Her blue eyes narrowed. "Not according to my surveillance. Now, hand over the brooch."

I complied.

She examined it, turning it over in her hand several times. "If this is a fake, you'll be very, *very* sorry."

"I'm already very, very sorry."

My sarcasm earned me a slap across the face. It felt as if someone had thrown a boulder at my cheek. My eyes automatically welled with tears.

She duct-taped my wrists behind my back. It felt as if my arms would pop right out of their sockets. "This really isn't necessary," I pleaded. "I can't identify you, and I know Becky and Ellen will keep quiet."

"Then let's make it necessary. I'm Gretchen Howell, most recently of the Mass Women's Correctional Facility. Before that I was Ellen's stylist, until she killed my brother."

My mind was trying to stay focused. Nothing I read indicated Ellen Becker was a murderer. I looked over at Ellen as Crazy Gretchen was duct-taping my ankles together. Ellen vehemently shook her head.

"She won't own what she did, so she has to be taught a lesson," Gretchen said just before she slapped duct tape over my mouth. "I'm taking this to be authenticated," she said as she held up the brooch. Then she looked at me. "This wouldn't have been necessary if you hadn't put Ellen's things on eBay."

I knew then that I was looking at Tiara64.

"I'll be back, girls. Make yourselves comfortable."

When she closed the shed door all the way, we were plunged into darkness. I made a noise, and both Ellen and Becky moaned back. I'd kept my legs up higher as she'd duct-taped them to the chair. Now that she was gone, I did my best to work the tape free. All the while I was terrified that she would come back and find me.

I'd worked up quite a sweat and hadn't made any headway. Then I remembered the row of tiaras along the wall. I knew immediately I was in Ellen's storage unit. This is where she'd stored her secret past. Half hopping and half sliding, I worked my way over to the shelf. The crowns were about three inches above my bound hands.

Becky and Ellen were moaning at me, but I couldn't make out a thing they had to say. I didn't know if Gretchen would be gone for ten minutes or ten hours. I just knew I needed something sharp, and I needed it right then.

I hopped and scooted along the wall until I finally knocked one to the floor. Only problem, I couldn't see where it had fallen. I cursed in my brain. There didn't seem to be any solution except the obvious. I began rocking until the chair turned on its side. My head hit the concrete hard enough for me to lose consciousness for a few seconds. I rolled around until I finally hit the crown.

This was taking too flipping long. I had to move around until I had the right position. With my fingers gripping the tiara, I began sawing at the duct tape. It felt like an eternity before I freed my hands.

"Ouch!" I cried as I ripped the duct tape from my mouth. I made quick work of freeing my ankles, and I was on my way to free my fellow captives when the aluminum door began to slide open.

I dove into the gowns. It was the only place to hide and not a very good one at that. She'd left the door ajar, so I knew she'd find me in a matter of seconds.

"Finley!" Gretchen called, clearly irritated. "You have ten seconds to show yourself, or I'll stick the pin in Becky's eye. Your choice."

I stepped out and found Gretchen with the blade of her knife between her thumb and fingers. In a quick movement, she threw the knife, and I felt a burning sensation in my shoulder. Before I could process that she'd stabbed me, she was yanking the knife out. "Learned that in prison," she said.

"Too bad you didn't find Jesus."

She lifted the bloody knife tip just under my chin. "No one likes a smart-ass."

"No one likes to be stabbed, either." I pressed my hand over the wound, and hurling seemed like a good idea. I gagged twice, then splattered Gretchen's shoes.

I cried when she punched me in the arm close to my wound. "That wasn't nice."

"Sorry, I don't know the etiquette when speaking to a psycho."

"You have no idea. I've had twenty-two years to plot my revenge against Ellen. I dreamed of this." She yanked me with her, then took the knife and made a nasty slash across Ellen's forearm. "And this time I won't miss," she snarled at Ellen.

"You missed something?" I asked, assuming the more I kept her talking, the more time I had to be alive.

"After Barry died, I went to Ellen's house and shot her. She was supposed to die. Instead, she played dead, waited for me to leave, and then called the police. I was arrested, convicted, and served twenty-two years of a twenty-five-year sentence. Twenty-two years. Do you know how long that is when you're stuck in a nine-by-six cage?"

"Why did they let you out?" I asked.

"Curious thing, aren't you? Well, truth is, I became a model prisoner. Earned my bachelor's and master's degrees in computer sciences. Came in really handy when I had to track Ellen down. Didn't take me long to find her new identity."

"I read the article about your brother's death. It was an accident."

"No, it wasn't. She knew Barry had had too much to drink, but she still let him drive."

Again Ellen moaned against the tape.

"She had no right to—"

Before I could process what was happening, I smelled the acrid scent of gunpowder, and Gretchen was on top of me. I felt a sharp pain in my left side, then everything went black.

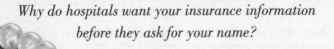

*Why do hospitals want your insurance information
before they ask for your name?*

epilogue

I opened my eyes and saw Liam sitting in a chair on the right of
my bed. I knew from the beeping sounds and antiseptic smells
that I was in the ER.

"Welcome back," Liam said.

I started to get up, but I felt a nasty pinch at my side and
shoulder. "Ouch!"

"You might want to stay still. You've got forty-seven stitches."

With my good arm, I raked my hair back off my face. "I'm
a little fuzzy."

"No, you're a little wacko. What were you thinking?"

"If you're only here to chastise me, go away."

He smiled. "After you called me sweetheart?"

"That was a clue."

"I figured that out all by myself. Figured out that you
wanted me to find your car and a key, and that there was something on the Crime Stoppers tape you wanted me to hear."

"The ship's bells in the background."

"Got that. Victor Dane was confused at first, but when I read Jupiter, I figured that's where you three were being held."

"How are Ellen and Becky?"

"Becky is taking a shower, and Ellen is getting stitched up as we speak."

"Liv and Jane?"

"Took a walk."

Tony and Izzy pulled aside the curtain. Tony had a beautiful spray of roses. "How's the patient?"

"I'll live."

Izzy looked terrified. I plastered a smile on my face. "It's not as bad as it looks. They charge based on how many machines they connect."

Izzy relaxed a bit. "Seriously, you were stabbed and everything?"

"Just grazed," I lied. "Come here."

Izzy moved to my bedside. I patted her hand. "I'm really okay, and luckily, so are my friends."

"I was scared."

"I was too, but it's over now."

She gave me a gentle hug, then said, "We brought you flowers. Dad says they're your favorite."

"Your dad is right. How was the dance?"

"Lindsey Hetzler and her boyfriend got caught making out, and she got suspended and—"

Tony stepped in and placed his hands on Izzy's shoulders. "You can tell her everything later. Finley could probably use some rest."

"Sorry," Izzy said.

"Don't be sorry. I'm glad Lindsey got hers."

"Can I see you again soon?" Izzy asked.

"The minute they spring me from this place, I'll give you a ring."

"Feel better," Tony said. There was an awkward few seconds when I sensed he wanted to do something. Squeeze my hand, hug me, kiss me? Something.

Once Tony and Izzy left, it was only Liam, me, and some tension.

"Who shot Gretchen?" I asked.

"Does it matter?"

"Yes. It does to me."

"Leave it alone, Finley. It isn't worth rehashing."

"Was it you?"

"Izzy looked really worried. Maybe she should come back and sit with you for a while."

"Why won't you tell me?"

"Because I don't want you to be grateful."

"Why not?"

"I want you for a whole bunch of other reasons."

"So what are you waiting for?"

"Well, you to get off the morphine drip for one."

I smiled. "And since I'm sure my face is all scratched and horrid, you'd probably like to wait for that to heal, too."

"You're beautiful, scratches and all."

"Then how about giving me a kiss?"

He stood and came to my side. "Oh, don't worry. I will. Often. Get some rest."

"I'd rather have a kiss."

"You're making it tough for me to walk away."

"That's the point, Liam. I don't want you to walk away."

He bent down and brushed his lips across my forehead. "I don't want to walk away, but the cops have been waiting to talk to you."

"They can wait a little longer."

"So can I," he said. Then he kissed my lips and walked out of the room.

Turn the page

for a sneak peek of

the next stylishly entertaining

Finley Anderson Tanner novel

BARGAIN HUNTING

from bestselling author

Rhonda Pollero

Coming soon from Gallery Books

My road to happiness is under construction.

one

I had forty-three seconds left. My fingers were perched over the keyboard as I watched the time slowly tick away. eBay bidding is an art if you know what you're doing and I was a maestro. I was bidding on the innards of a Rolex Ladies DateJust watch. If I won the auction, I'd make tremendous strides toward my build-my-dream-watch-from-scratch project. I desperately wanted the watch of my dreams and I'd spent two years gathering parts on eBay. At the rate I was going, I would have all the parts by the time I was thirty-five.

The clock ticked down below thirty seconds and I was not the high bidder. I was lulling my competition into submission and the plan was to swoop in at the last second and hopefully enter a bid high enough to win the auction.

My attention was on the computer but I became distracted when the security lights switched on and I heard a car pull into the drive of my Palm Beach cottage. If I had to guess, I'd assume it was not one of my friends. No one I knew would drop by without calling. Especially not when it was nearly midnight. There was a knock at the door. "Hang on!" I called, my eyes fixed on the clock. There was a second knock, louder and more impatient.

Shit. "Just a minute!" Or more accurately, seventeen seconds.

My front door, which I knew I'd locked, suddenly burst open. I looked up from my screen and found Liam McGarrity standing in my foyer. Liam was tall and handsome in a bad boy kinda way and I'd spent the better part of a year tamping down my attraction to him. I hadn't been very successful. Only this time, my heart skipped a beat for a different reason. Liam was covered in blood, holding an equally bloody beach towel.

Forgetting that I was dressed in a pair of Victoria's Secret boxers and a pair of layered spaghetti strapped tees in complimentary shades of pink, I stood when I read his expression. I'd never seen him looking anything other than sexy, arrogant, or amused. But now his piercing blue eyes were narrowed and etched with concern.

"I need help."

"What happened?" I asked. "Did you hit an animal?"

Suddenly my eBay alert avatar announced, "Your auction has ended." The comment barely registered.

He stood stiffly, his stained free hand dangling at his side. "I found a body."

"So you came here? Shouldn't you call the sheriff's office or something?"

"The deceased was a member of the sheriff's office. He was shot with my gun."

My brain was spinning, trying to fit the pieces of his conversation into place. "Back up. What happened to make you kill a deputy?"

"I didn't kill him."

"But you said it was your gun."

"It was. But I haven't seen that weapon for five years. I don't know how Paul Lopez was shot with it."

"How do you know it's yours?"

"Serial number."

"Did you lose the gun?"

"In a manner of speaking. Look, I know this is asking a lot but can I hang here for a while? I'm sure the cops will go looking for me at my place. I doubt they'd come here."

"Am I aiding and abetting?"

His eyes met mine. "Probably. But if it comes to it, I'll swear you knew nothing about Paul or the gun."

"What's with the towel?" I asked.

"I used it to wipe down my car. I'd like to wash it, along with my clothes."

"But if you didn't do anything—"

"It won't play like that. Trust me."

The thing was, I did trust him. Liam had saved my life on more than one occasion so the least I could do was wash a towel. "Give it to me," I said, walking over to where he stood.

"Can we do my clothes, too?"

As inappropriate as it was, my mind flashed the delicious image of Liam standing gloriously naked in front of me. I dismissed the thought and remembered the bag in my guest room. "Wait here."

I dashed down the hallway and returned carrying the bag. "Is there blood on your shoes?"

"Probably. After I clean up I'll take them outback, rinse them and then hit the soles with some bleach."

I nodded. "To screw up any presumptive test for blood."

He offered a half-smile. "Very good. I see Tony has taught you a lot."

Tony Caprelli was the latest and hottest addition to the law firm of Dane, Lieberman and Caprelli. Even though we had a mild spark, Tony'd blown me off with the single-father excuse. He was, however, coming around. Thanks in large part to my close relationship with his daughter, Izzy. Izzy liked coming to my place to enjoy the beach, and more and more frequently, Tony hung around as well.

Liam looked in the bag. "Do you always keep a bag of men's clothes in your house?"

"Tony left them this afternoon."

Liam's expression darkened. "Oh."

I really didn't owe Liam an explanation. Screw it; he could just let his mind wander on that point. "The guest bath is the first door on the left."

"Thanks," he said as he slipped off his shoes and dropped the towel on top of them.

In a matter of minutes, I heard the shower start. I used the time to rinse and bleach his boat shoes, then placed the towel in the washer while I waited to add his clothing.

Liam emerged towel-drying his black hair, carrying his bloody clothes. He was dressed in khakis and a blue polo shirt that did magical things for his eyes. It was quite a change from his cargo shorts and Tommy Bahama shirts. As attractive as he looked, it just didn't feel like Liam. He wasn't the dressy casual type, hence the reason he'd left the shirt untucked. Other than at my sister's wedding, I'd only seen Liam in his signature attire. While he did wonders for a tux, this ensemble made him look like a Ken doll.

I added the clothes to the washer, along with the towel he'd used to partially dry his hair. "There's a comb in the guest basket in the bathroom," I said.

"No need," Liam replied as he raked his fingers through his hair. All that did was give him a tousled, just-out-of-bed look that made my stomach clench. Even in the midst of a crisis I couldn't control my hormones. God, am I ever lame.

"I took care of your shoes," I said.

"Give me the bleach so I can rinse the traps in your bathroom."

I handed him the bottle. As he walked away I got a sinking feeling. While I was happy to give Liam aid and comfort, and probably more than that, I felt as if I was getting in over my head. Liam didn't need the help of a paralegal who had worked exclusively in estates and trusts for eight years before adding criminal defense work to her repertoire. He needed a lawyer. He'd probably get pissed, but it seemed prudent to call Tony. He'd know the best course of action. Besides, the two men had a friendship that went back more than a decade.

I reached for the phone and dialed Tony's cell. I didn't want to call the house phone in case Izzy was sleeping.

"Caprelli."

"It's Finley. I'm sorry to bother you so late, but something has come up. Liam was—"

"Who the hell are you calling?" Liam demanded.

I placed my hand over the mouthpiece. "Tony. You need him."

"No, I just need a couple of hours. Then I'll be out of your hair."

"Finley?" Tony asked into my ear.

I looked at Liam, tilting my head to one side. "Please?"

"Gimme the phone."

I handed Liam my cell, then twisted my blonde hair up into a messy knot at the nape of my neck.

Though he was speaking to Tony, Liam surveyed my now-bare neck, then dropped lower. A shiver tickled my spine, and I was reminded that I wasn't exactly dressed for company. While he was on the phone, I went into my room and grabbed a bra, panties, T-shirt, and shorts. I changed in record time.

When I returned to the living room, Liam was off the phone and on the sofa. The slosh of the washer just off the kitchen echoed in the quiet of the room. The layout had been the brain-child of my friend Sam Carter. He'd taken the dilapidated shell and turned it into a white, coral, and teal thing of beauty. There was no wall dividing the kitchen from the eating area or the living space. It was open and airy, and the focal point was the triple sliders leading out to a stunning strip of beach I considered all my own. In reality, it wasn't mine. Florida doesn't allow for individuals to own private beaches. But Palm Beach got around that rule by building a succession of sea walls that took claw hooks and a hefty amount of rope to scale.

Liam's large frame made the room feel smaller. I sat at the opposite end of the sofa with my legs tucked under me and one elbow resting on the padded top. "Going to tell me the whole story?"

"Not much to tell," Liam said. "Got any beer?"

I went to the fridge and got him a beer, then placed a new pod in my Keurig and made myself a cup of hazelnut coffee. I opened the bottle, added cream to my coffee, then rejoined him.

"Someone was killed with your gun. Seems to me there's a story in there somewhere."

Liam shrugged. The action caused a strain on the seams of the shirt. Apparently he was more broad-chested than Tony. I really needed to stop making these comparisons. Attraction or not, Liam really was the wrong man for me. For any woman. Well, except for his not-so-ex-wife, Ashley. As far as I could tell she was the only woman who was a constant in his life, and I'd often seen the two of them out at restaurants or clubs in downtown West Palm. It bugged me that he still had some sort of relationship with his ex, but I was in no position to challenge him on that one. Plus, there was the issue of my always picking the wrong man. A habit I'm trying really hard to break. Tony, on the other hand, was definite boyfriend material. Except for the instant-family thing. But I was getting over that, thanks to my good relationship with his daughter. But there's always a danger associated with dating a widower. Tough to compete with a ghost. Tony's wife had died when the towers went down, so he'd come to Florida for a fresh start. I wouldn't mind being part of that start, I just had to find a way around the single father thing and the fact that, technically, he's my boss; interoffice dating is a huge no-no at Dane-Lieberman.

"Paul and I used to be partners."

"Is that how he got your gun?" I asked.

"The last time I saw that gun was just before it was put in the evidence locker. That was five years ago."

I fiddled with a strand of hair that had come loose from my messy coif. "I'm assuming things don't normally go missing from the police evidence lockup?"

"Not usually, no."

"Could Paul have taken it out?"

Again he shrugged. "Maybe, if he was taking a second look at the case."

"What case?"

Liam took a long pull on the bottle. "It was five years ago, and the case was closed. I can't think of a valid reason why he'd be wasting his time on it. Besides, he was transferred to traffic division after the incident."

"What is this *incident*?"

"Let it go, Finley."

"You brought me into this," I said, irritated. "I think the least you can do is fill in the gaps so I'll know why I'm risking so much."

"I've done the same for you."

"I know that. But you've always known why I was in trouble. Now the proverbial shoe is on the other foot."

"They took my gun five years ago."

"Why?"

"Because I shot and killed a kid."